DUNCAN'S
COLONY

DUNCAN'S

COLONY

Natalie L. M. Petesch

Swallow Press
Ohio University Press
Chicago Athens, Ohio London

Swallow Press Books
are published by
Ohio University Press
Athens, Ohio

First edition
First printing

Library of Congress Cataloging in Publication Data

Petesch, Natalie L. M.,
Duncan's Colony.

I. Title.
PS3566.E772D8   813'.54   81–14188
ISBN 0–8040–0401–3   AACR2

For Carlos and Ana María

*The very nature of truth alters
according to our perceptions.*

Ortega y Gasset

DUNCAN'S COLONY

The Place
The American Southwest

The Time
The mid-sixties

The Characters
Duncan, former seminarian
Klara, (b. 1900) arrived in U.S. from Russia before World
War I
Michele, a young poet
Pinosh, a puppeteer
Andrea, Malcolm's wife
Malcolm, a mycologist: married to Andrea
Jennifer, a student, aged fourteen
Carillo, a revolutionary, formerly in Vietnam

The Scene
During the nineteen sixties, following the missile crisis and during the Vietnam War, communitarian societies began to reappear
in the United States. Those who were of an invincibly optimistic
nature gathered together in agrarian or utopian communes remi-
niscent of the nineteenth century. Others, who believed that
these crises and wars augured the end of modern civilization by
nuclear warfare, gathered together for a brief season of love in
colonies where they hoped to survive the destruction of the
world.

This is the story of eight people who lived together for nearly a
year in such a colony: Duncan's Colony.

Michele

It used to be one of those games people played: If you had to live on a desert island with only a few dozen people, whom would you choose? Ah, but we did not have that option. We were obliged, from among the numbers who wanted to be here, to let them choose us.

This, of course, is not an island, not even a desert. It is only a spot between the vast Southwestern desert and the sea. But this is the place that was chosen for us by Duncan, partly because of the special talents of our colony, partly because Duncan's private history leads him to think of the desert as a place of temptation: but also of salvation. Though the desert itself is several hiking days away, we feel close to it: like the Magi of old we watch the stars and dream, not of the rise of a new kingdom, but of the fall of the old: not of our life to come, but of our lives as they were.

The only obstacle to the perfecting and inscribing of our Past, as though it were a hieroglyphic tablet which we meant for future generations to penetrate, is our curiosity about the Present. In spite of, or because of, Duncan's ban against newspapers and television, we are curious: curiosity is the one emotion among us which has not been weakened. In theory, when the time comes, the news from beyond our compound will be so utterly depressing as to cast us all into despair: but meanwhile we are still afflicted with the habit of curiosity, with "the itch for the 6:30 news" as Malcolm calls it: we want to know just how bad things are Out There. Thus, Malcolm continues to operate his short wave radio; his trained mind continues to record all that is happening to us—all this with the passion of a scribe who is convinced that his chronicle will be of enormous interest to postlapsarian historians. How we cling to the old terminology. I wrote *postlapsarian* as if I were some theologian still dabbling in arguments over Eve's guilt. But what word must I coin from the now irrelevant art of word-making to describe the chronicle of events in this, the last Garden? Thus we have in our ready vocabulary, *postfluvian, postpartum, postmortem*—even *posthumous*: but for the death of a world, a planet, we have not yet discovered a form, but speak in terms of outworn eschatologies.

One would think that, having come together here, in this apocalyptic embrace, we would either cease to care about what is going on Out There or cease to make rules regarding our access to news (among other things). But so entrenched is the habit of harmony through proper rule(s), of the illusion of Order created by penalties, rewards, prohibitions, that in spite of the absurdity of doing so, we have laid down a new Decalogue. Duncan points out that, of course, there is no way of enforcing these rules, but adds, as though it were his special role to make ethical comments: that "true" morality is not achieved by force but is a condition within the individual. We sit silently while he forages among these philosophical relics, dry bones of a Judeo-Christian ethic never to be fleshed out again. The rules which Duncan hands out to us in his oddly ornamental script (everything which does not definitively contribute to our survival now seems ornamental) seemed simple enough till we thought about them. They were:

   i. The dead are to be cremated at once.
   ii. Persons suffering from shock will be isolated.
   iii. Any persons (including the above) inflicting violence on others will be kept in restraint (kind and degree to be determined by consensus).
   iv. There will be no pregnancies.
   v. No additional members will be admitted to the colony.
   vi. Members of the colony are to refrain (voluntarily) from listening to news broadcasts.
   vii. Our combined effort must be to survive; and failing that—to die without criminal acts against each other, and in possession of our sanity. . . .

Nobody asked what Duncan meant by sanity. We looked everywhere but towards each other, fingering leaves, making trails in the dust, like children tying their shoes, wishing their playmates not to notice that they were suffering an invisible assault—a weakness of bladder or bowel. Each one of us in the silence took inventory of our character, marking the tender rotting *locus* which we meant heroically to conceal from the others. I thought at once of Mark; our bitter, severing quarrel over these events had forced me to reevaluate myself. If I was not fit company for him during these Last Days, could I believe he had ever loved me? I recall reading somewhere, while I was still in college, that de Beauvoir had said Sartre could hurt her only by dying before her. But suppose they had imposed upon them this choice: whether they were to die *together*, and Sartre had preferred, like Mark, to go off alone . . . to do it his way. What then?

Mark's decision to let me come to the Colony alone has rendered our marriage meaningless; and now only my death, which I must achieve *alone*, has become significant. What this says about love and marriage is terrifying. Have 'They' been lying to us all these years? Only a short time ago (but it was years, actually!) I remember seeing a documentary on starvation in Africa (how prophetic that seems now): after numerous political and geographical upheavals, fewer than a thousand persons remained in this particular tribe; there were no crops or animals left, each person was forced to forage for himself in order to survive: one saw that the wife of one of these starving tribesmen had that very day gone out to forage and had found food for herself. Yet she made no effort to save the sick and starving man who lay at her feet—her husband. On the TV screen she seemed no monster— indeed she appeared herself only barely alive, while her emotionless face seemed to leach a useless charity from our living room, as from our bones.

Perhaps that is really what Mark is fleeing. From the dread of some sort of psychological (or actual?) cannibalism. For this same reason, a teacher of mine in grade school once told me that he hated to fly in a plane with his wife and children for fear that his last thought as the plane went down would be how viciously, how despicably, they had all—*all*—in their terror, behaved.

But the reason Mark gave me was neither ethical nor philosophical. He merely said that if the prophets of doom had turned out to be correct, if what God, Baby Jesus, and the Snake had so cleverly initiated (he could never stop immunizing himself against his early religious training by heaping upon it his full measure of scorn) were all to end up in a great urn of ash, then he wanted to be out at sea when it happened. He said he had always had an abiding respect for the ocean. He said (smiling) that he had faith in the ability of the sea to renew life, even if it meant their starting all over again with a handful of friendly protozoans. At any rate the idea of being closed in by land filled him with loathing more than with fear.

So we had driven in a leisurely way, down to the Gulf, where the *Hebrides* lay offshore. In the last hour, I wanted to show Mark that I was not losing control, that I was still capable of doing something for him. I insisted on carrying his suitcase. I lurched forward across the dunes, his heavy bag striking my knees: somehow I had forgotten that Mark was a strong man over six feet tall and that, naturally, he would have packed a bag suitable for himself to carry. It was as if, since my mind had grappled with the absurdity of the universe, I now expected my body as well to be capable of absurdity. With the weight of Mark's bag falling on top of me, I plunged down the sand dune; it was ridiculous.

It was heavy because it was full of books. Mark said he'd also brought his bathing suit. "Like going on vacation," he said. "You read, swim, lie in the sun: *grow healthy*." He tried again to smile, but his mouth was closed. I could see the dry seam of lips, a pouch of weariness: no further messages, his mouth said to me. So I hunkered down over the suitcase, refusing to let go of it. We began to struggle for it in the sand, like murderers for a gun; but I did not relax my grip on the handle. Presently Mark said, as if I had won him over: "O.K. I'll stay here. It doesn't matter, really." He sat in the sand beside me for what may have been hours. I was not aware of time passing. He sifted the sand through his fingers, he watched me, he looked toward the harbor where the *Hebrides* lay awaiting her last passengers. As the twilight gathered and gulls crowed around us, I suddenly regained my "sanity." I released the suitcase which fell slantwise toward the rising tide. In another hour or so the sea water would have covered our feet. We kissed. The taste of his lips was salt; while we'd sat there, he'd been crying silently.

When he was out of sight, I stumbled back to the car and in the morning I got in touch with Duncan at the hotel where he was staying while interviewing Klara Kleist.

So, I already knew that Duncan's Last Commandment was not relevant. As for the Fourth—not to admit new members to the colony—he had already broken it by accepting Carillo, who had survived a long struggle alone in the desert and had finally wandered into our camp—the first or perhaps the second evening of our arrival here.

But at this first "official" meeting of the colony, we were silent while Duncan read *The Rules* to us. Only Pinosh, perhaps wishing to break the spell of terror which lay on us all, demanded in his light, lively actor's voice if love affairs were to be permitted. And if not, he said, he wanted *out* this minute, because, he explained with a calm comic lucidity, "I'm already in love with Michele there, and I've only seen her twice since I arrived."

I looked at the man who spoke so lightly and unbelievably of having fallen in love with me. What could he know about me? What could he see in my face? We had barely spoken ten words together. It could only be the climate of Last Things: what more amiable way to pass one's time than fucking in the grass while the rest of the world fell into space like a meteor?

We call him Pinosh because, from the moment of his arrival, he has insisted that he is the original Pinocchio who, "If we remembered, turned out to be a real boy. Which hasn't been much fun," he added with a grimace. He is certainly one to die laughing: shall I go with him and giggle absurdly when the final light streaks down? Or choose another? I look with the appreciative detachment of a housewife buying love-apples at the fruit stall: "too hard," "too soft," "too ripe," "too green": but there is Carillo, in the heart of whose discontent there must be desire, if only to forget the failure of his "Revolution." Or Malcolm— who of course is married—but what do such alliances mean under such conditions? Or perhaps even Duncan himself, from whom one gathers exquisite signals such as radiate from the lunar moth: a sensuousness lying upon his very skin, like the sheen of silk.

So why not? Yes, Pinosh's question is an honest one. When one's time is measurable, the decision—with whom to spend those last hours—becomes terribly important, striking all one's actions with the impact of existential choice.

But though Pinosh was (perhaps) being more honest than any of us, we pretended to smile at his childishness as if to say that the time for love had died with the whale and the wolf. As he asked this question, I noticed that Pinosh was whittling a figure. He turned to me: "Who shall it be? Alice in Wonderland or Lady Jane Grey? History or fantasy?" In spite of myself, I felt pleasure at perceiving that what he held in his hands was to become a puppet. Of course, I thought, Puppeteer: part clown, part actor, part madman.

Pinosh held the stalk of the unfinished body very gently between left forefinger and thumb as he posed his question to Duncan: "When you wrote to us, you mentioned a lot of stuff we'd avoid here: firestorms, fall-out, infection by contact. Now what in the name of heavenly puppetry do you mean by Infection-by-contact? I'm looking forward to bodily contact. Lots of it, in fact. Compensation, you know. . . . And I've picked out me-own-true-love already." He looked at me in a way that indicated that I was to have little to say about it: he was accustomed, among his puppets, to creating the responses he wanted.

Duncan threw more wood on the fire. The sun was beginning to set. The colors of the campfire blent with the expanding sky: there were no clouds, but the sky tautened, became a thing alive, skillfully winding about us great swathes of twilight the color of mead. Slowly it drew the light upward from the campfire in long amber streaks.

For some reason, all of us, Malcolm and Andrea, Klara, Jennifer, Carillo and even Pinosh, and, of course, myself, were very anxious to hear what Duncan would say on the subject of "love." Not of course that any of us believed an edict could be pronounced on such a matter: but we were very curious to hear what Duncan would reply. It was he, after all, who had conceived of the doctrine of survival, the antithesis of martyrdom, as a religious act.

But we were to be disappointed. Had we hoped for some commandment which would lead directly to heaven via the short route? He gave none. Kneading the palm of his hands like some rehearsing St. Francis tracing his stigmata, he declared with emphasis that he had not brought together his colony in order to indulge in futile, hair-splitting disputes concerning 'sins of the flesh.' He wished only to save a 'remnant' to do the work of God.

"Of the Devil more like, I'd say," retorted Pinosh.

Jennifer groaned with exasperation, as though she were on her way to an exciting basketball game at her local high school, and these absurd delays on the part of the adults were "too much!" She and Malcolm exchanged glances: Andrea looked deliberately away from her husband in the way one avoids answering an importunate question by pretending not to have heard it.

MICHELE

I think we were disappointed at the possibility that Duncan may have selected us for his colony as a merely religious act: we had persuaded ourselves that it was on the basis of some personal merit, the strength of our characters, perhaps, or some report he had received of our courage or ingenuity: even perhaps some metaphysical Reward for Past Services. So now our spirits were dampened—or rather our vanities were piqued—by the knowledge that we had not been selected like epicures to savor the last delights of survival, but merely as communicants in some private religious rite of Duncan's, himself the chief cleric. Yet, because his was the energy, the force which had brought us together, we deferred to him—this would-be Believer, more fit to be a courtesan or Petronius Arbiter than the disciple of any new doctrine of faith.

He claims to have chosen us from among thousands of replies to his advertisement, which both Klara Kleist and I read in the Detroit papers. How odd to *advertise* Survival as though it were a new cereal, or a way of improving your tennis backhand. But absurd as it was, we replied, he answered, we came.

We women range widely in age (was this part of Duncan's plan?). Klara Kleist, for instance, serene and meditative as a Dalai Lama, must be at least eighty, whereas Jennifer is less than a child —that is to say, she is bursting with the need to declare herself a woman, an equal among equals: and surely Death is the great democrat. Just why Jennifer did not follow her parents to whatever faraway place they moved to is not clear to me. Nobody explains anything.

Actually it was not Duncan's, but Malcolm's, first statement which made most sense. He has already been reconnoitering in the caves, preparing to work with one of his old hobbies, the cultivation of mushrooms. "The way for us to do this," (he seemed to speak with an authority surpassing Duncan's—but derived from whom?) "is to act as if it's not happening. Take notes. Keep on with your profession. We're the lucky ones, it seems to me. We don't need operating rooms, football stadiums, klieg lights and television channels to do our work. So whatever we dedicated our life to before we came to Duncan's colony, that's what we ought to do. And keep a record. For our time-capsule, you know." This, with a smile.

But to what had I truly dedicated myself before coming here? Ah, that is the question I must answer above all.

JULY 10

And that is the problem. I did not sufficiently dedicate myself to anything or anyone but Mark, and since he has left me to die "alone" (as if at any other time, one died any other way), everything that I've done has been rendered null and void. It's as if now I have before me a vast debit sheet, asking: what did you do? what did you do? Above all: *why*? And when I have added and subtracted and embezzled a few meritorious acts here and there, I discover that somewhere along the line I had meant to become a recluse and a poet (in that order), the Dickinson of the twentieth century. I had the talent for long silent days, the solitary's precious ore. I did, in fact, become a recluse, did in fact write some few poems; but all for the wrong reasons. I did not *choose* isolation, it merely happened because I followed Mark wherever in the wide world it was necessary for him to do his research. I was happy to follow him, not remembering who I was; and women who would have offered me friendship in strange lands, in lonely towns, must have sensed in me that glossy billiard ball of marital happiness, of conjugal delight, of female uxoriousness—because they would merely touch me lightly in conversation, then ricochet out of sight . . .

So now when I must, as Malcolm suggests, dedicate myself to what I had previously dedicated myself, I find a vacuum. I can write the few poems that have occurred to me since arriving here; but I feel in them a void at the center, a lack of intensity. I have been accustomed to wait for inspiration from some ironic impact of Mark's body or mind upon mine, from which, in bitterness and pride, I would take to my pen and feel I had transcended his cruelty by writing about it. I wonder now how many poets have dulled their art by sharpening it on one edge only, making of their gift an *ars talionis*?

That was my error—is it too late to mend? This evening, Pinosh, true to his warning, approached me in my tent (we are to live in these tents until the prefab is put together).

"Michele," he called from outside the tent, as though we had been comrades for years. "I'm coming in. I've a new puppet to show you. Of course that's not even supposed to look like a pretext," he added, coming in and lying down at once on my canvas army bed.

I didn't protest. In our situation, what would be the use?

He had in fact brought a new puppet. "Othello," he said, without waiting for me to identify the princely figure resting on his hand. "I figured the one thing we lacked here was a token black."

I sat stiffly at the edge of the awkward little folding chair beside my writing table. There was very little room in the tent, and in order to stand by the exit I would have had to pass his out-stretched body. I stayed.

"You know that you and I are to be lovers."

"I heard your pronouncement. And how did you arrive at this conclusion? Statistics? Sooth-saying? Or merely a serene and steadfast self-love?"

He held the puppet upright: "*And bade me, if I had a friend that loved her/I should but teach him how to tell my story/And that would woo her. Upon this hint I spake.*"

In spite of myself, I smiled. Nostalgia gripped me like lust. Mark and I at the theater, Desdemona's dainty body lying head downward, dead, dead, dead: it was not possible that the play could end with so much death.

"And to what do I owe the honor of this election?" The arch set of my lips revolted me. A stupid, coquettish thing to say: *only yes or no, lady, this is not the time for the antique vanities. If not you, it'll be another—it may even come to acts of jealousy, rites of combat, confrontations—*

Pinosh deftly removed the figure from his right hand and began counting on his fingers. "One . . . " I knew at once what was coming and felt humiliated in the old way, the way Mark knew so well how to render me sick with self-examination: was I *enough*? (Clever enough? Passionate enough? Eager enough?)

"*Que voulez-vous?* Klara is so ancient, she'd fall apart, though I do confess it, she's had such a long, *intriguing* life, I'd be willing to fuck her if she'd tell me all about it. But she won't. Women like that die without an immodest tale (*tail?*)," he shrugged, "to leave behind for their great-greats. Jennifer is hot for it, but I don't want to get into one of those big-buck fights with Comrade Carillo for screwing privileges: he's got an M-1 rifle and can shoot the worm out of a bird's beak. After all, this is a survival game, not a screwing contest. O.K." He was still counting us off on his practiced fingers. "That leaves you. And Andrea. If you were me, who would *you* rather—her or you?"

I was stunned by the tone, a deliberate blow to my self-esteem which doubtless he sensed only he would be able to heal: an old skill, I recognized Mark's technique. Wound you, pillage you, then nurse you tenderly back to health. The terrifying thing was that it worked. I felt hurt, I felt my own market value plunge out of sight: he could choose someone else, Jennifer perhaps, and who, then, would lie with me on my bed during the long terrifying nights to come? Pinosh had simply asserted, in spite of the new order, the old order of things: he had chosen and subjugated me —without even a struggle on my part. It was a kind of mental abduction. Within the hour we became lovers, hardly troubling to undress. Except for his sullen, almost angry climax, it could not have been called what we once would have referred to as sexual *pleasure*: it was rather a new kind of chore, like vacationing city dwellers being obliged to bring up water from a rural well: hard work but novel and therefore still interesting. When custom had begun to stale us, perhaps then we would try nudity once more, with all its posturing. For the moment, we merely sealed a bargain.

Duncan

The people of San Luis Rey were brought together, according to the story, by the will of God. Slowly, ineluctably, the author frees them from their earthly preoccupations, and from their huckstering egos, and launches them into holy Grace as into a seaworthy vessel. Then they fall through the air and we are to believe that, like every falling sparrow, the waiting hand of God caught them as they fell.

But Who will catch us as we fall? Why are we here? *Here.* I sit looking at the round period with which I ended the thought: Here. This speck of atoms, this dust, this microcosm: this Earth.

I prefer to believe that God did not will these events at all, but rather that the Devil was victorious: that Genesis was wrong, the Apostles, Aquinas, and of *course* Milton—all were wrong: that like an Aristotelian hero, God, too, had his tragic flaw and has been overcome.

His flaw, perhaps, was that he believed too readily in His absolute power over the universe; that, having created Death for man's "punishment," He believed that he could, like Sinbad, neutralize this monster by invoking a hypostatic Jesus. But Death, instead of being merely punitive or even morally rehabilitative has become the Final Solution: the Devil saw how he could work his will by it, though he too would be destroyed.

Thus: Death was God's Frankenstein. I say, if this be heresy, let Him punish me for it. Let Him try.

But perhaps God is evolving too. Perhaps He is trying to find a way to overcome his weakness. Perhaps He needs help. Perhaps when He decides to remake His universe, He will need some builders. With these hypotheses in mind, it became "logical" that the only meaningful religious act I could perform was that of survival. I cannot know what God's intention is with regard to rescheduling the Creation: my only option is to help Him hang in there. It was with this in mind that I placed the ad in the *Press* and prayed for guidance. I fasted for over a week, hoping I would see visions: but none came. But on the tenth day, names began to sound in my brain. First came Klara (yes, I *saw* that it was Klara with a 'K'). Then one evening there was a storm. Knots of lightning, like barbed wire, separated earth from sky. It was as if, while I watched, they were barricading God. I had the urge to speak to Father Molinari about my Plan. He would (again) tell me, no doubt, that my idea was heretical, but perhaps he would find some meaning in it: even heretics have been accredited with significance, if only that of the catalytic opposition.

I slipped quietly into his office to wait for him: he often worked long hours in the evening and his chancery light was still on. He meant, obviously, to return to his desk shortly. I paced back and forth in his office, torn between the desire to speak to him and the sense that I was intruding on his privacy. Yet I was doing nothing but waiting alone in his office, as I had done many times before. Suddenly (was it accident or intention?) I glanced down at his desk where a single sheet lay spotlighted beneath his lamp: it was an application for the annulment of a marriage. Their names stood forth in the light as though embossed by a seal: MALCOLM AND ANDREA DELANEY who, after twenty-three years of marriage, were seeking an annulment on the grounds that neither side had made his marriage vows in good faith.

It did not seem to me odd at the time that they were seeking some Higher Authority to declare their union nonexistent when all along (they said) they had been deceiving one another as to their original intent. My religious training had accustomed me to accept these paradoxes which ran like parallel lines through all one's life—never meeting, never joining, yet inseparable. And I accepted this illumination of their names by the chancery light as a revelation. I wrote to them at once of my colony, and it did not surprise me that they accepted. Thus (ironically enough) instead of the separation they had sought they were reunited by the apocalyptic turn of history. Perhaps they had needed just some fatal challenge to their dull marriage to make them cling to it as their only reality, as one clings to worn-out furniture which relates to our Past.

But if Malcolm and Andrea were chosen by direct revelation,

I cannot justify Michele's presence in the colony except as a matter of personal taste, if you will. I can only say I was strangely stirred by her letter: egotistically, perhaps, I felt that anyone who could write such a letter would be an excellent person to record what happened to us here: every apocalypse must have its scribe. Yet now she tells me she is not interested in doing so, while Malcolm—whose vows, advice and sworn observations I tend to disregard—is the very one who has elected himself as colony scribe. For our time-capsule, he says.

My choice of Pinosh is what troubles me most. Perhaps in him I erred grossly. But what does error mean under such conditions? I assured myself it was merely an historical accident or even a 'clerical' whim. But more than likely it was my temptation in the desert—to which I have succumbed. After all, there were hundreds of letters from artists, musicians, actors, entertainers of every kind. But from among all these letters—for whatever 'reason'—but one puppeteer.

The Temptation, as I now see it, goes back to those early days when I wanted to be an actor: it was clear even then that for me the theater was a rich well of corruption. My moral sense was utterly lost among its swords and symmetries—its sensuousness, in short. Only a month before I entered the seminary (how I do recall it!), I saw *Hamlet,* and the beauty of his costume, the silver-threaded buskins—the very panache of it all—made my senses reel. I understood only too well what Father Molinari had meant when he warned: "You're not suited, Duncan. You don't have the vocation. Called perhaps, but not chosen. So why torture yourself? Look at me, after all these years. Nothing but a chancery priest, and even *that* is under a cloud. The Bishop may yet send me to Nova Scotia, where (I'm told) among old ladies and dying invalids there'll not be a single serpent to tempt me . . ." And when I'd told him about my reaction to Hamlet: "Ah, you're fit only to order the tomb at St. Praxed's. . ." And of course he was right.

Yes, the theater was an addiction, one could become as enslaved to it as to the Devil. And to think it was the Stuarts who reopened the theaters! Oh we poor forked creatures—what slaves to pomp we are!

I will confess it at once—it was not Pinosh's letter at all which tempted me, it was the show he performed during the interview. He brought with him three puppets, he played all the parts.

Himself invisible, behind a screen his voice alone carried the performances. What a voice! Thus was I tempted. I rationalized that we in the colony would need some distraction from our mortality, that perhaps puppeteer-Pinosh would save us all from madness—he with his capricious assault on reality (because Death is virtuous, shall there be no cakes and ale?). When the electric power had wound down, when recording and tapes were useless, I rationalized that we would bear this clown a ripe and seasonable gratitude for distracting us from Ground Zero.

Perhaps to punish myself for this indulgence, when Carillo wandered into the colony, I did not put up any resistance; they had each one agreed to the rules; they were simply *naïfs* who did not count the spiritual cost of admitting so angry, so *ideological* a man to our midst: it was not a time for political ideologies, I wanted to say. After all, he had not been praying in the desert, he had been hiding. With his hand grenades, his submachine guns, his rifles and his band of guerrillas (and a few women, no doubt), he and his comrades had been preparing for the death of capitalism and had found instead this most bitter joke: the death of us all. I saw Jennifer's eye fill at once with excitement at his approach and rationalized that the child, in her isolation, would soon be throwing herself at Malcolm (I concealed to myself that it was equally possible that she might lie in wait for Pinosh): I told myself that I wanted to save, if possible, what remained of their relationship (Malcolm's and Andrea's), and I let him in. It was not humanity on my part. I cannot make a body count of live bodies, as on battlefields they make a count of dead ones. So, for Carillo, I did not make any humanitarian case whatsoever; in fact, my ethical instinct (if there is such a thing) reversed itself and I found myself thinking: we have more than enough for survival now, but should our supplies become dangerously low, this guerrilla fighter will be more powerful than any of us: he will take what he needs, regardless of the others. But the others, in their innocence, all voted to allow Carillo to enter our colony (the first week, and already an exception to the Rule).

Our place is so far from what is sanguinely referred to as civilian defense areas that before coming here Malcolm and I argued fiercely over the "choice of environments," but when he saw that he could grow mushrooms nearby (and I think we also silently acknowledged the forlorn inadmissible hope that perhaps we could adapt ourselves when necessary to living in the Caverns) he consented to the spot. Also there is a mountain spring several kilometers away: how long it would be clean enough for use is not yet an empirical question. We will use it, that's all we can say.

I had one of three possible places in mind: one near the Mississippi so that we would have transportation on the river (but transportation to where?); one in Florida not far from St. Augustine, where ecologists had once told me that the area was one of minimal fall-out. A third possible place (for the same reason) was near Brasília: but it seemed unwise to try to 'survive' in a totally unfamiliar terrain. I explained to Malcolm that I did, in fact, choose this spot because of the limitless depths of the Caverns (of course they will be dark, and not likely to continue to be pleasant: but *pleasant* is a word, critics have noticed, which Milton rarely used after Paradise was lost). And Malcolm conceded that we were several hundred miles from any city worth destroying by a multiple warhead: he vowed as how it would have to be a major technological error for anybody to bother with a few people in our isolated spot.

All these intellectual explanations for our actions, and the *real* reason I chose this place was because I thought I saw an eagle or a hawk and I took it for a Sign. For twice in my life eagles were "sent" to me to reveal my true mission. If this is egocentrism, so be it: I shall not fail, I warn you, to earn the epithets I've received —of heretic, apostate, anti-Christ. I console myself with the historical fact that all new ideas have been promulgated by "heretics."

But let me try (for Malcolm's sake and for the "Martians" he purports to write for) to record my youth. . . .

My youth. . . to begin with, I'd like to say it's not my fault that I do not know who my parents were: they were sinners, obviously, and I was surrendered for adoption. But didn't Buck know that? Didn't he (even) have buried away somewhere the so-called shameful past of "The Poor Idiot" who had signed the papers and given me over to their perpetual care? And how well-intentioned they were, those hard-working Depression-hit little speculators of the human spirit, who negotiated my birth certificate branded *Illegitimate,* and then proceeded to devaluate it as if I had been issued in exchange for legal tender and somehow gone bankrupt. Of the two, Johnye was less restuctive, but she was also, I think, less intelligent, and choosing between them for companionship I discovered a third alternative: to linger in the barn, working and collecting eggs. It was Johnye's idea that we could supplement Buck's money at the filling station by saturating ourselves in baby chicks that would grow up to be money-producing fat pullets who would lay eggs in our spare time: but of course no such thing happened. All that occurred was that eggs plummeted to three dozen for a dollar, and frequently we fed them to the hogs, it was cheaper than carrying them around from house to house (there weren't all that many houses in Junieh, Texas anyway).

I think sometimes I wanted to be a priest because I could not bear the smell of the chicken houses. I wanted the smell of incense, not corn and farina. And as for Buck and Johnye, they were so starkly impoverished, heart and soul, that I often thanked God they were not really my parents. No, I was not grateful to them, not at all. They had come to the local baby exchange (in this case an allegedly interdenominational orphanage) intending to pick up a newborn waif, in order to stave off boredom, barrenness, and old age. But (being true to their Natures) they had bartered shrewdly and come home with a half-grown kid to help on the farm: I was old enough to be useful, but still young enough (barely seven) to be intellectually browbeaten. ("What do *you* know about the two Popes?—you're not but a child.") A child, yes, but strong enough to work: while Buck plodded away at the filling station in which he already owned a part-interest (investing meanwhile in a bit of property nearby which was to become a parking lot), Johnye and I worked the chicken farm, which she expanded. But when eggs finally hit a quarter a dozen, we switched to turkeys: at one time we had fifteen hundred turkeys craning their knobby necks across the barbed wire compound.

It was supposed to have been an interdenominational orphanage, but the Bucks (as they were known in Junieh) knew that their mission had been to save me from the R.C.'s: they estimated that a better part of their good works had been in saving me from Popish error. But what they couldn't save me from was an inner conviction, as ingrained, say, as Original Sin, that there had to be more to life than turkeys. Even allowing for the fact that the world was again plunged into an economic *débâcle,* I felt that if I could be released from the farm I'd be a well man; that on the Bucks' farm I would never find out what was meant by such oddments

of our language as *buskin, codpiece, tucket,* words which had begun
to fan my curiosity since coming across a little fly-specked book
of plays Buck had had since his high school days.

One rainy day before Thanksgiving I decided to put on my
own play for my entertainment. I shoved the turkey crates off to
one side of the barn and set up a stage. I had filched a green
velvet hat and some knee-high fishing boots from out of Johnye's
trunk and was grandly taking my bows, swinging the gorgeous
imitation ostrich plume of Johnye's hat, when she entered. She
began screaming.

It seemed she would never stop screaming. Between these
piercing outbursts, she would fall on her knees, weeping, "Oh
Lord. Oh Lord." I was frightened, not so much by her suggestion
that the Devil had entered my soul but that I now felt myself in
the sole care and protection of adults who appeared to me raging
mad. I do not know how I had the courage to set my mind against
them; I only know that I felt it was their intention to destroy me
if necessary in order to destroy the Evil within me, and like a
baulking mule, I stood as if mute and impassive—it was my only
resistance. They beat me and prayed, prayed and beat me; Sun-
days the whole congregation echoed their prayer: save this boy
from the corruption of the flesh, from the filth of Sodom and
Gomorrah. It took me a while to realize that with the unsullied
instinct of the pure for the impure they had instantly interpreted
my improvisation of stage attire as a kind of transvestism. Thus
I was prayed over as a thief and a degenerate. Whereas my
mother (they said) had been a mere sinner, gulled by the man
who had abandoned her, the "Poor-Idiot's" trespasses could be
forgiven even as the Bucks forgave those who trespassed against
them: but, and they asked the question aloud: what was this
Duncan?

The question echoed in me for months: what was I? I pondered whether what they accused me of might be true. I studied
my reactions, as though sexuality could be registered to the nearest tenth of a degree. When the paper boy delivered the newspaper, I watched his movements through the blinds, recording
mentally my own impression: he seemed a skinny fellow. But he
reported that he had seen me spying on him, and before I could
make up my own mind about it, it was common knowledge in
Junieh that physical contact with me was to be avoided at all costs.
Although football was the *ars poetica* of our high school, I played
no football: my mere presence in the locker room caused an

absolute silence to reign. Finally, one day, I bound up my knee and declared I had fractured my kneecap: I never again tried out for any team.

It was perhaps no great loss, but the gnawing question continued to corrode: who was I? Buck's contempt for me had turned into a hardened despair: he spoke to me only to send me out to the barn or to order me to take root beside the telephone to await phone orders.

What does a person do under conditions of house arrest? He learns to divert himself to avoid going mad. In my case I could read, and so long as it was a recognizable volume from the World Classics borrowed from the local library, they thought such reading would save me from bad company. From bad company! From Moll Flanders, Falstaff, Madame Bovary, Richard III . . .

The inevitable climax came when, of all places in the world, a traveling repertoire group came to play *Le Misanthrope* in a town about ten miles from Junieh. There was absolutely no question in my mind but that I must see this performance; but the problem was to get away from the farm for the entire evening. When I had hit upon a plan, I applied myself to all its aspects with the deviousness of an Iago: I lied, I stole. I created a crisis among the turkeys which would keep the Bucks busy in the barn most of the evening. Then I put myself to bed with a false fever and instantly made my escape.

The crowd at the theater was, it seemed to me, as different from those at the movie house in Junieh as French kid glove to razorback hog. The thing that struck me, most was that they walked differently, as if the oil of the earth had smoothed their joints: they moved without fluxion. The women (to me) were like figures on an antique vase, their gowns as elegant as chitons, their hair in coiled pyramids. I did not know at the time that Molière had died penniless, so I did not consider the irony of attending his play which was being performed in clothes that would have paid for his lodging for a year; I was simply struck by their fashionable elegance. Only their voices marred the vision: rather like sediment at the bottom of a jar that needed shaking up. In their voices I sensed the same power as Johnye's; to work their will upon me because in some way I was weaker than they, and I had the feeling that they would not hesitate to tell me to *go on home, boy, before you get into trouble.*

Trying not to look overwhelmed by it all, I bought my ticket, climbed up to the balcony, and looked around. The chandeliers had been polished, their facets glowed: when I looked up at them a desire, like lust, gripped my bowels. The voices of the audience had become hushed and eager, their eyes gleamed at me through the gradually increasing darkness. A braided coil of rope drew the blue stage drapes together: two trembling velvet stalks of blue pulled by a finger of gold. The last thing I saw before darkness surrounded us was a young priest in one of the loges; he looked very much like what I was later to recognize as a Bronzino—his hair in a modified tonsure, his eyes like two black-birds. He leaned forward and rested his hands on the balustrade; his delight was so obvious, so *permissible.*

Like some sort of palimpsest, I saw another image superimposed upon his dark form in the loge; that of a monk in a medieval monastery pouring water from a carved cup into a bowl of brass. There he sat, a study in chiaroscuro, the perfect whiteness of his occasional smile illuminating the darkened theater.

Throughout the performance this priestly portrait remained in my line of vision: when he laughed, I laughed, when he breathed, I breathed. And yet there were more wonders to come. The actors seemed to me absolute perfection—though in retrospect of course I recognize that many bits-of-business were aimed to amuse the provincial audience. But their sheer elegance, their daintiness, their seventeenth-century costumes as iridescent as birds, that needs no description. Every child has experienced this anarchic joy, every adult knows he has tried to forget it, contain it, lest it run riot . . . But for me that night there was no real world I wished ever to return to, and if Mephistopheles had wished to bargain with me that I was to sit entranced there for another twenty years and then render up my soul, I would have flung myself upon him in gratitude.

I walked all the way home to Junieh; perhaps nine miles it was, but I barely noticed the hour or the time: Alceste and I had banished ourselves to some lonely island.

The inevitable occurred; my absence had been noted. Buck, in a great hurry to catch me, had hurled himself into a truck which we used to carry turkeys to market. On the truck were the huge crates large enough for a dozen turkeys who were wont to crane their necks as if watching for the rifle which, later, Buck would use to blow off their heads for his customers (he preferred it to chopping or wringing).

Buck was a huge man by anyone's standards; he was so heavy
that he rolled from side to side as he walked, using the weight of
one side of his body to throw the other side forward. And I was
still an adolescent—barely a hundred pounds or so. So it was no
astonishing physical feat for him when he spied me on the highway—Alceste's final speech running through my brain like rain—
to seize me by the scruff of the neck and shove me into one of
the empty turkey crates. Then he locked the crate by winding the
wire through the padlock exactly as he would for the turkeys: he
was relying on my sense of humiliation to keep me impounded.

"What kind of varmint you think I caught me 'side of the
road?" he yelled out with bitter derision to Johnye as soon as the
truck stopped in the driveway. He set the crate down in the road.

Johnye, to her credit, was not amused; tears ran down her
cheeks at my condition. But it was clear that she thought the
punishment a just one as she knelt down in the dusty road to
speak to me where I sat, ostensibly impassive and incorrigible,
but actually so stunned by the turn of events that I found nothing
to say or do but sit in the turkey crate hugging my arms as if I
were cold. Yet it was a warm, soft, summer night.

"Whatever made you do it? What did Buck ever do to you that
you do him this way? Were they drinkin'?" she asked of Buck,
pressing her wet handkerchief to her mouth. I could just see in
the rim of moonlight that a leaf had fallen into her hair: the leaf
was soggy and afflicted with mold; the hair was dry, clean and
grey. For a second my heart split between pity and rage. But like
a captive animal concerned only with its own pain, I turned my
back on her. With a sob she made motions of unwinding the wire
around the hasp.

"Let him be," Buck ordered. "It'll teach him what jail's like,
that's for sure." He lifted the crate to the screened porch.

Johnye protested, but it was, after all, a warm night; stars like
steel in an onyx sky, not a cloud anywhere. We were well protected against night predators, I knew, since I had myself stopped
up every breach in the screened porch. So I was physically safe.
Before they left the porch Buck thoughtfully rolled down the
rattan blinds which would screen out the early morning sun. I
heard them ascend the steep stairway to what had once been an
attic storeroom, but was now their bedroom. For a while I heard
voices, then Buck saying loudly and firmly: "No use arguin' about
it till all hours of the night. We'll talk about it in the mornin'. He'll
be cooled off by then too, most like."

There had been no threats, my crime had been too "unspecified" to be labelled juvenile delinquency; but there was an atmosphere of anticipation, of threat: one serious infraction and they would not hesitate to put me away in the local detention—for my own good, of course.

Even now as I write this I am certain that I did not weep a single tear. My sense of humiliation was so intense that I can recall only the fury of a trapped animal: I would have gnawed off my leg to free myself from the crate. I did not have to do that . . . but it did take me several hours to get free. By a steady but irreversible pressure against the sides of the crate, I managed to crack the slats sufficiently until by bucking my shoulder against the wood with all my force I splintered the cage. Then I emerged: rather like an awkward baby chick.

I managed to get a ride with a truck driver heading South. I didn't even remember to ask him how far he was going, and perhaps that aroused his suspicions. He seemed an amiable enough person, driving (he said) to Mexico on business. He didn't ask questions, but I felt him observing me. I felt relieved to think that I was still wearing the clothes I had worn to the theater: I was too keyed up to think that I had no sort of luggage. . . .

The guards on the United States side were casual enough (perhaps they didn't care how many wetbacks were smuggled *back* to Mexico) but when we had driven about two hundred miles into the interior, I was placed under arrest. The trucker, as it turned out, was part of a dragnet designed to pick up young Americans dabbling in quickie marijuana deals while apparently touristing in Mexico. Although I had no marijuana on me, I was—first of all —an American, and I had no visible means of support. I had not yet even thought of a reason for having crossed the border. My only aim had been to escape from the Bucks forever.

I was immediately hustled into a detention cell where I was to soon learn that even a broken tie of respectability is better than none at all; that it was better to be an incorrigible runaway, convicted of ingratitude to his family, than a powerless suspect picked up in a foreign country—doing what? Pushing dope? Fleeing from a mass murder? Pimping? Rounding up wetbacks without visa papers to be smuggled to L.A., Chicago, and all points East? I discovered that I could be accused of any or all of these: far safer to be a recalcitrant minor, a fallen sinner. I sat in my cell, stunned by how quickly I had fallen from working-class honesty

into becoming a "dangerous criminal" who could be smashed in
a Mexican jail as calmly as a bug crushed up in a book. For the
first time in my life I felt truly grateful to the Bucks: they were
afflicted by a sense of sin so pervasive that it was, to my mind,
deforming and grotesque, but they would not mindlessly kill
anyone. They had been trying to save me from certain punishment after death. My Mexican jailers, however, would have been
happy to snuff out my life. They had decided I was part of "a
criminal element," a "degenerate" and their system of justice was
expeditious: it meant I could be kicked in the kidneys for an
awkward joke, or even a mistaken use of the language. I was
instantly classified by my particular jailers as a sort of vermin,
living at the expense of the Body-social, and therefore it would
have been no sin on their part to exterminate me. They did not
need a legal trial to decide this, nor was there anything of religious prejudice in this—my jailers, in their innocence, were incapable of asking themselves whether the Pope would have
approved of contempt and hatred. So I was forced to choose
between an arbitrary and overzealous Authority, which at least
believed I was personally worth saving, body and soul, and the
mindless brutality which permitted the excesses to which I was an
unwilling witness and (occasionally) victim. For days I sat in my
cell and listened to the screams and curses of middle class teen-
aged Americans who had been out on a joy-ride, discovering for
the first time in their lives that all the last minute rescues of
American citizens *(per se)* which they had seen on television were
a means of selling breakfast cereal, not liberty or freedom. There
were even some who cried out that the American government was
encouraging this brutality in order to stop student trafficking in
marijuana.

At any rate it did not take me many weeks to opt for Parental
Authority. I truly "repented" in a manner which would have
thrilled the Bucks' evangelical hearts. And, at last, after I had
surrendered the Bucks' name and address to the authorities, I
began to count the days till they would come and I could be
released into their custody. Never had I felt so truly their son, and
I vowed I would mend my ways and try to understand a moral
rigor which made crimes of social differences in taste. Meanwhile,
a fellow-inmate had handed two books over to me with a great
sigh of boredom (one was in Spanish and the other was in
French) donated to him by a village priest. The books were *The*

Curé of Ars, and *The Confessions of St. Augustine* (likely subjects for the son of Buck and Johnye!). Unlike Montesquieu, I could not forget all my chagrins in a quarter of an hour, but I found the naughty life of St. Augustine before his conversion a matter of personal interest. The fact that he could so graciously repent and feel forgiven, start afresh without hallucinations of Hell and per- petual damnation, seemed a very cosy thing: a sinecure which a youth such as I, lately grown in wisdom, ought to be getting into. . . . I set the idea aside for a moment and glanced out the window through which I could clearly see the Mexican sky: clouds like pearls in a ring of sky. Even the shadow of the bars which cut across my vision could not mar the spectacle. Then I saw, from what I realize now must have been a great distance, the wings of a hawk or perhaps an eagle swooping southward toward the mountain range, and by a strange distortion of time I could suddenly see myself in the bathroom at home in Junieh. . . .

I had just finished bathing in one of those clawfoot, porcelain tubs which the Bucks, like just about everybody in Junieh, still had in their bathroom. (No showers yet, either.) I was in a hurry to dress, as it was a chill October night and the room was un- heated. Quickly, I jumped from the tub and, because the floor was cold, I stood on the toilet seat, drying myself. At that height, almost for the first time, I think, I saw myself naked. It was a strange sight: it was almost as if suddenly there was someone else in the room with me. I discovered that I had a lithe, lean, muscu- lar body; beneath the skin, like antique horns, lay two breathing instruments whose ribs I could see when I exhaled. In addition, when I leaned over I could create perpendicular lines which reached around my side like a pleated stage costume, moving wherever I moved. I was extraordinarily pleased with my dis- covery: I felt anyone would have been pleased to see me, and I posed shamelessly before the mirror—as a discus thrower, a de- cathlon runner, a swimmer, as The Thinker. While I was enjoying myself in this way, through the transom above me, as though arriving on invisible wings, came an announcement from the Audubon Association: ". . . let us speak out and tell the truth about eagles . . . Eagles *belong*. . ." followed by an explanation of the contribution of eagles to the ecology. But what impressed me for some reason was their conclusion: "Your National Audubon Association is *dedicated to the preservation of birds of prey.* . . ."

And I thought, as I fanned the sky of the bathroom with my

arms, how marvelous it was that they wanted to preserve birds of prey, that they were spending time and money to let the world know that some creatures, however predatory they might seem to the ignorant, were splendid in nature and contributed some mystic wealth to the world. With a sudden sense of freedom and gratitude (to God?) that I was not twisted and deformed, not a hydrocephalic nor blind nor halt, but this free-flying animal with wings of skin, I felt a great wave of joy. Indeed, I think what I experienced was a kind of transmigration of soul: the story of the eagle and the hawk was mine, I must be preserved. Like that of eagles and hawks and other birds of prey, the human form (including mine) was sublime (I decided) and those detractors who feared it as the repository of sin and reproduction had fallen victim to mankind's most vicious lie against himself.

And now as I stood in the Mexican jail there again passed overhead, like the words of that radio announcement rendered into a vision, a gliding hawk or eagle—I really could not tell which from my cell, and again I felt that sense of fitness—of the irrevocable order in the universe of which I, too, was a part and must be saved. Mainly, it was a naive belief that All This Beauty could not have been conceived by a mad Creator merely to divert himself by watching it destroyed: eagles, whales, humans, gods, all.

While I stood there transfixed by the spectacle of dark wings winnowing shadow from light, like some Aztec God in the sky, I heard footsteps and voices outside my cell door: Buck and Johnye had come to take me home.

They did not speak at first. But when the guards had left us alone, Buck raised his fist and knocked me to the ground: "Damned fool!" he said, his voice breaking. Then he picked me up, brushed my hair back with a fierce but somehow caressing gesture and took me out to the car. He shoved me into the rear seat exactly as he had locked me into the turkey crate: he had, I suddenly realized, learned nothing by my experience except that what he had suspected all along was true—that I was a body corrupted in a spirit corruptible. . . .

Perhaps it was a subconscious desire to repudiate them at their deepest religious level that inspired me to become a seminarian at nearby St. Luke's. Or perhaps it was my recollection of the priest who had seemed to be enjoying all the good things of this world while looking forward to the rewards of the next one as well. Whatever my "reasons," it was clear to Father Molinari that I was not meant to be a seminarian; and since the super powers were testing their nuclear weapons, busily preparing for their great confrontation, it was not difficult for me to give it up: it seemed to me that in any event our most venerable institutions were soon to become casualties of war.

Michele

The following day, Carillo entered my tent. It was as if he had been waiting for precisely that moment when I had succeeded in giving myself to Pinosh (or the latter had succeeded in taking me: but what do such verbs of possession mean anymore?). It was as if, even if seismic tremors had wrenched the world apart, he reserved for himself this rule: that he touched no woman belonging to a comrade, that such inroads, overlapping of ownership, etc., were divisive, counterrevolutionary, were (one smiled) the weapons of the CIA. Although the ultimate struggle for power is now over, and his rifle is now useless except to shoot an occasional snake or rabbit, he leans on his old values as upon a "sheperde's crooke," quaint and nostalgic as the print in an antique almanac: "Shearing the Lambs on Allhallow Eve."

And he stood there, not respectfully, but merely silent, not-yet-having-decided-to-speak, and as though wishing he had for me some direct command from Che Guevara or José Marti or Emiliano Zapata which would restore a proper perspective to the absurdity of this, our world. I wanted to weep. My eyes rested on his broad fingers which had now begun plucking at my blanket.

"Army issue," he observed dryly. "Serviceable, long-lasting. In an emergency, excellent for snuffing out fires." It was as if he were reading from a service manual.

"Carillo," I said. I noticed how I rolled the "r" on my tongue, with a delicious sense of prohibited caress. I suddenly felt I could never win this man's respect except by dying bravely. Sexuality on my part would not repel him, it would mean merely that I had deceived him: that instead of loyalty, fearlessness, blood-oaths, I offered him instead a spasm of pleasure like a jellied dessert: glittering a moment, warm in one's mouth, then liquid nullity.

At the trill of his name which came from me involuntarily like a bird call, he scowled. Not displeased, but as if annoyed at something within himself, he continued to smooth out an invisible wrinkle in the army blanket which lay across my cot. "I've come to thank you," he said, "for voting for me. You must realize, I wanted to stay. At the moment there are few alternatives. If the vote had gone against me . . ."

"Carillo, this is not a cadre. The vote was unanimous. Why should we have voted for the death or injury of one more person? There will soon be enough death for everybody—"

"One more person is one more to struggle for the available resources. In simple arithmetic: before there were seven, now there are eight to feed."

I spoke as lightly as I could. "Of course—Malthus was right. There was a time when we could have stopped growing people and started growing soybeans . . ." I shrugged: it was altogether too obvious. "But we've stopped counting people now. Even by your own terms you're a valuable asset."

"What do you know about my terms?" Stern. Defensive. As if there were still secrets he had to hide from "us."

"You operate in a moral system—or did—where some lives were worth more than others. I can't accept that . . ." Yet even as I said it, I felt I was lying. At the moment I would have traded off Jennifer, Malcolm, Andrea and Klara for him. I was glad he was there; it would, I thought, make it all at least . . . interesting. I would even throw Pinosh into the scale! I added to myself wildly, as I waited apprehensively for him to answer me; and I began to worry about whether I had been so stupid as to go mad when Mark left me only to fall in love with this—child.

"At any rate, you've nothing to thank me for. Everybody wanted you in. You'll be useful to us. . . . Isn't that the ultimate value?" I knew it wasn't, but I didn't want him to leave. I wanted the conversation to continue . . . I wanted, I realized, to wipe out what had taken place between Pinosh and me by imprinting upon my memory what I was convinced would be a blindingly brilliant experience: I had become an epicure of caresses . . .

He looked offended. "I weigh life for life, like everybody else. Hierarchy was not our style, whatever propaganda you may have read about us. Or perhaps I should say: whatever you read about us, it had to be propaganda, therefore lies. You could not have known the truth unless you had lived with us . . ." For a moment

I thought his voice would break, but he stood up, busied his hands with something in his shirtpocket. "Will you come to breakfast with me?" he asked, as if in a conciliatory manner.

"Honored, I'm sure." Again, that stupid self-mockery. I was not honored, I was afraid: afraid of doing something that would reveal to him my need of his approval. But at the recollection of Pinosh's counting off on his fingers, I crumbled inwardly.

As if to avoid any such revelations on my part, he said bluntly: "There's no time left for party invitations and R.S.V.P.'s. Would *you* like to join *us*?" The change of pronoun seemed in itself a laying out of lines: I felt like a branded heifer.

As the morning was cool, I began hunting through my suitcase to find a cardigan. Carillo watched me as I turned toward the small mirror affixed to the tent-pole; I patted down my hair (as if I were going to a picnic, I thought). I tried to find a handkerchief, but I was not yet sufficiently organized in my tent to lay hands on one quickly. For some reason (decades of responsibility to cleanliness and hygiene—what lady could blow her nose into a locust leaf?), the inability to place my hands on what would once have been a commonplace item unnerved me: were we to degenerate into filth and snottery? I began flipping through the neat pile of sweaters, slacks, blouses, as through a deck of playing cards *(for god's sake, I had brought an umbrella!)*: no handkerchiefs.

"Jesus, what are you looking for?" He sounded impatient, and when I explained, he looked at me with a sort of amazement.

"You're not going to believe this, but it's sheer agony to me to go to breakfast without a handkerchief." Then I doubled over, laughing till tears ran down my face.

He stood there in a kind of a shock for a moment, as if according to his service manual, at this point the comrade should be restored to reality by a hard blow to the head. But in silence he offered me his handkerchief: a piece of red flannel, neatly cut into a size approximately 10 X 12.

Carillo

He handed her his piece of flannel rag, which was still clean enough to use for a handkerchief, although he had already used it this morning to dust his binoculars (perhaps they, too, would turn out to be useless, but he had been unwilling to discard them). He experienced a pyrrhic sense of pleasure in shocking her: did the overprotected middle-class esthete think that in the jungle and sprawling hideouts of the cities one carried boxes of Kleenex and rolls of White Cloud? Still, he was relieved that her face revealed no physical distaste for the rag, only a kind of surprise. She made a show of using it, and the tip of her nose seemed suddenly to shine with a faintly ludicrous but very natural energy. He smiled.

"Don't laugh at me, please. I can't help my upbringing. I like hot tea in beautiful cups too. You should try to understand . . ."

"It's hard. . . ." he admitted. "We never had the time and energy to understand you. What we want . . . we wanted . . . was to eliminate you—people like you, that is."

"Me? Like me?" She looked hurt; he resisted the impulse to take her hand as if she were a child.

"As a class." He tried not to sound either overpatient or irascible; yet it was hard to believe: this woman, who had attended school most of her life, understood nothing of class conflict. She feels, he thought, that because she was sympathetic to the poor and gave to United Fund that she should be "forgiven," "understood." Like the Germans who requested a "deNazification trial": *they* never collaborated with the enemy—not *really*.

"Well, *try*," she said with artificial brightness. She spoke like a child that had decided to be clever and winsome because that was the best way to keep the adults from destroying you. In the past he might have said, with an effort at patience, "This is a *meeting*, not a beauty contest." But now her desire to please (or appease) him merely made him feel sad. She lit up another cigarette.

"I thought that Duncan . . ." He shrugged. Her supply would run out soon enough, he guessed. Enforced austerity. Not his business anyway to care whether she smoked: she was not likely to have time to die of lung cancer.

"Well, I'm not really a chain smoker. I mean, I don't smoke more than . . ." She stopped, perceiving that she had angered him again. He told himself that he must be more patient with these people, it was not their fault. Yet he sternly believed that it *was* 'their' fault; that by their self-deceptions, their rhetorical distinctions between being and doing, between "passive" evil and "active" evil (like owning stock in Dow Chemical was not the same "evil" as shooting a Browning automatic), that they had brought the world to this pass: capitalism considered as though it were the bubonic plague and they were still in the Middle Ages and the whole thing, against which they were totally helpless, was in the hands of God. Yet their God had been a truth-sayer: "yea or nay, all else is evil."

He managed to say, in spite of his annoyance. "Well, it's not important. We should go to breakfast, I think."

"Yes, yes." She had at last found the sweater in her packing case. As she moved about he noticed that she was carelessly dropping ashes. Strewn about were magazines, all with subscription labels: *Atlantic Monthly, Harper's, Fortune, Holiday.* It was as if they never expected their subscriptions to Pleasure Inc. to be interrupted. He had known a man in Texas who subscribed to twenty different magazines, the cost of which would have fed an entire family for a year in India. It had been the guy's perpetual lament (or the boast of conspicuous consumption?) that he never had time to read them: too busy taking pictures for skin magazines, going to ski resorts in Colorado, flying to Amsterdam, Prague, Lisbon, The World.

As if the word 'Texas' had reverberated across the tent, she asked:

"Fantastic coincidence, don't you think?—you and Duncan coming from Texas. I mean, if you *were* going to drop into just any old survival colony in the country, wasn't it pretty nice of Fate to arrange it so that the place was owned and operated by someone virtually from your home town?"

He smiled: he and Duncan, had, in fact, been born hundreds of miles apart. Himself near El Paso and Duncan somewhere else near the Mexican border, Duncan had never said exactly where.

As she smoked, she held an elbow in the palm of her other hand—a posture which he had always disliked: it was almost a mandarin pose of leisure-class conversation (what to do with one's *hands?*).

"And did you get a chance to live on a ranch? Like Duncan, I mean. I don't mean to suggest that everybody in Texas lives on ranches. I don't mean to fall into that stereotype—I know you were already suffering from *urban sprawl*—" She laughed, sensing perhaps that her very denial revealed her cultural ignorance. It was rather like those women who, when they invited him to eat at their homes, would ask, when he said he was half-Jewish (he wasn't at all sure this was true, but he liked to say so), if he ate pork. Others, more curious, would want to know if he were circumcised.

"I'm afraid Duncan and I have nothing in common. Duncan was *adopted.*" A distinction, he knew, which was meaningless to everyone but him.

Carillo's first memory . . . Swaying birds, with black wings; in the center of their boiled-onion faces a starched whiteness, lenses of unframed cut glass, blue eyes, and a cleanliness which he already knew contrasted with the stench of his crib, even as the light of God contrasted with the pitch of hell.

He had to learn to control it, the nuns would send him straight to hell if he didn't. That much was already clear. All the nuns were his blessed Mother. His father . . . only His Father Who Art in Heaven could be his true father, so he was not to think that he had been born of any dirtiness. Indeed they assured him, though his body was filthy, his soul was clean. His soul belonged only to God, but his body belonged—for the moment, at least— to them; and so they collected what came out of his body into a little brown clay pot with birds painted on it in blue and orange, and rewarded him with a blessing and he became clean. Only, he held his Thing, which was forbidden. He complained that his pee itched and burned. Indeed, it made him feverish at night and, until he was five, he dreamed almost nightly that he was lying in a hot bath into which Sister Sophía had poured an entire box of epsom salts, which was slowly corroding him. He would feel how the salt burned through his Small Hole. (They didn't know that he knew that he'd examined every opening in his body with a rude and inquisitive finger: sniffing himself afterwards, he'd decided he smelled rather like Otto the dog.)

Finally, they had realized that he had some sort of kidney ailment and they argued among themselves as to whether he could best be cured by (1) water purgation, at least a gallon a day or (2) complete abstention from fluids or (3) prayer. Luckily for him, the consensus was Prayer, and the infection cured itself. Perhaps it was the coconut milk, he afterwards thought. He had discovered in himself a passion for coconut milk, and would manage to control or relieve himself for the reward of a piece of white coconut or a sip of the broth which streamed forth from the tri-form orifice of the coconut as from the mouth of some underwater god foaming up the lip of the sea. Because for a while he ate virtually nothing but coconut and bananas, the Sisters of Mercy called him Monkey. *"Mono pequeño,"* they would say. "Take all the shoes for us to the Plaza. Give them to Señor Díaz to clean for us. Can we do *every*thing ourselves?" So, he had been carrying their shoes to Señor Díaz in a large coarse laundry bag when one day he noticed a Mexican boy no bigger than himself carrying a small shoebox and a couple of brushes: he was earning money shining the shoes of a handsome dude wearing a suit as smooth as a horse's behind (it was called a sharkskin suit, but he didn't know that at the time). So Carillo had started making money cleaning the nuns' shoes (he had split the profits with the Mexican kid for the use of his box). It was the first and last time he was to be a capitalist.

According to the Sisters, from among the twenty kids at the orphanage he had been in the "worst shape." This was because he had had neither mother nor father (nor crocodile) to call by name. (Sister Sophía was full of odd sayings. She made them up herself, he thought, and pretended they were ancient apothegms; a kind of frustrated literary urge, perhaps.) The reason for his extremely low status ("worst shape") was that he had not arrived on the doorstep of the Sisters in romantic 19th-century style, complete with lace booties and linen swaddling bands. Rather he had been discovered naked in the garbage can, with the afterbirth like saliva or the drool of a hydrophobic dog soaking through the newspapers in which he was wrapped. He had been conspicuously placed on *top* of the garbage can, to be sure, so that if he were lucky and God was on his side, someone would hear him cry. And if he had failed to cry? He wondered even now how he had had the good sense to cry out, he barely an hour or two old, according to the doctor who came to feed him with eye dropper, like a bird.

Soon, Mono learned to seize the bottle himself and could suck up six ounces with scarcely a breather, like some old drunk taking his first drink in the morning. Then, according to Sophía, he would cry with gas pains for hours. The Sisters thought it developed a manchild's lungs to cry, so they let him cry. Besides, he was the youngest infant they'd ever had at the orphanage, so what did they know? Sophía opened her empty hands in reply to her own question.

So, because God Himself had been a Jew (or so at least, Sister Sophía had confided to him) and because he had liked the looks of Him as he sank, with his strong face and agonized body, on their Cross in the chapel, Carillo had decided he would be half-Jewish on his father's side (ignorant of the matrilinear line in Jewish law, he thought he had opted for the one with the power, so that when he prayed he might have a conviction that His Father would fight for his cause). Later, though he understood this to be mere fantasy, he never quite relinquished it as a viable hypothesis and went through his adolescence asserting that he was half-Jewish ("and the other half nigger, I reckon" would come the challenge).

In fact, no one ever knew who or what he was. The only clue was the newspapers in which he had been wrapped, which Sophía had thoughtfully cleaned and saved for him and which he, Carillo, had saved until they fell apart in his hands.

The newspapers had been filled with stories about a madman named Hitler who was murdering off the Jews, and later, Carillo created a myth in which he explained to himself that it was for this reason that his mother ("Mary Doe") had abandoned him: she was somehow saving him from Hitler. After this, Carillo had always had a special sympathy for the "blood" tie he himself had created, and therefore believed in; and once he had let a political prisoner escape because of his, Carillo's, ignorance of his "own" symbols. He had thought the prisoner was wearing the Star of David. Only later had he understood the guy had been wearing a Satanist's pentacle. The consequences could have been too grim to be laughable. After that, on guard against his own sentimentality, and feeling that he had exposed his cadre to danger merely by his personal weakness, whenever it was his turn to interrogate prisoners, he would carefully snip from their necks their last link of defense: the stars, crosses, crescents of their religions, their military dog tags and their hearts-of-silver on which had been engraved in italic: *I will wait for you forever.* Once, when he had been obliged to share in the execution of a prisoner, he had personally wrapped the i.d. tags in leaves and by a system of relays had contrived to leave them at a news station in the prisoner's home town. . . .

He sat up on the blanket which Jennifer, in her passion, had thrown down from his bed to the floor of his tent. He felt such sadness, he was not certain his chest would not collapse; it was like an illness. Not fatigue, not satiety, but an unbearable burden of knowledge. What did she want from him? He had tried to fathom it, and the deeper he went into it the sadder he became, till he thought he realized that what she wanted was an identity, however shadowy or brief. She had not lived long enough to achieve one: not yet wife or mother or mistress to anyone, she wanted a title, a rank in the colony, if only that of Carillo's Woman. It was something, after all, like being the *mama* in a Puerto Rican gang. It was an odd use of his sexuality; he wondered if she had truly wrung as much pleasure from it as she appeared to, or if it were only one more role she clung to—a form of ownership, an attempt to assert by feigned delirium that *she* was the one for him.

But he was not so vain as to believe that it was his hand alone on her naked body which gave her the crises she crooned for. He imagined that it was merely the only form of communication They had taught her in her fourteen all-too-brief years. And now she would never learn any other form of communication, she had run out of time.

As if he were telling her a fairy tale, he would try to explain: "Have you ever heard of Marx? Engels? Trotsky? Che Guevara?" Her eyes would at once glue over with boredom and insult; she only wanted him to want her, and the moment he ceased groaning with what she believed was perfect pleasure (he could feel himself torn apart by the pity and insanity of it all), she felt she was "losing" him. To what? he wondered. His attempts to instruct her had created fits of petulancy, her cravings were utterly alien from his own. For hours, she would describe how in her room, in her *own* room, she had had at least thirty stuffed animals, and black-glow posters which did "fantastic" things to your mind while you lay in the dark watching them, how she had had over a hundred rock and roll records (did he dig The Joppers, The Screams, the Ultra-Violet Electric Guitar?, and she frowned with irritation when he repeatedly confused all groups with the only group he could recall by name, the Beatles).

"Besides, who cares about that fuck-up Marx anyway?" she would demand. And she would suddenly become furious with him for wasting his time with her, discussing an ideology which had *obviously* been all wrong (where was his dictatorship of the proletariat, whatever that meant anyway, she jeered: what the hell had Marx known about a cobalt bomb?). Then she would try to wrench memories from him, like scorpions from under a rock; she insisted he *must* remember some of the things she remembered, he wasn't as old as that fruitcake, Duncan, or those two anti-people, the Delaneys. He was young, young, young: like her. *What did he remember?* became for her a favorite game, a sustained effort to bring them together into a common past. Its failure would end in her exasperation, till at last she would begin to kiss and bite his lip till it bled. If she could not succeed in making them of the same generation she would at least, she seemed to be saying, make him drunk with her flesh, so that together they could forget the whole goddam world, the planet.

Then suddenly, she would accuse him of being hardly human, hadn't he done *any*thing but tote his gun around like some Texas cowboy? "Teach me to shoot your rifle," she demanded unexpectedly, and heavy with relief at being able to do something practical, at being able to teach her *something,* he dutifully arose and got his rifle and began instructing her first of all on how to carry it safely. . . .

"Oh Jesus!" she exclaimed. "Not *now.* I didn't mean this very minute!" And she began to sob like a middle-aged woman whose life has been a total misunderstanding.

And yet she had a beautiful young body, especially when compared to the hunched, broken bodies of the sugar cane workers, to the wrinkled faces of the wielders-of-the-short-blade, cutting tomatoes in the San Fernando Valley. A healthy body, with short legs making a small childish V, as the thighs joined to the plump knees: rather like his sister Estelle.

Of course, Estelle was not really his sister. How can a man claim to have sisters when he knows nothing about himself? But Estelle was the 'sister' he remembered most clearly because it was she who had explained it all to him: how he had really no sisters, now that the Sisters of Mercy had been absorbed by the Sisters of Assumption, but he'd have *her* parents for foster-parents.

He had been altogether delighted, imagining that this was a kind of adoption. Adoption had been at the very heart of the system of the Sisters of Mercy, and every kid in the place knew that adoption was based on charm, cleanliness and the ability to seem loving. Carillo had never, he had understood from the first, possessed any of these qualities; and on visiting days, when social workers from adoption centers would arrive, or on days when a man would come to deliver fruit or the Sunday paper, all the orphans were instructed to be "good" and to be sure to go up to the stranger and kiss him and give him a long, long hug and call him *Daddy*. The instructions were so conscientiously followed in the hope of finding some permanent *Daddy* that visitors found themselves cornered by a buzzing little swarm of kids, till at last the visitors, without even a show of politeness, would reassert their freedom by scuttling out the back door. But Carillo, knowing that he was charm-less, knowing moreover that at night he must bear the shame and burning of his Thing, would merely stand under the lintel while the other children cried as lovingly as they could, *Daddy! Daddy!* He would wonder what *adoption* was like the way the poor wondered about Mediterranean villas: who lived there? how did one buy one? *Adoption* was the talismanic word, proof that someone had decided to love you and put it down in writing: a contract. Anything less was a waterway of good intentions, promises and perfidies in which you could only drown but never escape. . . . So, one after another, Carillo watched as the youngest, sweetest, cleverest and (often) the most cunning little liars cuddled up to their new owners, quivering like puppies in their eagerness for the ultimate word of love. Years later, whenever he saw a story for the Animal Rescue League or the Humane Society, with a picture of some blissful beagle being hugged by an adoring child with a caption reading "Barney finds a home" or "Irresistible puppy makes a new friend," he wondered about the dogs who didn't make it, the mongrels whose parentage was too obscure, or whose kidneys too weak, so they were sent off to the crematoria or to have their hearts experimented on, so doctors could save lives.

Thus when Estelle had said that the Vacas were to be his foster-parents and that he would live with all of them, her eleven brothers and sisters, he thought he had become lucky at last (it was true that for more than a year now his Thing had been better and he waked up in the night to do his Duty, which made him infinitely more acceptable to everyone: he understood that: his market value was higher because he had at last become housebroken).

He had not really grasped at first that the Vacas were living at subsistence level themselves and that only two of the "family" were birthright Vacas: Estelle and her brother Victor. The rest of the children were the Vacas' sole means of support, a group of little *bandidos* as Feliciana Vaca called them, who ate too much, grew too fast, wore too many clothes, and all of whom she would send to the Devil, except that she loved them (she said) like her own flesh and blood.

Feliciana loved like a saint, but she could count like a broker. She could calculate how much bread fourteen people would eat by looking at their bellies. She never took in a fat child, she said, because either he would eat too much to stay that way or he would begin to lose weight and the County would say she was starving him. She was not really miserly but merely cautious: bankruptcy sniffed everlastingly at her door. Indeed, Carillo considered in retrospect that they must have all eaten like scavenger birds: they ate till there was not a potato left, after which they would all sit around and drink Koolaid by the gallon. The amazing thing was that they did not quarrel about food, because of Feliciana's singular talent: Estelle said she could divide a pinto bean into four equal parts.

Shoes and blankets were another matter. For these, the children fought like tigers. Shoes were as precious as a land-grant or an immigrant's visa; with shoes you could perhaps get to school every day and get free milk and (sometimes) a lunch; you could get to Church and be saved; you could go to baptisms or even wakes and be invited to a piece of cake (no *bandido* of Feliciana's would have known that the cake was slightly stale). Only once had he seen all Feliciana's *bandidos* arrayed in (borrowed) shoes: when they had lined up for a photograph for the County—a blurred photograph which nevertheless he had stolen and still kept in his possession, referring to them all afterwards as his First Family. For when Feliciana died suddenly, his "family" was broken up, their diaspora began. He and Estelle were separated, it was the only unforgivable thing that had ever happened to him, he sometimes felt. Because he had truly believed that Estelle was his sister: how could the County take his sister away and give her to the first dumb brute (the man who took her for a few months had decided to marry her) so she would have a place to live and something to eat? She was only fourteen and he was not yet ten: it was an agony of misplaced history. *Wait for me, Estelle, wait wait wait.* But of course the County knew that Estelle needed to eat, she did not need a brother. Later, when he had begun to hear stories of children fucking for chocolate bars and Chinese girls (before the revolution) dead in the brothels before they had begun to menstruate, he understood that Estelle had made a good bargain: she needed to fuck only one man per day, not twenty or fifty, she was well-fed and clothed and beaten only occasionally.

Staring at Jennifer's face streaked with tears while she sucked the edge of the pillow like a baby its *biberón,* he said suddenly, harshly: "You're old enough to be married, really."

She kicked her feet violently, not turning to look at him, thinking perhaps he was making fun of her.

"Yes, you are," he insisted. "You're old enough to have kids, and to be fucked by every man in the colony if he wants . . . Who would stop them?" he asked vaguely, rhetorically. He thought of the women who had been his comrades, some of whom had wanted to marry him, to whom he had patiently explained: A revolutionary must be like a priest, free of ties that the Enemy could use against him. Suppose I had to choose between letting my comrades die and seeing my children exploded by a bomb? So he had never married. Now he said, partly to see how she would take the idea, "You should be married."

She sat up, looking at him with suspicion. "You're crazy," she said. "What would be the point?"

He shrugged. "Just like I said. It'd protect you—maybe."

"OOooooh," she said as if mortally wounded. "You don't *like* me at all!"

"But I do. I do." He soothed her, wiped her tears. "Let's get out of this tent. I'm going to show you how to shoot this thing, so that if anybody attacks you. . . ."

Tears ran down her cheeks (he had no handkerchief, he realized suddenly: nor did she), and she shook her head morosely: "I'd never *use* it."

"You have to use it. If they're coming at you, you goddamn well *got* to use it." Then at his look of rage, she turned her back to him, he touched her apologetically, sighing: "Didn't They teach you *anything?*"

She sat up then, cupped her hands like a golden-haired doll baby in a Woolworth Christmas sale. "No," she said, puckering her lips. "Not one thing."

Following the dispersion of the Vacas, he lost track of the numbers of applicants who came, who looked him over, who tried him on, who rented him for a week, a month, a year, and paid themselves off in the rebates he earned for them in the field or milking cows or even (the most pleasant) picking beans, berries and squash and selling them at highway stands (every box of beans, berries or squash sealed and accounted for). Years later he had tried to calculate how his childhood had been spent, how many "families" had pawned him and (occasionally) redeemed him until finally he could add up enough years to be called "of age"—and he had had great difficulty recalling the names of the "families." Then, suddenly, he was too old to be kept in the County Home: no one had adopted him, even though he'd been offered to the world in Open Court. So, since he was "of age," the administrators, with no evil intent but merely to safeguard the younger children from ambiguous influences, sent him off to the County Reformatory: there were no other facilities for una-dopted teen-agers. It was there, at the Reformatory, after he had been thrown into solitary confinement (known to the trade as "the hole") for fighting with the big bruisers who stole shoes and blankets from weaker inmates, that to give himself some sense of reality in the spaceless dark, he had finally wrenched loose from his memory the names of the "families" with whom he had spent, say, at least six months. As a further discipline, he had arranged them alphabetically (it was at this time he had decided permanently on his own last name) and had come up with Benson (or Benssen, he was not sure of the spelling), Carpenter, Chelekian, Delano, Vaca, Villareal and Woodruff. As an added inspiration, and to further the shaping of reality in the darkness, he played at silent Anagrams with the letters of these names—cheating a little with the Ben*ssens* or *sons,* as he needed them.

He could not bring himself to include the Buells, though they belonged in the list. The Buells came into his life just before he was finally sent to join thieves, runaways, incorrigibles, and drug peddlers for his crimes of having been charm-less and not-getting-adopted.

He had been farmed out to the Buells for what was supposed to be a more or less permanent period (until he became "of age"). The Buells lived in Piñata City, so-called because the town had been started as a birthday gift by a man who believed he had sprung a "gusher" in oil, only to have the well go dry in a few weeks; so the piñata, rightly enough, was empty. Nevertheless, Garvin Buell, his wife, and her thirteen-year-old daughter by a former liaison were left behind while the town quickly evaporated. How Buell earned a living, Carillo never learned; perhaps for a while Buell won more than he lost at the weekly poker games in the kitchen. Certainly the "dairy" farm with its half-dozen lean cows was not supporting itself.

During these poker sessions, Buell's stepdaughter Carrie and her mother, Eula, and Carillo stayed out of the kitchen for fear of incurring the wrath or ridicule of the other farmhands who came from miles away to drink Buell's homemade liquor and "have a ball." "We're gonna have us a real ball," Buell would inform them, "so stay out of our way." Carillo sensed that the two women were relieved to be let off so lightly. Since Carillo slept on the sofa downstairs and was the last to go to bed at night (as well as the first to rise in the morning), on these nights he would sit upstairs in the only bedroom playing checkers with Carrie while they waited out the party below. Before Eula had finally left the farm, she would pretend to occupy herself with a bit of sewing in the corner while they played; but by the time he and Carrie were witnesses to the Big Buell Bet, as he afterwards called it, Eula had already disappeared from the farm. . . .

On the night of the Big Buell Bet, he and Carrie were playing checkers as usual. Carrie was already a woman grown, bigger than Carillo, whose ribs still showed like multiple lashes across his sides: he was barely tall enough to kiss her, even if he had thought of it. But he was not yet suffering from that longing which he thought of as a kind of generalized loneliness, a twilight area between flashes of lightning and seizures of darkness in which he dreamed of faceless girls kissing him or of himself, grown to manhood, touching their breasts. More frequently, he simply dreamed of Estelle: he was not old enough to substitute one emotion for another. He grieved for Estelle in a manner too deep for him to understand, it was a physical loss, a perpetual absence-of-love, the way he felt when he saw strangers embracing their children and would realize that never, never, had anyone touched him in that way, except perhaps Estelle, when in the coldest nights of winter she would let him curl up beside her to keep warm. . . .

So, when Carrie had introduced herself to Carillo the first day on the farm and had begun cursing her stepfather, Carillo had at first thought that perhaps she was reaching around to Love or Sex by starting out with Hate, as he'd seen so many folks do (they'd begin scolding and beating a foster child, then end up seducing her). He had even thought that perhaps it was a kind of perverted jealousy: of her mother, perhaps. But he soon understood that the hatred was real, and that what she was telling him was no fantasy but truth as bitter as bile.

It had all started in the barn. Buell, who had been milking a cow, yanking its udders with the ferocity of a man dying of thirst, had suddenly turned to her and begun, not playfully but with terrible intensity, pulling at her breasts. She had fought wildly, but her struggles had only excited him the more, and for fear he would kill her, she had ended up by pretending she had wanted it all along. She wished now that she had pulled out a knife and killed him, she said, looking at Carillo as if she hoped he might offer to do it for her. But by this time, Carillo had learned that violence could only be overcome by silent endurance, at least until he was grown. At that time, although he appeared nearly as tall as Carrie, he was a scrawny seventy-five pounds . . . In silence, he had turned his gaze away, feeling he had failed her.

She had folded up the checkerboard. "It's time we went to bed," she had announced irritably. The laughing downstairs became louder. "You pig," she said suddenly to the floor. Then crouching down as if she hoped they would hear her through the thin ceiling below, she repeated like some crazy rosary, "Pig, pig, pig, pig." Then she threw herself on the bed, not sobbing or crying nor moving but staring at a crack in the plaster as though it were a kind of map or a canyon which she could, by an act of will, leap into.

Soon after that night, Eula Buell had simply gone—disappeared as completely as if the fourteen years between her involuntary infliction of life upon Carrie and the hungry, brutal years in between with Buell had never existed. Buell claimed she ran off with a nigger, but Carrie whispered to Carillo that her mother had found out what Buell had been doing in the barn at milking time all these months. Carrie had pleaded with her mother not to go, but Eula had packed her little bag, the one which, years ago, Buell had used for bowling, trying, with the tears running down her cheeks, to explain to Carrie: "He don't want me, honey, he wants you. A man like that, he gets tired of a woman, he gonna kill either the one or the other of us, y'know? An' it ain't gonna be you. I ain' fightin' for my own kid to be slept with. So you keep him tied up good, y'hear? Make him fight for it ever' time, that'll keep him hotted up like a buck stud. Then he'll never turn you out like he could me." Practical, cynical, teaching sexuality as a survival text.

And it had worked for Carrie, he understood that now. For a while she had had a warm blanket when he had none, she could lick the foam off Buell's beer glass every night, and if the bees left honey along the wooden walls of the barn, old man Buell would scrape it up, and laughing boisterously, would have her lick it off the scraper, every bit of it. It worked till, having lost more in rodeo bets and poker games in one bad night than he could have earned in a year, he was obliged to tap his heretofore untouchable savings account—only a couple of thousand but considered as sacred as seed corn: Buell had already seen one farm dry up during the '30's and he kept this sum for what he called his "Last Chance" stake. When he had driven into El Paso to withdraw his "Last Chance," Buell had discovered that the bitch, Eula, had forged his name and had run off with every cent in his account.

After that, there had been nothing either of them could do to appease Buell. What he wanted, he said, was cash, so he'd "get shut of the place and go down to Mexico where he'd get a couple of girls to work for him." Every day Buell accused them of driving him to bankruptcy—Carillo because he was too dumb to shovel cowpads out of the barn, and Carrie because she was nothing but a cunt like her mother: the two of them did nothing but eat.

They had grown inured to Buell's insults which, like clever beasts, they had learned to flick from their skins like flies: they feared not vituperation, but the whip. And they lived from day to day with the illusion that each performed a service which was somehow profitable to Buell and thus they could hope to escape destruction.

But Buell was cleverer than they, with a shrewd eye for his investments. One night when he had staked all he had in cash plus most of his cows, he had begun offering the services of his two "employees" upstairs, Carrie and Carillo. Buell had really hoped on that night, the night of the Big Buell Bet, to recoup the losses which the bitch's mother had inflicted on him; but he kept losing. The drinking increased with every loss, and the losses increased the drinking. By midnight, the four poker hands were no longer singing and smashing bottles; a terrifying silence had descended on them. Carrie folded up the checker board and signalled to Carillo to retire on the floor. She folded herself into a khaki blanket as into a grave. She wanted to melt into the darkness, Carillo could see. Her eyes blinked with terror.

It did not take long to happen. Buell came up the stairs, not roaring, not joyous, but rigid as a blade, one could smell the sweat on him. What seemed somehow ominous was that he had removed his boots and was padding across the cold floor to the bed; his woolen hunting socks, curiously red, cushioned the sound of his feet. Carillo, as he lay on his pallet on the floor, feigning sleep, was always to remember the sight of the naked toe thrusting forth from the sock, like a gun in a holster. "Okay, girlie. It's your turn," he addressed Carrie's form, curled up into the feigned bondage of sleep. Like a pillbug, Carillo thought, pretending to be a thing without attraction and of no more use than a curd of dirt or a stone. But Buell was not fooled. Besides, it would have meant nothing to him anyway if she had been asleep. He yanked her from the bed, holding her suspended in the air for a moment like a butterfly by a single wing. "Come on down. You can for once be of some use to me. Them bastards are gonna kill me if I don't bring you down. And damn if I'm gonna get my head blowed off just to save a little pussy."

She began to plead with him but he cracked her across the cheek with his fist: her skin bled at once, smooth and vulnerable as a tomato. . . . Buell began shoving her down the stairs. She tripped on the last stair, whether by accident or design would have been impossible to say—perhaps she threw herself, hoping to break her neck; and when she landed a cry went up from the other three poker players: "Olé! That's the spirit. Fight'em, girl."

Carillo lay trembling, undecided. Then he rose and slipped his jackknife into his pocket (he never got a chance to use it, it was merely an instinct: even at the time he realized that it was a hollow gesture like something he had seen on television: in real life a scrawny kid with a knife didn't attack four brutes testing the weight of their groins like murder weapons).

Carillo glided down the stairs like a somnambulist, he could not believe it could happen; yet by the time he had crawled, barefoot, to the bottom of the stairs one victorious player had already collected his bet and was wiping himself with a handkerchief. With the eye of a deer for survival, Carillo noted the blood on the handkerchief, but Carrie's eyes were closed and she did not struggle. "Have at her, Cloutie," he said. "We ain't got all night. And maybe I'll have me another try. This one waren't too good, she's bloody as a bitch with a litter."

Carrie's eyes remained closed. What amazed Carillo was that she neither screamed nor fought: perhaps she knew that if she did they would surely kill her.

There was money on the table—Carillo had no idea how much, but it was all in cash and there was a lot of it in large denominations, such as he had never seen. Later, trying to put it together, Carillo came to the conclusion that the entire farm, including Carrie, had been sold or lost to the three poker players; and they were dividing the spoils.

He had often asked himself afterwards: if he had known the outcome, would he have leaped as he did on Cloutie? The answer, most likely, was *no*, he confessed to himself. But at the time he had thought, if he had thought of anything at all, that perhaps his useless attack could serve as a distraction, like the barking of a dog, and that in the moment's pause, Carrie would rise up from the floor and run away. Or the men would come to their senses; or God would intervene . . . Had he not even heard it said that God protects fools and children? He had lunged at Cloutie screaming, *let her alone, let her alone* when suddenly it had occurred to a couple of the victors that they could double their spoils—that here was excellent sport indeed, with a taste of the illicit, like venison during days when hunting was illegal. What they had in mind was experimentation: when would they ever have such a good chance to plumb their own minds and desires in an atmosphere without restraint, bound to secrecy by the guilt of accomplices? Within moments one of them had grabbed Carillo's head, the others were bearing down on his arms. Spread-eagled, Carillo could feel his vomit rise; and at the very moment when he was going to yell and resist and die fighting (he didn't want to die but he was too young to be frightened at death), from where he lay, his face ground into the floor gravelled with the grit of the men's boots, he saw Carrie, saw the blood on her thighs, and her eyes open now, like almonds peeled white with terror. And he thought, I'm only a guy not a girl and it won't kill me. I can hate and despise them and still be me (whoever that is); but Carrie will bleed to death, or worse: they will decide to get rid of her body afterwards, claiming she just disappeared, like her mother . . .

Cloutie now began to blame Carillo for his own pleasure. It was too much for him, it had become serious, it was something he had wanted and was enjoying, as Carillo could see by the mad look of licence on the guy's face, and so Cloutie began beating him in retaliation, claiming that Carillo was nothing but a damned dick lover anyway, that's why he'd come down here, to get it, and now he *was* going to get it, and he punched Carillo straight in the eye, so that Carillo understood why Carrie had lain silent, passive, unresisting. He too closed his eyes while the pain enveloped him in a cloud, pain so dense that it was a kind of armor. He learned that when you are suffering you have nothing left for shame. And so he endured.

They lay sobbing in each other's arms, he and Carrie. Gently she bathed his broken skin above the eye, then without looking at him handed him a sort of ointment or maybe it was only baking soda, he didn't remember, which he applied to the painful burning area which, fortunately, he couldn't see. Then, exhausted, they fell asleep. Although ordinarily Buell spent the night with Carrie, and Carillo slept below, this night Buell abandoned them together.

In the morning Carillo was awakened by their dog, Klondike, barking. He was alone. He listened for sounds below but there were none. He could not imagine what Carrie might have done at breakfast time. Had she prepared Buell's grits and eggs as she did every morning? How did one continue to face one's pimp every day? Carillo lay there, every bone and nerve aching, thinking about the girls in the County Home: would they all, every one, live like Carrie? And he vowed, he vowed to God or Somebody that somehow he would change this one thing, if nothing else. . . .

The flutter of the curtain as the wind changed aroused him to the fact that he must rise somehow and do his chores. It was a grotesque sense of obligation, like picking up toothbrushes, paper clips and hair pins after a mass murder. Still, he managed to slip on his tee shirt and slowly, a step at a time, it was so painful to walk, make his way to the bathroom (a knot of fear dissolved in him as he relieved himself: he had had paralyzing nightmares during the night of never being able to do so again). The water in the basin as he washed up seemed to echo in his head with a faint *whoooshing* sound and he realized that during the struggle last night something in his ear or head had been injured, but he had no time to think about it. Where was Carrie?

Downstairs there was complete silence. The kitchen was devastated, dishes smashed, broken bottles littering the floor; on the spot where Carrie had lain there were bloodstains: no one had troubled to wash them away. Buell and Carrie were nowhere to be seen. The car was gone, so apparently Buell had gone off somewhere. Could they have driven off together? His gorge rose at the thought.

He sat there a while, mulling over the possibilities should Buell never return; he, Carillo, could run away. . . . But he knew to the depths of his aching bowels that they would catch him, and then he would not only be an orphan but a delinquent and he would be shipped at once to the Reformatory. He decided to wait it out for a while, to see if Buell would return with Carrie.

He heard Klondike barking again. He slipped on his sneakers and jeans and limped out to the field. Apparently, Buell had gone without giving a thought to the cows, who were lowing plaintively in the barn. Klondike never ceased her barking. Cautiously, Carillo followed the sound of her barking to the rear of the barn, where he stopped, seeking some explanation: the door was unlatched, but the cows had not been watered or fed, and they were restive. Klondike barked more insistently than ever, as Carillo crossed the threshold. He gazed around in confusion; he now saw what had aroused the dog: from the upper hayloft a steady trickle of blood was dropping from the wooden planks into an empty

48

milk bucket below. Slowly, efficiently, it trickled into the bucket, almost as if the pail had been placed there by design—a bitter gesture of thrift in a world where nothing could afford to be wasted. Carillo trembled from head to foot; as he climbed the ladder to the loft a vertigo seized him and he nearly plunged eight feet below to the floor of the barn—an aerialist who had missed the pail . . . As he drew his legs up to the floor of the loft, he heard a hen clucking, and in his inner vision he saw an egg, warm and fresh, fall into the softening straw . . .

All the way up the slow ascent he had prayed that he would find Buell or even that all four of the winners lay in a mass grave beneath the bales of hay; but God did not, after all, protect fools and children, but led them into bizarre acts in which the victim atoned as if she were guilty and the guilty went laughing-free. He saw, with an exploding light and fragmentation of his heart that was worse than pain, worse than any beating or hunger he had ever endured, the motionless girl, her quick-creeping blood flowing now softly, like a heartbeat, into the pail below. In her lap, as if she were about to take up her kitchen chores and peel her veins as though they were the white flecks of potatoes, lay the serrated kitchen knife, and Carrie rested her head against the bale of hay, not breathing, no, but neither suffering nor enduring: beyond shame. They did not even wait for her to be buried before they returned him to the County, and in a few weeks he was offered up for adoption in Open Court.

Buell turned the dairy farm over to his creditors and went to Mexico.

Jennifer

I've only been here twenty-four hours and already I can see that they are a pack of fools. What makes me angry is how they can *accept* this sort of situation. They are all so resigned, so noble. I want to *howl.* It makes me furious. I want to scream at them: "It's the benign assholes like you who sat around being patient, looking at both sides of the question, wanting a limited kind of war, who have let this happen. Fools. Fools. Fools." And now there's this *priest* (that's the ultimate humiliation) deciding what we're to do with the rest of our lives. As if the priests and clergy ever did anything to stop it.

And it's no use blaming it all on Science either, it's just the filthy people who did it. And when I think of all the things I've never done... The bastards have cheated me of everything. When I was twelve Mom said, "You're too young to go out with boys." Too young! I wish I'd slept with every guy in high school, I do. I *do.* When I think of them, I could die ... There was Sean and Larry and Aeneas and the one they called Bartleby the Scrivener (I never knew why, and now I'll *never* know!) who used to *always* show up behind me in the cafeteria, always order just soup and would sit opposite me, just looking, looking, looking and blowing on his soup, cooling it with his breath. Oh God, if I'd known then what a mess they were going to make of it all.

And I'd never wanted to have a baby ever at all: but *now!* Just to have that *trans* whatever-you-call-them in a priest's collar tell me I'm not *allowed* makes me burn to get pregnant. Where does he come off at, telling us women what to do or not?

We're supposed to go right on doing just what we were doing: that's all right for *them,* they've already lived most of their useless lives. But what about me? I hadn't yet got around to doing anything, I hadn't even got started!

Like I just learned how to swim, *really* swim only three summers ago. I decided then that if I tried hard, if I kept up my practice I could be in the Olympics someday. And how am I supposed to "just go on" swimming in a place that's surrounded by the desert on one side, by the mountains and caverns on the other? In fact, if that priest is so smart, I wish he'd tell us where we *are* going to get water?

The fact is, I can't believe it. I can't believe it's happening. I look down at my body: the hairs on my thighs are golden, when my hand rubs against them there's not a sound: smooth as velvet. I am so beautiful. How could I die? Will all this disintegrate? I've seen horror films of how you look at the end, worse than the VD films they used to show in the auditorium (meanwhile the guy behind you would be sliding his hand under your seat, most like). In fact, when I saw Duncan's ad in the *Press* I thought, he's *got* to be kidding. But I answered anyway because deep down inside of me there's a desire to survive this shit, it wasn't my fault, it wasn't our generation, we didn't do it, we tried to stop it, everybody said preparedness was everything, ABM's and all that: and now here we are a crop of losers.

But I came anyway, just in case.

JULY 9

This is nutty. I'm beginning to keep a diary, just as if I were still that silly girl I used to be, confiding: "Dear Diary, My period came around. What a relief . . ." Or: "We drove to the cabin at the lake. Barry forgot his XXX's so we had to drive into town. There were a couple of village creeps there, who saw Barry go into the drugstore and started making dirty noises. I called Mom at midnight to tell her that Diane and I were babysitting and watching the late, late show. . . ." *That* kind of silliness that used to fill "Dear Diary": all in code of course, because I didn't trust Mom when I was out of the house, she'd go through my hair shirt, hair by hair, looking for fleas.

And now Diary-games are not games. This is for real.

Dear Diary, how did I get bottled up with these losers? One guy's an historian or a sociologist or something—one of those phonies who start believing their own statistics. Like they said it'd take decades for China and Russia to make weapons big enough to destroy our major cities. O Major Cities, wherefore art thou now? And then there's that blonde woman with glasses, Marcie? Marcelle? Michele? Something like that. She writes a lot too, so maybe she's another historian or something. These cats think they can beat the rap by putting it down on paper. Me, I'm just talking to 'You' to keep myself company, the only company *worth* anything around here, with all these idiots. *She* won't be much company, that Marcie-or-whatever, I think she's already shacked up with little Pinocchio. (He *is* cute, though he's too swishy for my taste.) Andrea's a drag, she's been saying 'yes' to her husband for so many years it scares her if she's smiling and he's scowling: she immediately drops her mouth and tries to look troubled. Though I must say it's a mystery to me what there is to smile *about.*

It seems to me I've given up everything to gamble on this one-shot thing. It's like I can't win unless everybody else loses. If everything goes *boom,* then I'll have made the right choice, the choice for survival. If not, I'll have wasted the best time of my life. But Malcolm says, "Don't worry, it won't be 'wasted.' My computer gives 'em a couple of years at the outside."

XXXXXXXXXXXXXXXXXXXXXXXXXXXXXXXXXXXXXXXXX
XXXXXXXXXXXXXXXXXXXXXXXXXXXXXXXXXXXXXXXXX
XXXXXXXXXXXXXXXXXXXXXXXXXXXXXXXXXXXXXXXXX
XXXXXXXXXXXXXXXXXXXXXXXXXXXXXXXXXXXXXXXXX
XXXXXXXXXXXXXXXXXXXXXXXXXXXXXXXXXXXXXXXXX
XXXXXXXXXXXXXXXXXXXXXXXXXXXXXXXXXXXXXXXXX
XXXXXXXXXXXXXXXXXXXXXXXXXXXXXXXXXXXXXXXXX
XXXXXXXXXXXXXXXXXXXXXXXXXXXXXXXXXXXXXXXXX
XXXXXXXXXXXXXXXXXXXXXXXXXXXXXXXXXXXXXXXXX
XXXXXXXXXXXXXXXXXXXXXXXXXXXXXXXXXXXXXXXXX

I X'd all that stuff out above: I don't want anybody to know about that. Not even 'You,' dear Diary. And then Carillo had the gall to ask, "Didn't they teach you *any*thing?"

"No," I said. "They didn't teach me a thing. Why should they?" My sarcasm was quite lost on him, though. Actually, for some crazy reason I wanted to take his hand off the rifle and kiss it (his hand I mean, not the rifle)! But I was scared to. How can you act that way with a guy who's some sort of combination guru, nark and summer lifeguard? O.K. Carillo, you asked for it: What did they teach me? (See answers below, smartie.)

First of all: never to sit with your legs apart, it wasn't "lady-like," not even if you were only four years old and didn't have any idea yet that you loved Daddie and hated Mommie, and besides that, you preferred to play kickball to fooling around with Ken and Barbie and all their assorted wardrobes (Mom thought Ken was a little too old for me, but that Barbie-doll was super). Anyway, it was not allowed: thou shalt not sit with your legs apart; and you couldn't play kickball *either.*

Bunch of hypocrites, all of them. While they were worrying about us skinnydipping and smoking pot, *they* were getting ready to blow up a couple of billion people. Ideas like that, and we couldn't even arrest them: it wasn't illegal.

The next clear message (in What-I-Learned) was that once you've started menstruating, you can get pregnant. *Therefore* you were never to dance too close to a boy because he might think, "oh-you know-what." *"What?"* I used to ask Mom, and she would turn her back to me and pretend to be looking for something in the fridge. Also, another message: you were not to go in swimming when you were menstruating because you would catch cold. I'm not sure how this was supposed to relate to pregnancy.

MUCH LATER

Yeah, they taught me that there was an enemy under every bed. Meanwhile the enemies were gathering in the sky in great nasty clusters of radioactive fallout. The liars, the bastards.

They taught me that it was wrong to be cruel to animals, and so I did volunteer work after school for the Animal Rescue League. Meanwhile, they were destroying the rocks and rills and the purple mountains' majesty—everything they could lay their greedy hands on.

They taught me (Christian) selflessness and sacrifice and moderation in all things. Meanwhile, they were stockpiling poisons in the bowels of the earth that could eat out the lungs and nerves of man, woman and child in a matter of minutes.

They taught me never to lie. Meanwhile, their whole fucking lives were one long lie—from the time they first dropped me off at nursery school and said, "Now Jenny, you be a big brave girl and don't cry and we'll come get you at noon." Then later, never even saying they were sorry they came three hours late . . . They didn't know I could tell time.

What else did they teach me (Dear Diary)? I learned how to

conjugate a verb, and how to solve an equation, and how to put together a dress, and how to let my eyes go soft when a boy talked to me. Meanwhile I learned on my own that if I slept with my thighs pressed together very close I could dream in an exciting way which took care of everything that I was not supposed ever to be even thinking about. And meanwhile, I learned too that you didn't have to get pregnant, that they had lied about that too; so, I went on the pill and after that it was a ball from weekend to weekend and I went to every "football game," only of course it wasn't the football game that was so groovy, it was Sol and Andy and Izzy and Bart and Aeneas (his real name was Bruno Antonius!).

And what *that* taught me is that every guy is different in a lot of ways you'd never suspect until you have sex with them. But one way they were all alike: they all wanted to be *the* one you liked to do it with the most. What they didn't half-way understand was that it wasn't a sex thing with me at all! Honest! I just needed the company. Being home was a drag, and I got sick of listening to all their lies. One way of breaking through lies was to get them in bed. It's hard to be a hypocrite when you're fucking your head off.

Even so, some tried. Some thought they were *better* than me because I was a girl they had fucked, whereas they. . . . Oh well, it's hard to explain ("Dear Diary!"). There's nobody to explain it to anymore, anyway. Certainly not Carillo. He's as moral as a Baptist preacher; he doesn't understand *pleasure,* only pain, sacrifice, some kind of morality between comrades. He doesn't really want me, I think: he just doesn't want anybody else to have me, that would be so *upsetting* to the group. It's a kind of dog-in-the-manger-thing, in reverse. He's a sort of Puritan, really. I think I hate him.

I can't help it, can I? if we owned a few goodies before it all went smash. Sure I could use the car anytime I wanted to (all I had to do was get my date-of-birth changed on the license) and it sure beat trying to check in at motels. Sometimes the guys just plain *looked* liked kids, whereas I always looked mature. "My body," I always used to say, "never gave me any trouble, it was my head that got the hard knocks" (playing dumb was the rule, you never let on that you had straight A's, it was like having V.D.).

After all we can't all be lucky like *him,* ha ha, and be left at the orphanage like the morning paper. I had plenty to eat: is that immoral? I had a nice sweet pink bedroom which was air-conditioned in the summer and *too* warm in winter: is *that* immoral? And I had plenty of clothes, shoes and records and my own bike (two or three of them—they were always getting stolen) and all-wool cardigans, at least a dozen. But I worked too. It wasn't all given to me. I helped Mom do the dishes, I did my own laundry (at least my undies and things), and every Saturday I put on a smock and covered my hair (it was real long, even when I was a kid in elementary school) and we cleaned the house from weathervane to potato bin (well maybe that is an exaggeration— we didn't *have* a potato bin). But I did my share, and we never killed anybody or threw rocks into buses when they had busing, and I know my parents were as ignorant as a blind horse tied to a millstone about the Real Facts of life; but they weren't *criminals* or anything, Jesus, they worked all day. Mom was kind of a teacher, she was a volunteer teacher's aide, she did a lot of volunteer work and she was thinking about going into social welfare only there wasn't enough time to get a MSW or whatever she needed, somebody had to cook supper and Dad didn't like her to leave him alone evenings, especially since he was gone a lot anyway on trips: he sold bricks—not just your ordinary garden-variety kind of bricks for houses but for whole projects—government buildings, arsenals, condominiums, Golden Age Retirement Communities, that kind of thing; and he made money, but it cost a lot to live, there was a lot of inflation, and he was also "insurance poor" as he called it.

Is that all my fault? Is that any reason for *him* to just sit staring at me, without saying anything, as if I were a drug addict and he was praying for me?

And so I hate him. It's true that sexually he turns me on, *really* turns me on, not like those kids at Tech, or even the older ones at Community College, but there's something deeper going on here, if you know what I mean. (Hey, who's '*You*'? Ha, ha.) What's funny is, he's not even my type! He's sort of skinny and his face is full of scars and his hair is kind of *not*-color, a kind of neglected blond which is almost brown, and he's had so much metal put around his teeth, it's almost—but not quite!!!—like kissing a kid with braces . . .

When he offered to teach me how to shoot his rifle—MORE LATER. . . . (Bet you can hardly wait, eh, 'You'. . .)

He doesn't have to act as if I were an absolute nincompoop, does he? Because I *did* learn something for real before we came here. I learned that I was a neat swimmer, I mean, I was *good.* I'll bet you that in another four years I'd have made the Olympics. Even Mom, who always hated to see me with my hair dripping wet and my skin full of goose bumps, even Mom had to admit that I could swim better than Uncle Dobbs who won every prize in the book. Dobbs is Mom's brother, and she didn't like *him* to swim either. Sometimes I think she didn't like anybody to want to be that good at anything, I mean to really care. It was like she thought it would hurt you to care.

I *also* learned a little bit of French and a lot of biology (in more ways than one, ha ha) and was trying to decide whether I should learn to type and all that—just in case I never did anything really *great* in swimming. But if I didn't make it as a swimmer I was going to be an airline hostess anyway, so I wouldn't need all that clerical stuff. To tell the truth, the thought of being indoors all day instead of in the water really turned me off most things. Mom just wanted me to be a nurse, for instance, so I could marry a doctor and have nothing to worry about after that.

It's the water I miss most of all in this damn place. So when C. asked me if I'd like to come with him to the creek to wash the dog, I felt as excited as though it were New Year's Eve and *anything could happen.* So we made a nice leash for Tikki from one of my best belts (it cost me twenty dollars, counting the silver buckle). C. looked at it and said with a sad, wry smile: "You want to save the buckle?" I said "No, what was the use? Would the Martians be trading in silver?" He liked that, I think. What I tend to be careful of, and it's something I'm not used to, is saying things just because I know they'll please him. Like with Andy and Bart and all those guys, it was so easy, it was like rolling off a log. You'd just say, with "open admiration," *Oh Andy, you're too much! Oh Bart, you're something ELSE!* and that was it. It meant anything: that they were tall, handsome, clever, witty, strong, desirable, that they fucked like crazy. *Anything.* But with C., if I think of something that will make him smile even a little bit (God, how did I get mixed up with a guy who never laughs? Though I got to admit there's nothing to laugh about), it's like moving a mountain. So the funny thing is that if I think of something that I think he might *want* me to say, I don't say it. (That about the buckle took me by surprise.) I get angry, just thinking that he's hoping that I'll say this-whatever-it-is, and instantly I clam up. Now isn't that *something else?* (God, this is all so crazy, sometimes I wish either Andy or Bart or Aeneas or one of those losers were here with me, at least I always knew what was going on.)

So anyway, Dear Diary, "You," the Martian, or the Jolly Green Giant, he asked me to go down to the creek to wash the dog. This was after they'd been digging all day to lay the foundation for our new House and I said, "Gee, looks more like you need a bath than *he* does!" He looked at me strangely as if he thought I meant something sexy or something; but it was simple truth. He was as dirty as a coal miner, like you'd always see on TV coming out of the tunnels. Even if he'd tried to, I wouldn't have kissed him. I mean there's a limit. Last *couple of times* (you know what I mean) his body smelled like sweat, I mean real sweat, not just working up a little moisture in the summer heat. At first I was really turned off, but then I forgot about it. What was strange: I tried to pretend he didn't smell that way, that he smelled like Bart who always used wonderful kinds of soap and creams and stuff; but I couldn't *remember how Bart smelled either*!!! What a funny thing, that you can't remember smells. But that smells make you remember.

Anyway, who else was there to go with? Andrea's O.K. She's really been awfully nice to me, but there's no s-u-s-p-e-n-s-e. I feel I always know what she's up to. With C. well it's a guessing game: I have to figure out what he's thinking. I'm so busy trying to scope him out and trying not to sound like an idiot and still trying to be "myself," not some bubblehead he wouldn't look twice at, that I forget to be scared. Forget why we're here and that tomorrow or the day after or next month or next year, all these crimson leaves will glow not with the sun but with real fire.

I had to stop after *that.* I can't take too much of *that.* It's not really real anyway. It can't be going to happen. It's like when they tell you every fifteen minutes in the U.S. some woman dies of breast cancer, you think that's a shame and how lucky you are it won't happen to you, *probably.* Anyway, you think, they've lived to be forty or fifty and they've had their lives, whereas me, Jennifer, I've only *had* breasts three or four years. . . . So of course I figure the statistics don't make any sense applied to me. What I can't adjust to here is that it applies to everybody. It's like those True/False questions that are False if there's a catch word like *everybody, at all times, never, always.* (Still, there were some dumb

teachers who never figured you'd take that qualifying word seri-
ously and the answer turned out to be True after all. . . .)

Anyway, "Barkis was willin!"Carillo removed the silver buckle
and dropped it on the table in my tent. (*Our* tent? It's getting so
he's here whenever he's not out there: not that I mind, but there
are sometimes you know when you need to pluck your eyebrows,
shave your legs, etc.) But he doesn't seem to think of that, seems
only to think he needs to protect me from: Pinosh, Malcolm,
Duncan. Or is he really *jealous?*

They walked down to the creek, not hand in hand, not even
together, but simply plodding, as if they had a long hike to make
and were saving their energies. The dog pulled at Carillo, but he
merely tightened the leash and kept Tikki at his side: the dog
became a kind of barrier, Jennifer thought. The sound of the
stream made her long for water, for a real pool into which she
could plunge like a dolphin. She pictured herself for a moment
flashing in the sun, a white satin bathing suit just barely covering
her bronze skin; her long blonde hair hanging upside down as
she plunged (no bathing cap for this one) and then soundlessly
moving her body under the marine-blended colors of the pool:
the coral tile, the aquamarine water, the sun entering from above
like a knife. Then out she would come, her arms and shoulders
dazzling with water and Carillo would say . . .

Only of course he would not have been there, she could not
have known him, he would never have been lying poolside with
all her friends—Clarisse and Larry and Aeneas and Barbara and
Bart and . . .

"Did you bring the soap?" he asked, his arm flexing against the
pull of Tikki who seemed as anxious to get to water as she was.

She nodded. She pulled the brown soap for Tikki out of the
bag in which she also carried a towel, a comb, some hair shampoo
and sunglasses (as if they were going on a picnic instead of to hell,
she thought).

Through the dense foliage, the summer sun came down in
waves, glimmering across her eyes like water. She squinted as
Carillo bumped past her now with the racing dog. With a tremen-
dous pull Tikki yanked both himself and Carillo into the water.
Carillo dropped the leash and turned toward her, questioningly.
What he seemed to be asking was whether she would help him

rub Tikki down with the soap. She shrugged negatively and began peeling off her clothes. For a split second she felt herself in competition with the dog as she flaunted her beauty (she knew she was doing it, but she didn't care) before him: who is more beautiful? upon whom will you lavish your love? her breasts seemed to ask as they moved forward of their own will toward him, toward the water.

He pretended not to notice her. Or was it real? Did he really not care that the sun was burning, that it was a morning in the very sinews of summer, that there was soap on her skin and water on her lips: she sank herself into the stream as into a baptismal font. It was no accident, she suddenly thought, that salvation came with water: in the name of the stars, planets and universes to come, I baptize thee, Jennifer the Immortal. She giggled.

She rolled over and rested her head upon a rock as upon a pillow. "Want some help?" she asked rhetorically. He had started at the dog's head; its russet coat had turned dark in the water, and it now lay patiently across Carillo's knees while he massaged its ears, neck and the triangle above its nose with soap.

"You know, there's a story—" he began.

"A *real* story? I mean a *story*-kind of story, not something that really happened to you?"

"I don't know whether it happened or not. But I've heard that it happened."

"Well, that makes it kind of real. I mean, how do you know whether anything really happened? Like I think about a hayride I went on once: ten kids in a wagon singing like crazy, and a horse with this crummy hat on his head, and everybody ticklish in the straw and acting like they've never kissed anybody in their lives: was that real?" Hardly pausing for breath, one arm akimbo for balance, she clung to the pillow of rock at her back. "And we weren't thinking about war and things like that. What we talked about sometimes was about the lake getting polluted, and whether we'd get to see Europe before it was all parking lots and skyscrapers, and some of the older guys talked about joining the Sierra Club to keep investors out of the Canyon, though I can't say I really had it all clear in my head at the time, what they meant. But those were what we thought were the *problems* and in a way it was kind of fun bragging about how good we were going to be at solving them. Not like our parents who had goofed so badly

—" She stopped, realizing she had forgotten the cardinal lesson, one of the things they *had* taught: be a good listener. Instead, she was rattling on like a four-year old demanding an audience. Incredible. Stupid. She looked at him guiltily: was he bored? To her surprise he had paused, his hands still full of soap while he scratched and caressed Tikki around the collar area where the fleas were most likely to root in.

"You had time to think about that, at least." She was not sure whether he meant that she'd never had to dig ditches and scrub floors on her hands and knees, but rather had spent her time thinking about whether Venice was going to vanish into the sea before she could get there; or did he mean that she had, at least, lived long enough to experience the "reality" of the problems of her generation: a half-life, but better than none. She decided not to ask him to explain; they might start quarreling, and the one thing she did not want to do was quarrel. It was the effect of the water, it always made her feel good-natured. She smiled at him to prove it. Her smile was meant to say, You are *not* going to make me mad, I am going to be Jennifer the Benevolent, the Imperturbable, the Immortal: it was the Law of Conservation of Energy or Something.

"The story," she reminded him.

But he was looking at her, his eyes taking on the color of the water. She tried not to pose, tried to look *naturally* beautiful, but the craving for his admiration got the better of her, and she pulled herself up and put her hands behind her head. At once her arms felt like stones weighing down her shoulders, and she knew she had goofed again: the light of interest she had seen for a moment died, and he returned to washing the dog.

He spoke as if to himself: "When Che and his men had broken camp one morning, they realized they were being hunted by a very well-trained, disciplined company who were not far from them. Their dog, whom all the guerrillas loved—he was their companion, he was more than a mascot, he was their *friend*—anyway, their dog began barking: it was a warning for *them* that the enemy was close, but it was also a clear signal to the enemy of their own position (they were in the mountains . . .). So . . . they were obliged to . . ." His voice broke and he thrust his hand into Tikki's coat as though he meant to disappear into the russet brush of hair. ". . . kill the dog. 'This time, we must kill our friend: whom must we kill next?' Che said. And Che wept."

If Jennifer had not believed Carillo incapable of it, she would have said he was sobbing. But of course he could not be; it was only that she herself was so shook up all the time that she imagined everybody else was falling apart too. She wasn't even exactly sure who this Che was, or what he was doing in "the mountains." She knew about Castro, of course: everybody recognized him with his beard and cigar. Once, when she and Mom and Dad had spent the holidays in Miami, nearly every second *really* good-looking guy was a Castro-cursing Cuban. One of them, a guy who owned the restaurant in which they were eating, had explained to them, Jennifer and Mother and Dad, why they left their country. And "Che" was involved with, or working for, this bearded madman, she understood *that* much. But there was still something very weird about a guy setting himself up to knock off a whole class of people and crying over a dog.

She sniffed incredulously. "I hear they played music in the concentration camps too," she said. It was supposed to be a kind of compromise statement, not intending to make him mad at her, but showing her refusal to agree with any of his "stuff" merely to gain points with him.

He jerked his head around at that. For a long time he sat staring in the creek while the water rushed around Tikki, rinsing the soap in a haphazard way. There were a few fleas nuzzling in at the tip of the tail, but Carillo ignored them.

She felt contrite, it was his trip after all, so she could, in an odd way, sympathize with him precisely because of her lack of sympathy: he was alone in his obsession, the way she'd been alone always, even when the whole gang was there. Most of the kids she knew would just chalk him up as a weirdo and forget it.

"I'm sorry," she said, feeling sorry *for* him, but not really sorry for what she'd said: it was true, wasn't it? The Germans, too, had been nuts about their dogs, and they had kept a few Jews alive, artists, to play for them the world's most beautiful music. It was better than a stereo . . .

Without looking at her he observed: "You've heard it said that a revolutionary is inspired by great love."

"Love of what?"

"Of the people."

"People? But I'm people: and you don't love me."

"I do love you. In revolutionary love."

"That's b— that's *bunk.* Calling it something else *makes* it something else. I've been in love lots of times. It's not like you say—it's not this slow, steady, calm, dedicated *friendly* kind of thing."

He studied her as if she were about to reveal some great truth which he had always meant to have time to consider: "It's not friendly?"

"No." She rubbed her bare feet against each other, feeling the softness of her inner sole. "No. Sometimes you absolutely hate the guy. And then sometimes you're jealous. You want to scream when he looks at another girl."

He shook his head. "That's nonsense. It doesn't make any sense to me at all."

"Well, what does?" she demanded with irritation. "Popping grenades and kidnapping ambassadors and lining The Enemy up against the wall: you call that love?" She hung on the phrase just long enough to censor it in her mind, then unleashed it: "That's nothing but murder."

She could just faintly hear him over the water which trickled beneath her in triads of sound: *run, chuck, run; dip, dip, dip; wood chukk chukk,*

". . . the other side."

"The other side of what?"

"I can't explain it to you. Only somebody who's been through it can understand it, can believe it. Suppose I said to you that in Greece, in Portugal, in Spain, in South Vietnam, they use torture and imprisonment; that in the developing nations hundreds, thousands, have died at the hands of their corrupt governments? Would *you* believe me?"

She shook her head violently.

"You see, these are the horror stories no one believes till their history has been written."

"Yeah. Well, *some* histories have been written, and I've read a couple of horror stories: like your 'successful' revolution under Stalin."

He was silent. She felt for a moment she had vanquished him in argument but that she had not played fair. Like getting a good grade on an exam because you got hold of the questions beforehand.

"Of course," he said aloud. "They would teach her about Stalin. Not about the others. Not about Franco, Trujillo. Not about Ky."

She kicked her legs in the water as if she were practicing in a pool for the backstroke: energetically, rhythmically, toes relaxed and slightly inward; the water frothed up around her in small bubbles which reflected the light.

"Do you really think," she said dreamily, "that They will destroy . . . all this?"

Carillo released the dog, who rushed pell-mell into the water, leaving a wake of soap behind him. In a few seconds he emerged, shaking water everywhere, barking joyously.

Carillo rose from where he had been kneeling beside the dog, and balancing himself cautiously on the rocks and pebbles of the stream, moved toward Jennifer. He stopped, silently contemplating her bare feet before replying: "No, not yet. But this will teach us something."

"What will it teach us?" she demanded, her legs no longer swimming, but smooth, pliant, waiting.

"How to take a bath!" he said with a grin which quite surprised her. It occurred to her that it was the first time she had seen him smile at anything. It was strange that it was facing up to Armageddon itself which had wrought this wonder.

"Now it's your turn: Tikki's clean."

"Ah, but so am I. You saw—"

"But not the way *I* do it. I've been trained, you see. Special assignment for my cadre. Poor village woman comes along: maybe she's never used pure American soap before. I have to show her all the secret places of her own body . . ."

She felt the color drain from her cheeks. She was positively frightened, she could no longer say any funny thing, she was no longer in control: and she feared him. An hysterical laugh began deep in her throat but never became the shattering sound it should have been.

It should have been a teasing, chattering joke between them, culminating in joyful caresses, a leap from the water, a skirmish; then, according to the movies, sunlight and leaves and lying under the trees. Instead, it was an aggrandizement in which he took no part but was a sort of spectator, as if asking himself could he make *Pleasure,* and if so, what was it? At the same time she felt herself wound slowly, slowly, into her own pleasure as the soap waxed and waned beneath his hand and grew into rippling bands, quick glissandos of performance till she lay covered with soap as with unguents. Then with the hands of a slow, careful worker, he

found his way into all her agonies until she fought with his hand
on the rock as if his hand were the enemy and were destroying
her; then she seized it and pressed it to her while the rock at her
back hurt her, pressing into her so that the pleasure she felt
ground into the rock and though she cleaved to the hand which
parted her, she cried out that he should, he shouldn't, she
wanted, and he stopped her mouth at last, but was it love? she
asked, like a drowning person going down for the last time.

Klara

I thought I would ream out my last days in the knitting of socks for grandchildren, and in making tea for a few old friends. But they have all passed away, one at a time, like petals falling. So long as a few remained, the flower was good. But in recent years, having lived through times that no one any longer treats as real —times so far in the past that I have lived to see them romanticized in films and autobiographies (many spurious)—I felt I had at last come to the end.

Thus when I went to my room on the evening of the eighteenth of this month, I said, "Lord, now let thy servant depart." But He, cruel and demanding as ever, refused me a *non-historic* death. It was as if He said plainly, "No, Klara, that's altogether too simple. What do you think I planned for you after all those wanderings. A *quiet* end?" Then He must have laughed. "Don't be foolish. *I* write the script here, and you've been one of my most reliable characters. Why should I let you go yet?" So He sent me this Duncan. . . .

Yet it is a mystery to me why they have chosen me, an old woman. When I stood at the bottom of the great granite steps watching terrified and amazed at the spectacle of the Czar's soldiers firing on the people, I was a mere child, still cautiously resting both feet on each step downward, as I made my descent. It is a wonder that no one photographed me then at the foot of the steps as later they were to photograph children doomed to die in successive historical apocalypses. Doubtless they did not photograph me because I was not meant to die then (wormy meat for the sailors of the *Potemkin* not being sufficient cause for the death of Klara Kleist, eh Lord?). Only He knows what photographs, diaries, embalmed mummies shall be selected as testimony of His recurring wrath.

Perhaps, after all, some of this will survive. Malcolm has promised us that he will bury these papers in an "impregnable cylin-
der" which will safeguard the stories of our lives for posterity.

But for me, which story? which life? Like those who say the
body changes all its cells every seven years, I have changed myself
every decade though still disguised in this body.

Still, through every change, the basic catalysts were three; that
I was a radical in Russia (how promptly Galina and I were sen-
tenced to exile for the mere possession of those mimeographed
papers!); that I was a Jew at a time when of all times in history
it was most dangerous to be one; and that I was a woman. Perhaps
for these reasons also, I never properly specialized in anything,
though I felt from my youth that I wanted to know everything:
the usual weakness of the radical intellectual who wants to change
society. Results: chaos, ignorance, dilettantism.

If one of those newsmen or policemen who seemed omnipres-
ent at the historic demonstrations Galina and I participated in
were to show up here at Duncan's colony and ask: "Now, Mrs.
Kleist, what do you think of this experiment in survival?" I would
answer. "It's very amusing. But I think there's been some mistake. They should have taken some other in my place. I only take
up room. Somebody for the Jennifer girl, to keep her company.
She needs a lover. I? Do I need a lover? No, what I need now is
an uncrippled right hand to write with, and a memory like steel."

Life in Russia, even with the Czar, was like a dream compared
to the realities of Detroit. The Czar did not visibly affect our life
except in his permissiveness toward *pogroms.* He was like the
absence of air: one might suffocate there, but there was no one
to blame. There were no anti-Czar signs in those days you may
be sure. So whose fault was it that the very sight of a small boy's
yarmulke could strike superstitious fear (and therefore hatred)
into the hearts of peasants? We feared the random violence of
schoolboys more than we worried about the abuse of imperial
power.

It was not until, at fourteen, I joined the underground that I
learned that, however invisible, corruption began at the top, and
like certain theories of wealth, trickled down, down, into the
muddy culvert of death. The erosion of ethics at the top resulted
in imprisonment for us at the bottom. It was as simple as that.
We, Galina and I, tried to be brave, we swore like cultists writing
in their blood that we would educate ourselves and be free. We

had no idea what we were swearing, it was the mere rhetoric of adolescence.

Adolescent or not, they were preparing to send us away to the steppes, into a thousand miles of deserted, unpopulated tundra. In short, Siberia. Mother wept, Father wound his phylacteries with trembling fingers, rather as if they were a sort of sacred noose in which he wished to hang himself; and suddenly the decision was made, and we two adolescents, like a pair of Muhammads, had moved the mountain of indecision. To save us from exile in Siberia our parents were ready to abandon all they knew and follow us to freedom—to America.

I say, *follow* us. By uprooting themselves, by leaving all behind except for a pair of Shabbos candles and a box of hand-stitched towels which had been part of Mother's dowry, they were now to be forever dependent on us, their children. If a sign were to be read, a legal paper to be filled out, an interpretation to be made, either Galina or I had to be at their elbow. At Ellis Island it was I who was summoned to sing out to the immigration officers my parents' devotion to America and to list their identities ...

When we arrived at Ellis Island, Galina and I, we were not afraid; they combed through our hair for lice; to Mother's horror they pushed aside our shawls and examined the vaccination scars on our bare (!) arms (several years later we were again vaccinated, this time on our thighs—never dreaming that the time would soon come when these immodest scars would be as visible to bathers as toe nails). They asked about our measles, our mumps, our gingivitis (Galina and I knew that there would be an uprising of the working class, but we did not know why our gums were bleeding). It was the first time I saw Father helpless—the beginning of countless such views, beginning with his total inability to keep our food kosher on board ship and ending with endless failures to keep our family from poverty, his daughters from working, his wife from despair and himself from madness.

For Galina and me even the ride on the dirty train from New York to Detroit was thrilling. We were not altogether lost in the new language, we had begun to absorb English like a sponge. Galina, several years older and light years cleverer than I, had, with ruthless practicality, bartered her *gymnasium* ring for a tattered English dictionary in which the only word she recognized was *aardvark,* because one of her friends had told her, jokingly, that all English dictionaries begin with this wonderful word. And the queer thing was that in this case it turned out to be true, although it was only a simple little dictionary she could have bought in any dime store for ten or twenty cents. But Galina always insisted she had not overpaid for it: she had purchased it, she said, in an economy of scarcity (it was probably one of the few dictionaries for sale in steerage). All our lives whenever we were alone together, telling a story or reminiscing, if our memory failed us and we could not recall the name of a person, we'd call him *Aardvark,* which—no matter what our mood—would bring laughter, or at the very least, the warm tears of nostalgia and shared experience.

And how is it that this New Land, which only a few decades ago was able to succor the world, can now no longer even save itself: or *any*one? That is an enigma to me.

It startles me now to realize that what I have been describing, what Galina and I shared, was *happiness.* And this happiness lay in continuity, a sense of direction and meaningfulness: we believed that by our personal actions life could be changed. When we marched for women's suffrage, when we stoically refused to pass a picket line or did without coal during eight long weeks of a Detroit winter in order to support a miner's strike in Pennsylvania, we believed that our actions would be written large in the book of history. So during the strike, I remember, we shut off the two bedrooms of our four-room frame house on Chene Street and sat in the kitchen, warming ourselves by the gas jets—Galina wearing gloves and clumsily turning the pages of a biology book. Father would return from work, his round hat and earmuffs covered with snow, stamping his feet with cold as he entered the kitchen. At the sight of his unmarriageable, unmanageable daughters sitting there reading, wasting their time, he would make a sound in his throat that was like a howl of rage, only a howl that had been swallowed and was still burning and choking in his throat.

Father had begun in the New World by selling pushcart produce from house to house, but sometimes it was so cold the fruit and vegetables would freeze and the housewives would complain. Father hated the business, so he tried house painting instead, but the lead paint sickened him so that he was hospitalized for a year. When in the Spring he came out of the hospital, he tried selling insurance to other Jews, but he was a wretched salesman: the fact was that he hated to talk to people. . . . Galina and I were casting about for some way to supplement the family income, but it was harder for Galina. She was attending night school—intending, she said, to be a doctor, lawyer, merchant or chief. And that is what baffles me still, as I jot down these memoirs for Malcolm. I wonder how I can explain to those mysterious Martians who theoretically will transcribe these notes, how it is that Galina, with a mind like mercury, with an appetite for learning as insatiable as avarice, who laughed at the men in her class for being stupid clods—how is it that Galina dropped her learning like a poisoned cloak, married the stupidest of clods, bore four children and never again opened a dictionary? How is that? Why is that? That is a mystery, and that is the "story" I should like to write, and not my own, which seems altogether too clear to me. . . .

They came into breakfast this morning late. At Duncan's request I sat at the "head" of the table. Ironically, the setting was so primitive that it reminded me of my childhood, of the summers in the woods when Mother, with a sigh of contentment, would seat herself on the stump of some fallen tree, awaiting our encampment for Father's annual vacation.

Now with a sudden insight I seemed to sense a significance in their physical placement around the "table." Between the married couple, Andrea and Malcolm, lay a space of nearly five feet —an area already heavily cluttered with wrapping paper, leaves, tinfoil (they ought to be saving it), a torn shopping bag, and a couple of jackets tossed carelessly on the ground (it is still very warm: we have not, like the pilgrims, survived our first winter). It is as if Malcolm and Andrea are both actively constructing a wall of things between them, a wall of trivia, meant to block each other's view.

Duncan sits on my right, enthroned in a tree from whose trunk Pinosh had spent a long time whittling out a benchlike seat. He himself, Pinosh, that is, sits on the sparse grass alongside the young man who lately joined us—a Cuban or Mexican, I think, though very fair-haired: at any rate an unequivocal revolutionary of the kind we used to grow like giant sunflowers in our Russian soil.

Accustomed in this last decade or so to watching and listening, to survival by silence, I take in what seems to me an active if premature hostility: why are they angry, these three on my left? The Cuban (or Mexican) points to a place for Michele to sit.

Pinosh glares at them: they have arrived quite late to the meeting. It is astonishing to see Pinosh glare: the crackling amiability suddenly stretched into an immobile muscle. His gaze rests curiously on the young man's uncombed, ruffled hair, as if inspecting him for roll call. But there is nothing amiss with the young rebel —he is clean, orderly; his courtesy to Michele has nothing (or so it seems to me at any rate) personal in it, it is the direction of a guide. Pinosh tries to elicit a response from Michele who is now sitting at an oblique angle, but her eyes are upon the ground. She has given up smoking in order to be a member of the colony (another of Duncan's "rules"), but her fingers fidget mechanically, in a pantomime of a woman searching through her handbag, looking for her cigarettes, but she has found nothing but a handkerchief, into which she quietly coughs. There is a faintly apologetic smile around her mouth: it is a soft apology to the air, and to no one in particular. She has, in fact, interrupted Duncan who is telling us *What We Must Do.*

"First of all," he says, "we must pen in the few goats and chickens. Then we'll put together the prefab. Then, last, but not least, we'll dig a foundation for the bomb shelter where we'll place our stockpile of supplies: drums of water, boxes of biscuit, candy balls, vitamin pills, medical kits. . . ."

Malcolm scoffs at this. "It's useless," he says. "We don't have the technology. Let's just . . . live and let live."

He means, of course, *die and let die.* As he says this he stretches his arms sensuously. The light from the live oak tree seems to bend around his bare arms and shoulders. I cannot quarrel with any of his assumptions: if I were young, I think I would . . . what would I do? I envy the sensuousness of Malcolm's arms: it has been years since I have touched my body with anything but amazement—that a thing so wrinkled can have thoughts, memories, burnings in the brain as intense as wildfire. Malcolm's hair glistens; his self-love radiates. I smile tolerantly. If youth cannot love itself, who can?

The meeting this morning is to distribute the work; but what work can I do? Already, although I am quite comfortable in my armchair, my back is weary, my arms feel tired though they have held nothing this morning but a cup of tea. I look at Duncan with what I believe is a mildly reproachful, ironic smile: what would you like me to do—chop wood? tend the babies, like some English nanny? Duncan is saying that with four strong men (Jennifer

protests that's she's as strong as any man and gives Carillo a kick
to prove it; he rubs his ankle, without raising his head) we should
be able to construct the house in a month. Meanwhile, he hopes
for good weather, and strong tents. He wanted to remind people
that there was to be no smoking in the tents. Michele looks up
guiltily and explains, though no one has even looked at her till
then: "Don't worry, my supply will give out. Then I'll chew barks
and leaves." Pinosh smiles and nods agreeably: "You can suck on
my finger," he says. "You can suck—" begins Jennifer with exasperation. Carillo pats her on the shoulder, partly to silence her,
one feels. But she wrenches her shoulder away, like a football
athlete: she is trying not to cry. Malcolm says he has the plans
right here; he spreads them out on the "table"—a plank across
two piles of crating. It is a bit wobbly, and they decide to use the
ground instead. Carillo, Malcolm, Duncan and Pinosh gather
around the plans for the house.

We women, amused by the assumption that we can neither
read plans nor help build a house, exchange glances. "Well we
can always take in washing," says Michele with heavy irony.

"I get to stand guard duty," boasts Jennifer. And (perhaps
inevitably): "Carillo has promised to show me how to use his
rifle."

"Aah!" says Michele acidly. "Very nice of him!"

Andrea announces with unexpected practicality: "I think it
would be better if you learned how to fish. So long as there are
fish in the stream . . . Come with me, I'll show you how to use fly
bait. Did you bring boots?" It's as if Andrea has decided to make
a protegée of the girl. To instruct her, rather than fight her. Even,
if necessary, adopt her: the taboo against incest being stronger
than the taboo against (mere) adultery.

Jennifer senses a trap and is unwilling to abandon the men
positioned before their plans like Octavius, Lepidus and Antony
dividing up the world.

"Nobody'll steal anything while you're gone," observes Michele. But irony is too subtle a weapon for the child and Jennifer
stands frankly puzzled, indecisive.

It was at that moment that the dog came scrambling into our
midst. A starving animal, but still full of friendly madness. His
russet coat was torn from what must have been miles of scaveng-
ing before he found us. A dog quite without suspicion or distrust,
apparently well-treated before he became lost or abandoned.

Malcolm demanded to know, with unconcealed exasperation, if our privacy was "*again* to be invaded by an *uninvited colonist.*"

One would have thought the dog would growl at us: after all, it was starving and *we* were enjoying coffee and biscuits. But he he loped over at once to Pinosh, who promptly fed him a biscuit.

"You'd better curb those impulses," snapped Malcolm.

Pinosh made a strange sound in his throat—not quite an apology. "He won't eat much: look at him, he's a runty type and he won't get much bigger."

"He looks ravenous to me." Malcolm tapped his pipe on a nearby stone. What he meant, perhaps, was to show that he, at least, was observing the rules (the pipe had not been lit for days). This seemingly trivial action turned out to be of interesting consequence.

The dog, whom Pinosh had immediately begun calling *Tikki* ("as in Rikki-Tikki-Tavi—a name merited by his tremendous survival powers"), rushed to the charred pipe cleanings, thinking perhaps that Malcolm had set out some left-overs. Tikki began sniffing desperately; but when he discovered that he was being offered nothing but cinders, he began barking angrily. Duncan put out his hand, calling the dog to himself to soothe and quiet it. Perhaps he even intended to have a vote on the subject (there was some justification for Malcolm's complaint that the animal would be the equivalent of adding another member to our colony).

"Who will bathe him?" Malcolm demanded to know.

"He doesn't need bathing," growled Pinosh. "He already smells better than you."

"Here boy!" called Duncan. Reaching for another biscuit he held it lightly between two fingers of his right hand. The dog immediately leaped into the air like a fish, snatched the biscuit, and began running frantically around our table as he devoured the cracker. Then in his joy at having found succor, he raced madly around the circle of what he imagined to be his new friends. Laughing, Pinosh tried to catch him and quiet him, so that the meeting could continue. Duncan wore an expression of amusement and delight which tried to disguise itself as exasperation. Finally, as if drawn into the game by some irresistible clockwork of his own, Duncan feinted a downward movement and tackled the dog. Pinosh, unable to stop his momentum, plunged down athwart them both; within seconds an insane wrestling match had begun in which Duncan, holding the dog in his arms, pretended he would never release it, upon which Pinosh playfully drew Duncan's arms behind him in a wrestler's hold. Duncan began laughing with a strange hysterical delight, the dog was suddenly freed: Duncan lay on the grass, flushed and excited, a look of mingled pain, shame and pure delight on his face. His eyes became bright as enamel, he lay as if exhausted, Pinosh's arms now pinning him to the ground. Duncan giggled softly. . . . No one stirred for a moment, no one joined in their amusement. It was in fact not amusing, but somehow frightening. It was as if the stable leadership we had relied on had been pulled out from under us.

Meanwhile the dog continued to bark. Suddenly Pinosh released Duncan with a friendly and tolerant punch to the shoulder, and *began barking himself.* He pulled out from his pocket a puppet which seemed to be an animal, but was so nondescript it could have been anything from an ass to a unicorn. It had ears, though, and immediately it began a harangue in a barking voice which was nevertheless intelligible:

> . . . thou idle immaterial skein of sleave-silk,
> thou green sarcenet flap for a sore eye,
> thou tassel of a prodigal's purse . . .

Duncan rolled over on his stomach and lay with his face to the ground. We thought for a moment that he was injured; but he sat up presently, holding his skull delicately between the thumb and fingers of his right hand, as though worrying some inner pain. Then in a voice which seemed to be torn with real exasperation, he ordered: "The meeting will continue. And we'll vote on Tikki."

Perhaps it was the use of the dog's name which seemed to make Tikki already a real member of the colony. At any rate he carried the consensus; our votes were not secret, and Jennifer exclaimed petulantly, "Well, *I* want him!" Malcolm shrugged, raised his eyes ironically to Heaven, and made it unanimous.

Since this meeting, we have noticed that Pinosh contrives never to be alone with Duncan; when it is necessary for them to cut down trees or to damn the creek so that we can use part of it for the preserving of food among the cool stones (while at the same time keeping part of it for bathing and laundry downstream), Pinosh always manages to solicit the aid of a third person, even when it is sometimes clear that only two people are needed. No one has ever refused Pinosh this accompaniment.

And it is not, I think, because Pinosh "fears" what Duncan may do or ask, but because we care for Duncan, respect him; and we wish to protect him. Is that unfair, one wonders? Are we not, in effect, usurping Duncan's rights, restricting Duncan's freedom of courtship? What would my father have thought of such a question of freedom a hundred and fifty years ago? And yet, as Michele remarked bluntly while we watched the four men depart this morning (we have turned back the historical process: the men go hunting for food and the women remain at home in the cave), hardly seeming to be aware of what she was saying, "Well he has as much right to him as he to me." Or perhaps I didn't hear her properly. My hearing is not what it used to be.

JULY 30

I've been given too much credit, it seems to me, especially by friends and relatives, for having accomplished what most of the women of my generation failed to do. What they did not realize, these sympathetic observers, was that every action was inspired, not by a disinterested or selfless motive, but by the most ignoble of sentiments—*envy.* Envy, pure and simple. I could easily catalog the Desperate Efforts which made the significant changes in my life, which caused me to become, as one newspaper woman described, "a radical force in the labor movement, an astute political figure, and one of the first women to receive an advanced (honorary) degree from the University of Michigan."

But their praises were all lies. I did not become whatever I became out of freedom, but out of slavery: that is to say from malice and greed and envy and the need to heal old scars of humiliation. In short, the realization that an immigrant to America at the end of the Victorian period was not exactly like being a Henry James.

It was an old story: Galina and I dressed differently, spoke differently; above all, we thought differently. Having paid such a high price for our nonconformity in Russia, we were reluctant to begin aping a culture that demanded in essence total cultural conformity, especially among the Jewish women in our neighborhood. Their sexuality was disguised as virginal beauty, their intelligence concealed as a liability, and any physical development beyond sufficient strength to plant horseradish for the holidays and wring out the wash was considered alarming. I think Galina and I were spared this Procrustean bed only because we were forced to earn money: we were soon deprived of even Father's meager and sporadic income in a way we could never have foreseen.

It was a hot, steaming afternoon in June (summer had arrived early in Detroit that year). It was as if we had penetrated some murky underwater cave: at any moment, it seemed, small dark fishes of the sea would emerge. I could taste the soot of the factories on my lip, my eyes smarted with tears as I walked home from high school. I remembered suddenly that there was a doughnut store on my way home and that I was vaguely hungry: in those days I was so seldom hungry that I did not even recognize the feeling when I had it. For a moment I paused at the window of the bakery and looked, without actual longing or desire because I never had any extra pocket money to spend on such trifles, but with a sort of artist's detachment at the pyramids of doughnuts. Some were sprinkled with sugar and some with cinnamon, some were dipped in chocolate or frosted with honey, and each one was five cents, and it was like a hot poker in my bowels that I could not buy a single one, that the man who stood gazing at me from the other side of the window owned all those doughnuts and perhaps even then, as I swallowed my saliva and my pride, must feel faintly annoyed with me. I peered into the shop as if to check their wall clock, and for the first time noticed a sign strung across the wall in small frames. (I couldn't read the entire verse, which extended along the entire wall, but I caught the last two lines): Keep your eye upon the doughnut/And not upon the hole.

The irony of this sanguine philosophy on the part of the man, who, for the moment at least, seemed to own all the doughnuts of mankind, filled me with bitterness. I walked home asking myself: why not? why not upon the hole? It was the hole that was cheating me. In proportion as the hole grew wider, my hunger would grow, would become insatiable until the whole wide universe was only a black hole. . . . By the time I reached home I was furious. I threw my books down on the kitchen table and stalked out to the back porch to the icebox. I yanked open the door, determined to possess all that was mine, at least. I found that the fifty pound block of ice we had purchased yesterday was entirely melted away; the smell of spoiling butter assailed me: the butter dish had apparently slid down the melting block of ice and the butter now lay in a runnel around the tin shelf of the box. Under the box the ice pan was overflowing and a few roaches lay trapped in the runnel as in a dam. I was not shocked or sickened by the roaches; I had become inured to them, but Mother fought a perpetual battle against them, to her they represented the lowest dregs of poverty. "Even-in-Russia," she used to say, "we never had them." To which Galina would retort, "It was too cold there and you had nothing to eat." Which was not true. We had eaten there better than we did here, because here Father was *hors de combat.*

But I was thinking how upset Mother would be to realize that, in spite of our efforts, these vermin were still invading her household, when Father returned. He had lately taken up the peddling of what were called snow cones (that is, chipped ice in a cup with fruit-flavored syrup poured over the top, and eaten with a wooden spoon). But Father was handicapped because he was not strong enough to ride a three-wheeled bike such as many of the young men used; and he was afraid of horses. Yes, my friend from Mars or Venus, horses. It was possible to rent a small wagon, complete with horse from the I-Serv-U Ice Company and be "an instant investor in your own business" with only 50% of all registered sales going back to I-Serve-U (for overhead expenses, they said). So without a bicycle, without a horse and wagon, Father was doomed: all he could do was stand in one place just outside of Belle Isle and hope he could get the syrup into the cup before the ice melted too much.

On this day (the Day of the Doughnuts, Galina was to call it: she made fun of our sufferings as though she had read the play long ago, knew the ending, and could afford to poke fun at all the actors), Father came in through the rear door at the kitchen end of the house, which was in itself rather unusual. I was still standing in front of the icebox trying to decide whether to call up for an emergency delivery of ice (one had to pay extra for an unscheduled trip) or to take a chance on the rest of the food in the box spoiling by morning. Suddenly I was no longer either hungry or thirsty. I just wanted to sleep.

But at the sight of Father's face, fear tightened in my chest: something was happening over which the doughnut eaters and owners of the world had no control. Father was still carrying several jars of colored syrup and for some reason this made him look grotesque. Also, there was a long streak of blueberry syrup across his flushed face: it was as if he'd begun a make-up job for a clown's performance but had ended up tippling wine all afternoon and had come reeling home in his drunkenness.

But even at that terrifying moment I knew that this was mere metaphor: Father never drank, and if he had, it would not have made him violent, he would have simply sunk into a defeated, passive coma. But now, the blue stripe of syrup across his face seemed to blaze purple and red, he began shouting at me that all the food was going to spoil, why hadn't I ordered the ice, where was my Mother, he had three women in the house and the house stank . . . I tried to explain that probably Mother had gone to the market—the holidays were coming and the Kosher meat markets would be closed, something like that. But he had already raised his fist and struck me, he now began pounding at me, shouting that I was no better than all the rest, the world was a rotten sty and American women were the worst pigs of them all—and he would pound some sense into me. To say I was terrified is to reveal my weakness with language: how to express that I was seeing my father go mad, but at the same time I understood that he was perfectly right—that I was guilty, guilty, guilty—because never would I bring him joy, never would I restore him to his place of dignity in the world, never would I restore to him his youth, his dreams, his vigor. And it was true—the still-echoing, broken promises of America lay like a stench around the open icebox.

He was shouting unintelligible words in Polish, I realized suddenly that we were grappling together like assassin and victim. Would he kill me? Drown me, perhaps, in a pan of ice water? It was a laughable horror. He knocked me down now, for a second time and this time I lay quietly, looking at him, expecting a blow that somehow would finish me, finish us. From the corner of my eye, I could see the roaches now, gathering like a conquering army around the legs of the wooden icebox. Ah, so that was where they have been hatching, they are laying their eggs right before our eyes, I thought with a strange and tranquil clarity. Then suddenly Father began sobbing, his intention toward me (whatever he thought it had been) utterly collapsed. I now think his intention was total destruction, so that once he had assured himself of irreparable injury to those he loved he could go on to his true business; cancelling out his life. He picked up a chair, one of the few sentimental treasures of his life, a chair with a cane seat woven by his brother; and using the chair as a bludgeon and roaring like Goliath, he began smashing everything in sight. He pursued whatever vague end he had in mind for about an hour till I returned with a couple of neighbors who grappled him, still sobbing but also kicking and biting, to the kitchen floor. Meanwhile someone had called the police, thinking it to be a family quarrel, and a police car came and shoved my father, shackled at wrists and ankles, into the back seat. He lay stony and silent, his eyes staring at the seat covers. Then they drove away to the siren-sound of law and order. That weekend Galina and I began to look for work.

Andrea

Andrea knelt down pretending to pick up berries which had fallen from her basket. Through the thrusts of red bobbing before her eyes like Christmas apples, she could see them in the creek. As, shamelessly, she watched, she asked herself: at what moment does a fifty-six-year-old matron become a voyeuse? At the moment, perhaps, when she has looked into the void of her own life and decided there must be something better. She then begins to watch, to examine, to ask: why does one man smile at his lover, touch her hand, while another flees from her? Why do children mock one old man who sits in the park but the same children watch, chattering happily, while another man feeds pigeons a few feet away? These were the universal questions, the only questions, Andrea now felt sure.

The problem was that the questions were beginning to pour in upon her when she had fewer persons than ever to pose the questions to, and had run out of time with which to experiment with the answers. Michele, for instance, was learning something from that absurd Pinocchio. Even the old Russian lady had her chance for information, and Andrea noticed that Carillo would sit for hours, talking and listening to the old woman. What did they talk about? What she wanted, desperately, was someone to want to talk to *her*. Her sense of her own mediocrity was so devastating that it was all she could do not to apologize for boring people when she spoke, not to say *thank you!* as if they had performed a special service when they sat beside her at the big wooden dining table in the kitchen.

So long as they had eaten outdoors, with Klara still enthroned by the big tree stump and Duncan ensconced beside her, Pinosh and Michele still together, there had been no embarrassment for

Andrea, in the arrangements: there had been no *choice* on their part. Since the house had been finished, and they now ate in the big kitchen, she felt her isolation more keenly at every meal. All the preoccupations of her past (would the party go well? would Malcolm's trip be extened? would Malcom stay away so long this time that he'd never come back?) had become agonizingly simplified to a single question: *would anyone sit by her?* Since Time-together was all they had, the question of whether they found distraction in each other's bodies and amusement in each other's conversation had become the paramount issue: the deceptively simple question of *who would choose to sit beside her at the table* had become Andrea's daily ordeal. For weeks she had been consuming vast amounts of energy in a private charade: she would arrive at the dining table sufficiently late so that she could finally drop herself into a chair *inconspicuously, not demanding any attention,* after having idled her way along the route by pretending to check whether the stove worked, whether the bread had been properly wrapped to retain its freshness, or even whether the sweeping up after the previous meal had been properly done (if the positions at the table seemed "overstabilized," Andrea would occupy herself with sweeping the floor for several minutes). Or sometimes she would reverse this charade. She would arrive early enough so that she was the first one at the table, so that *she* was the one about whom they had to arrange themselves: some days she imagined it like one of those games children played, a game in which she was the Labyrinth out of which everyone was struggling to escape . . .

Her desire to please was so intense that she studied each person's face as if it were a map of Paradise; while she lay beside Malcolm (was he really sleeping? she never dared test his pose too far) she constructed conversations which she could use to draw a smile of interest or tolerance from The Others, as she found herself habitually referring to them (Malcolm sometimes included along with them, sometimes equivocally aligned with her). She did not know whether any of her ruses were obvious enough to be detected. Finally she had lost track of how much time she spent at these charades, and simply established a few firm rules for herself vis à vis The Others: never get angry, never criticize, never show sexual jealousy—*no matter what.* Her visual italics in this case were intended to cover as yet unenacted betrayals, humiliations which she had already years ago learned she could expect. Why should Malcolm change now, with less reason than ever? She was consumed by the conviction that she would die alone, no one would talk to her or soothe her last days: Malcolm would prefer to be with anybody but her.

She tried not to envy Jennifer. Indeed, she told herself that in all Christian charity she ought to feel more compassion for Jennifer because she had not lived her life; yet, like the rest of them, she would be called upon to surrender what was left. So at least the others said. But perhaps the whole thing was merely a hoax, a gimmick Malcolm had thought up so as to give himself another titillating experience: gourmet of experience that he was, always wanting something different. And how could she give him what he wanted when she was the same person he had married nearly thirty years ago? The lassitude of their marriage was like waiting for the end of a long trip: during the final hours you were so weary, irritable, deprived, exhausted, that you could only rivet your eyes to the black highway and count every sign, every mile until you were released.

She tried to consider whether she was truly the same person. Mentally she prepared a list: Andrea's physical attractions (if any) at their wedding; Andrea, when she had discovered she was barren; Andrea when she had begun to hide food in the basement, the attic, anywhere—like an alcoholic burying his empties; Andrea when she realized that Malcolm preferred to sleep with any other woman rather than herself: that indeed he preferred masturbation, if it came to that. The tragedy of the bedchamber: he had simply lost interest, virtually from their first efforts to consummate their marriage, efforts which had been about as exciting as the releasing of helium from a balloon. For her part it had been a ritual of disappointment and insult so pervasive that for weeks she had got up early every morning, fixed his breakfast and a neat little lunch he could take with him to the lab; then pretending exhaustion, illness, even for months an hysterical pregnancy complete with early morning sickness, she would disappear into the bathroom until his departure.

The truth was, she thought mournfully, as she sucked the berry juice from her fingertips (Jennifer had now wrapped herself in a towel and Carillo was leading her, supporting her; Andrea saw him raise his head attentively at the rustle of the berry bushes), the truth was that she envied the other women in the commune from the depths of her soul: they had had a *life,* while all her life she had been merely looking for one. They at least had some understanding of their fate, knew at least why certain things had happened to them, and seeing their choices now at The End, *chose.* Whereas she was now about to be dragged through her death as through her life—now, when for the first time, perhaps, she wanted ... what did she want? Perhaps it was only to know what other women had known. And the men too. Only, how did a woman her age learn anything anymore? She was cast out, unloved, denied anything except the memories of tormented nights, of turning and turning, reluctantly yet with a passion which even Malcolm could never have suspected. She would lie quiescently trying to will the thing with her mind: Come, she said to her body which hurried along without her, going in the opposite direction. That body which always, and in spite of herself, responded to Malcolm in a mixture of need and anticipated humiliation. But somewhere along the line the wires got crossed, Malcolm would lose interest, and she would begin to hate him again for having wrought the whole imbecilic performance, an actor forgetting his lines (*his* failure, she used to repeat to herself, over and over, during the early débâcles).

Yet she was more frightened of the women, Klara, Michele, Jennifer, than of the men. The men hardly knew she existed except when suddenly they became aware that she was sitting, huge and osmotic, beside them, like a comfortable cove from which they might have emerged without noticing that the water stirred at their movements. But at least to male indifference (she thought) she had become indifferent; she knew what they wanted: an understanding smile, a laugh at the right time, total motherly acceptance, but no, absolutely *no* sexual demands. She was to be a thing without desire, a eunuch, before whom one could discuss the most intimate details of one's life. So she merely watched and listened while they fitted the walls of the prefab together and assembled the portable bathroom—originally intended for a mobile home. The bathroom was so small it made her shudder, yet she would have died before confessing the anguish that beset her when she was obliged to use it during the night when all the house was silent: it was worse than trying to wedge into the tiny airless cubicles on the Greyhound buses, where one could with dreadful and obscene comicality, actually become stuck. While the men assembled the parts they laughed and talked, and now and then (condescendingly, she felt) tossed a remark or smile

her way. She was still one of them, the smile seemed to say, with
fatal *noblesse oblige,* still one of them, although she was too awkward, really, to be asked to share in this sort of work; but that was
all right, they hadn't forgotten her. . . . At such moments Andrea
wished only to be forgotten.

The women, on the other hand, were awesome because they
continually wanted to include her in their activities. They could
never ignore her, they invaded her mind, worried her body, made
her bitterly aware that she was the hull of a ship and they were
the acrobat sailors, balancing blithely on the ropes or the crow's
nest: they moved about, running, helping, dancing their way
directly into the eye of the hurricane which was about to engulf
them. If one had to die, she demanded rhetorically of God, why
couldn't one do it *gracefully?*

Sometimes she convinced herself that the only reason she had
followed Malcolm to the colony (apart from the fact that it was
impossible to conceive of *not* following him) was that she had
harbored the secret hope that the colony would run out of food
and she would die of starvation . . . *Laugh if you dare,* she addressed the imaginary creatures who would read this, her last will
and testament, everybody knows you're made of air and water,
you Martians, tiny as bonsai trees, ten-to-a-capsule for size, invisible gremlins, haunting UFO's: what do you know of flesh?

So in her despair and loneliness she had chosen berry-picking
as her major assignment, keeping the commune in fresh fruit.
And today, spotting Jennifer and Carillo ostentatiously headed
for the creek (though to be sure they were going to bathe Tikki
as well), had followed them: for she swore to herself that she had
much to learn and, like the black militants, meant to learn it by
any means necessary. She followed them, plucking berries all the
way, like some clever Gretel leaving a trail for her soul to find its
way back on: and she had witnessed what youth and fire could do
to light up the flesh. In spite of their bitter quarrels (she could
often hear them arguing wildly over "political" matters which
Andrea secretly believed did not matter at all), she saw how
Carillo half-carried the child back to their camp. *Her very knees are
weak from it* thought Andrea with a wrench of longing.

Actually, Jennifer had not made a sound, but Andrea had
recognized that desperate need, that shudder of pain and pleasure, an imitation of which she had experienced on rare occa-
sions, induced by her own efforts. Once it had happened by

accident almost, while she was washing and bathing: just as
Carillo had done for the child, only she, Andrea, had been alone,
and it was as if her loneliness had increased tenfold through every
seam of her flesh. She had stared down at the pubic area which
she could not even see: it was as if an invisible animal had invaded
her, gnawing at her; she gasped with pleasure, with surprise, then
the animal was gone. Was *that* it?

She waited near the creek now, about twenty minutes before
slowly wending her way back to the house. She had collected
barely a pint of berries although the area was filled with these tiny
edible berries whose name she did not know, and what's more,
she thought defiantly, did not care to know: what was the use of
learning such things? Idly, she plucked a few berries, nibbling at
them though they were sour and full of seeds. She barely noticed
how she returned to the camp, how her footsteps dragged in the
underbrush, her body colliding with the bushes. Then she could
hear Tikki barking just ahead of her, and she tried to delay her
arrival so that they could not imagine she had been watching. But
Carillo gave her such a look when she approached that she felt
herself go white, then red; a flush of shame enveloped her like
a mist. But thank God, he said nothing. She was so grateful that
he had not openly accused her, exposing her to the others that
she would at that moment have done anything, anything for him.

To her surprise, they were talking about children in the colony. They'd only been there a little over six weeks and already
Jennifer had missed her period. What was more, she said she
didn't care, she had done it on purpose, she wasn't going to let
any fruitcake priest tell her what to do. Carillo was silent, seeming
not to care, though surely he was the father? . . .

The summer was not yet over and already the girl had gotten
pregnant as easily as lighting a match. Andrea sat down at the
outdoor table, listening to their "group discussion" (at this, Jennifer snorted it wasn't any of their fucking baby); she sucked
absentmindedly at a piece of hardball candy she'd stuck in her
apron pocket, recalling now all the attempts she'd made to get
pregnant (in spite of *his,* Malcolm's "failure"). The doctors had
reminded her that scientifically she didn't need sexual satisfac-
tion to have a family, that so long as Malcolm could produce
sperm, he could produce babies; therefore it was her fault, not
his. So they had set to work on her as if she were one of those
mechanical dummies they use in hospitals to learn on—the Har-

veys, the Hals, the friendly, amiable Frankensteins and their Brides. They had blown up her tubes and spilled sperm into her as though they were making a sponge cake and needed twenty-one eggs. She took her temperature every day and waited for ovulation like a child waiting for Easter eggs. She had wearied Malcolm before work and waited for him at the door; it had been like a form of Aztec worship in which the cruelty of the sacrificial ritual cancelled out all the holiness, with the difference that both she and Malcolm were victims. She had read all the ads, all the sex hygiene books, and gone on crash diets, lost weight, gained weight, bought perfumes, colognes, creams, eaten certain foods which were supposed to increase your fertility; and had bored Malcolm excruciatingly with it all: the question of children became nauseating to him. She finally brought him to consent to a fertility experiment in which his sperm was frozen and at the proper moment induced to travel through her tubes. It was all useless; she became no more pregnant that a manzanita tree. "Not a calf in the carload," observed Malcolm one day with bitter malice, and since then she had not dared to touch him; they lived a platonic, asexual truce—border enemies—resentments only flashing up in trivia which had nothing to do with their true cause: money spent for someone else's baby shower, for instance; or the grossness of her avoirdupois, at which he never ceased to jibe, as though it were the layers of fat and tissue which prevented a baby from climbing into her womb. He said such bitter acidulous things it was as though he meant to scorch her into fertility by burning her with shame. . . . After that he began to pursue other women, any other woman. On one occasion he had even got his lab assistant pregnant. Andrea had been sure then she would lose him (but why did she want to keep him? she had asked herself, but could never find an answer. She only knew she was terrified that if he abandoned her she would be alone forever, alone on a sinking ship which even gnawing mice were fleeing. . .).

She fixed her fascinated gaze now on Jennifer's body, a body in which mysteriously a baby already grew. Jennifer had wrapped herself in a kind of shapeless terry cloth robe, but her hips and bosom bulged as if her very disingenuousness were calculated. The sound of a goat bleating in the nearby compound distracted Andrea's attention long enough to remember guiltily that while she had been watching at the creek, the others had been working, building a goat shed. Only Klara was where Andrea had left her an hour before, quietly inscribing in a notebook the tale of their lives . . . Beside Klara was an expensive camera, which Andrea recognized to be Malcolm's (why had he brought out the camera, Andrea wondered: was he taking pictures of their colony?).

Duncan was haranguing the girl. He sounded to Andrea almost irrecognizably savage. "It's crazy, that's all. You did it on purpose. You wanted to sabotage the whole thing. It's not too late for you to leave the colony, you know. You can go right on Back There and have your damned baby and live with them till the whole thing explodes in their faces . . . in your baby's face too."

"Take it easy, Duncan," said Carillo. "She needs this baby. Everybody needs something."

"*Nobody* needs a baby," said Duncan with icy denunciation. "Bringing babies into the world is the cruelest dumbest thing anybody can do."

Carillo shrugged as if to say: with so much death could one birth bring us closer to despair?

Michele stood tearing a cuticle; it bled and she looked down in fear as though she had just become aware of some internal hemorrhaging. "But nobody knows anything about babies here. Why didn't I take up nursing or something?"

Andrea forced herself to say, "I do have a book on childbirth. Tells all about it. The way it's supposed to come out. How to tie the cord. Everything."

"Oh God!" exclaimed Pinosh and began patting one of the goats (this one was named Nana and had become a sort of pet) so hard that she began bleating plaintively.

"For God's sake shut up that bleating animal before we make a sacrifice out of her!" Duncan snapped; then in the unnaturally calm voice of one reasoning with madness, "I move that we call a meeting together to decide whether Jennifer is to remain with us . . ."

"You're not going to have a meeting about *me!*" gasped Jennifer. "You've no right to decide *any*thing about me. I didn't come here to get pushed around as if you were my Father-Who-Art-in-Heaven."

"You broke one of the rules. And what's more, you did it deliberately."

"It was a shitty rule. Why can't I have this experience if I want?" Her voice rose into a sob, managing not to trail off into hysteria. "I may not even get a chance to see it born. . . ."

86

Michele said, trying to speak tranquilly: "Duncan, really, what do we have to lose?"

"Our sanity," said Duncan. "Everybody can think his way through to death quietly enough: but a baby? Who's going to decide whether he's going to be allowed to suffer. . . ."

"Still, I feel it's not our decision: it's hers. It's a crazy decision, that's true. . . ."

"Who's crazy? You're crazy yourself," snapped Jennifer. "Don't call *me* crazy. At least I have better sense than to get screwed by a faggot. I'm not as crazy as *that!*"

Michele stared, flushed, then silently turned away and began feeding one of the goats some grass. It nibbled at her hand peacefully as if they were merely gathered together in some communal retreat instead of quarreling over whether the death of a child born into their colony would demoralize them all. . . .

Duncan's eyes glazed over as if he were making a visible effort either to control himself or to reestablish his control over the others. It frightened Andrea, but her keen interest in Jennifer's condition, her sympathy for the girl in spite of her envy, compelled her to say: "I don't think we should subject Jennifer to a *discussion*. But if all you want, Duncan, is for us to *vote*, why Jennifer doesn't care whether we vote on her or not, does she?" She glanced placatingly at Jennifer. "She can still do what she wants. . . . I mean, to some extent anybody can do what they want. . . . " Her voice faltered: had she ever done anything she wanted?

But they seemed not to grasp or to care about the inherent contradictions in what she had said. Rather they agreed with her that they should vote on *whether Jennifer should be obliged to leave Duncan's Colony to have her baby.*

"While there is still time," added Michele.

"And with this proviso," said Carillo carefully, "that the vote should have the strength of a resolution only and not be enforceable. . . ."

Jennifer looked at him angrily.

Klara glanced up from her notebook. Andrea would have thought she had been indifferent to their dispute, but now she said as if equally summarizing it all: "Certainly no one claimed when we entered this social contract that all private decisions would henceforth be invalid."

Duncan grumbled: "I explained it all to her before she came here. She was supposed to *behave.* . . ."

"Oh Mother, another one of those holy hypocrites!" exclaimed Jennifer and walked off toward Pinosh who was still attempting to calm the frightened nanny.

"What did you explain to her?" asked Klara. "That she was not to have any further emotions?"

Duncan bristled. "This is a social collective, isn't it? That means that there are certain things nobody can do to destroy the equilibrium of the group: among these items are rape, murder, assault, malicious falsehood, and *bearing children*. . . . We're not the Massachusetts Bay Colony trying to found a new nation, we're just trying to figure out how to survive as long as we can. . . ."

"But since the girl is already pregnant," Michele murmured.

Suddenly Duncan turned on Carillo with contempt. "Fine revolutionary you are! Is that the way you guerrilla fighters did their thing in the mountains? Baby on one hip, submachine gun on the other?"

"It was not my decision. It was her decision. I'm not her commanding officer. I'm only. . . . her friend."

Duncan snorted. " 'Friendship. . . . friendship!. . . . What a perfect blendship!' "

Pinosh had sauntered back to their table; the goat was calm now and he patted her affectionately as though she were a dog. "Aw lay off, Duncan," he appealed. "The girl was on his tail right from the beginning. He's a sexy kid, can't you see that?" He laughed, a vague challenge in his voice. "Not everybody has to be in love. . . . Like me and Michele here. Ah, Michele,

> It is my lady O it is my love!
> O, that she knew she were!
> She speaks, yet she says nothing: what of that?
> Her eye discourses. . . .

Duncan stood glowering. "It's suicide," he said at last.

Pinosh looked sober. "So what?"

Duncan's voice quavered as if he realized the absurdity of what he was saying: "Suicide is against the rules. . . . Damn, let's have a vote on it anyway. Like Andrea said. Let's proceed with the procedures."

"Parliamentary procedure is at least better than gossip," said Klara.

"Where's Malcolm?" Andrea asked. It seemed to her she had been asking this question all her life.

Michele pointed in the direction of the caves where Malcolm from their very first week here had been trying to grow mushrooms. He claimed they could subsist for years on mushrooms, nuts, dried berries, and water: he did not say whether this would be deep in the cave or out of it. Andrea wondered if Malcolm actually believed in the possibility of anyone's surviving The Bomb or whether he was merely amusing himself—*carpe diem.*

"Go get him," said Duncan to Andrea.

Michele angrily blew smoke in the air: "Wait a minute. Why are you ordering Andrea about?"

"I'm not ordering her. I'm just asking her to go get her husband. He *is* her husband, isn't he?"

"You explicitly said: *Go get him.* I heard you. Everybody heard you."

Duncan waved his arms in exasperation. "What are we here, *l'académie française,* presiding over the purity of the language, or are we trying to get things done?"

"What do you want done?" said Pinosh irreverently, nuzzling his nose to the goat. "Say, when we eat this little nanny, save me the head: what a *marvelous* Greek mask she'll make!. . . ."

"Shut up!" snapped Michele.

"Michele is talking about freedom," observed Klara with unexpected loftiness.

"What?" Duncan seemed incredulous.

Michele took it up. "Well, perhaps I am. We're engaged, as Klara put it, in a social contract: we voluntarily give up certain freedoms for collective security, as they say: for survival. But now you're asking us to take orders—arbitrary, personal *commands.* So now we have to ask: why are you ordering us? We haven't elected you by any due process. . . ."

"Well of all the ungrateful. . . ."

Pinosh interrupted: "We're not ungrateful. We're just a bit worried. We're naive enough to wonder if, in order to save our lives a little, we're going to lose our liberty a lot. . . . Right, Nanny?" The goat bleated in reply.

"Very poetic. Very poetic," retorted Duncan. "But what's that got to do with me? Or with the facts. The fact is *I* organized this whole expedition."

"Aaaaah!" exclaimed Pinosh, raising his open palms upwards. "So that's it!"

"Oh quit it, Pinosh, sometimes you're a pain in the ass."

Pinosh waggled an obscene finger warningly.

Carillo said: "An elected officer takes on responsibility, but his first responsibility is fraternal democracy—toward his comrades."

Klara smiled. "Was that in your manual?"

"No—in our hearts."

There was an embarrassed silence; now and then Carillo's speech would resound with what had come to seem to them the most simplistic terms: honor, nobility, courage, truth, justice, as though he carried in his head a most precise definition of each.

"Oh shit. All this talk, when all I asked her to do was—Hell, I'll go myself."

Jennifer suddenly returned to the table, scowling and saying she'd never been so put down in her life: who the hell did they think they were, voting on *her?* Carillo removed a leaf, very gently, from her lap, but even this gesture seemed to irritate her: she promptly picked up another leaf and began shredding it to bits.

Klara picked up her notebook and glasses.

"We're due to make another batch of bread," Andrea reminded the women in a peace-making tone. Also, she liked them to think her memory for such details was excellent: she kept track of the perishable produce, made lists of every item—flour, dry yeast, powdered eggs, herbs they grew in pots, nuts and seeds of every variety—sometimes embezzling a little to nibble on during the night. For the most part the others seemed satisfied with her work.

"There's something the matter with the stove," said Pinosh. "You'd better wait till we fix it. No use filling up the place with smoke."

"Who's 'we'? Nobody really fixes anything here but Malcolm," said Andrea.

"Hey, hey!" Pinosh rattled a few dry leaves in her face. "Look who's protecting poor-baby-Malcolm from being maligned."

"Anyway, I think it's. . .crazy. . .to sit around quarreling about a baby that's not even born," announced Michele. "I'm going to mix the dough and get it ready to rise. Maybe by then one of you 'workers' will have got round to fixing the stove."

"I'll fix the stove," Carillo said quietly. "But I think you should wait till Duncan comes back. He wants us to vote, he feels it proper for us to vote. It doesn't matter that the vote is—"

"Meaningless. Exactly."

"—it's a symbol that he's in charge. If there's an election, someone is in charge of the election. It doesn't matter who wins."

Jennifer suddenly slid to the ground and, crossing her legs, began pushing her knees wide apart. "I've already begun my exercises. In natural childbirth the big thing is to keep your muscles in tone, and to relax. Breathe deeply and relax. I do these exercises twice a day."

Klara said, "I was pregnant three times. Apparently—there were no complications. Everybody said they should have been easy." After a pause she said with dry emphasis, "They were not easy. To *me* they were not easy. One—"

"I don't want to hear horrible old wives' tales. I don't want to be afraid . . ." There was a tone of supplication in her voice.

Klara nodded. "You're perfectly right. Absolutely. The main thing is not to be afraid."

Pinosh leaped to his feet. "What's that noise?" He began running in the direction of the cave.

The sound was rather like a police siren. They all stood up, ready to follow Pinosh. Klara began looking around for the cane she used in moving through the underbrush, but somehow during Pinosh's scuffle with the goat, the cane had got lost. She stood uncertainly now, not wishing to detain the others.

Carillo commanded: "Stay here. I'll tell you what's happening." The old woman sank back into her folding chair, glad to be relieved of the responsibility of action.

Within seconds they were all on their way to the cave. Andrea, in spite of her heaviness, managed to arrive there before either Michele or Jennifer. She felt certain something was happening to Malcolm, and she was somehow not surprised at the spectacle which greeted them: Malcolm and Duncan scuffling at the mouth of the cave. Malcolm was laying fierce punches into Duncan with no doubt of his intention: he was ready to destroy Duncan if necessary. Andrea screamed, Malcolm told her to go to hell and get out of the way. The two men exchanged several more furious blows before Carillo and Pinosh could separate them.

"The bastard tried to bust up my radio," Malcolm growled.

"Where does the sonofabitch get off smashing my radio? Is it any goddam business of *his?*"

"I said, *no radio.*"

"*You* said. Well just who the hell are you? You're just a clown who decided the end of the world was coming and now you don't want to hear another word about it. Well, I tell you there's still plenty of evidence of life going on out there—millions of people planning strategies, pitting their brains against the enemy, building missiles, multiple warheads—While you shitheads here are playing games with death, they're out in the *real* world fighting *real* enemies." He took a deep breath and looked at them all scornfully: "They're just going right on having elections, economic recessions, college graduation exercises. They're going right on fighting wars."

"I don't want to hear about it," Duncan yelled at him. "I don't want to hear about it. Their filthy wars . . . their band-aid efforts to stop the inevitable. When you joined the colony, you offered to abide by the rules and regulations. Well, *one* of those rules is that we were not to be distracted by the news from out there."

"But, fuck it, 'Out There' is still real, and so long as it exists it's our responsibility."

"*I make the rules around here,*" Duncan screamed.

At the sound of this naked scream, Carillo, who had been gripping Duncan's hands behind his back, suddenly released him: Duncan stood quietly chafing his wrists. It was as if Carillo thought it more important to hear what Duncan had to say than to keep him from *physically* hurting anybody. It was a long leash, Andrea said to herself, and glanced at Malcolm: he was all right. In fact, he was having the time of his life. She understood suddenly that to Malcolm the colony was a unit of investigation: he is observing us all, to see how we act, under stress, in isolation, under the threat of annihilation.

Michele

By this abdication of intelligence in favor of violence, Duncan has in effect ceased to be our leader. We now watch him suspiciously, waiting for renewed outbursts. And he watches us with equal suspicion, anticipating usurpations of power. His first test case came, surprisingly enough, in an encounter with Pinosh, in whose heart I'd not have suspected there was any such urge to power. It began like this:

Several weeks ago we finally gave up the idea of installing any sort of "modern" plumbing. Malcolm insisted that in order to install a real bathroom, etc., we would have to go to the city for the equipment, and besides that maybe employ real plumbers to do it. Here, no one knows anything about laying underground pipes. We do have a well for drinking water. The water assignment, which is extremely hard on the back muscles has been, so to speak, expropriated by the men. Although I do not find the winding of the rope and the lifting of the bucket too strenuous, the decision was made mainly in order to exclude Jennifer and Klara from this duty. Then for some reason Andrea also opted out, and to make it look like a "democratic consensus" they decided to exclude me from water-fetching also: the result—the four men are the hod-bearers and water-carriers of the colony. Just as they would be in the city, probably.

But to the incident which inspired these notations:

I am standing by the kitchen sink, preparing supper for eight. It is a bitter boring business; I have no interest in preparing the food, and I am, rather, remembering how Katherine Mansfield spent her numbered days in the kitchen, scouring pots and pans for Murry and their friends. An experiment in survival should be challenging, courageous, a chronicle of serendipities. Instead, this commune has been reduced to primitive roles in which the women have (again) begun roasting the wild ox and bearing the children (the sound of Jennifer's morning retching makes me retch and I flee into the woods to escape the sound). Andrea is now explaining to me why it is necessary for us to *peel* the potatoes; it has something to do with the sprouts. Impatiently, I reply that we can simply gouge out the sprouts—no need to peel all the damned potatoes. She tells me then that French Fried potatoes are not really *French,* that the French for a long time scorned them as a lower-class food, as being really *Irish* potatoes; that it was believed potatoes caused the *fertility* of the Irish (all emphases hers). I stifle a sigh and try to listen as if what she says has any bearing on why we are here. Then she suggests that instead of French Fries we have scalloped potatoes, that we may as well use up the goat's milk in the sauce for the potatoes as it will spoil, etc., etc. I feel she is tormenting me with all this useless information: does she realize she is tormenting me? I alternately glare at her to see if my gaze will stop her mouth and mumble my listless assent to anything she wants, anything at all if only she will be silent. It is like trying to think with the sirens sounding nearby. But now I sense some inarticulate longing in her, I riffle through my meager store of kitchen anecdotes, something to distract her from this all-consuming obsession, but it is of no use, it is like talking to an addict who is only waiting for you to leave the room so that he can sink the needle into his arm, a needle as sweet and bitter as death. If I leave her for fifteen minutes we will have scalloped potatoes: who cares? (Pinosh cares, I suddenly remember: he loathes scalloped potatoes, and like a *good wyf* I am compelled to say, "*please,* not for Pinosh." It is absurd, blasphemous: French Fries should be just as tasteless to those who now glimpse Death in all His rattling rags and bones as ... forsooth! ... scalloped potatoes.)

What I want to hear, what I am trying to hear is the conversation now taking place just outside our kitchen window, a conversation between Duncan and Pinosh. They are drawing water from the well in order to mix concrete; they are about to build a proper roasting pit which we will use for outdoor eating. It will be a relief to have such a place to gather around when the weather is good: indoors, one is bound by the sheer tyranny of space which means also the tyranny of having the privacy of one's thoughts mindlessly invaded.

At the recollection now of the many mornings in which my notebooks yielded scarcely a single private thought—to say nothing of a private poem—I am suddenly more resentful than ever of Andrea's presence in the kitchen, which is preventing me from hearing the conversation outside, which is preventing me from listening to my own interior monologue—that brooding self-consciousness Carlyle describes: a form of selfishness, really, but poets are addicted to it.

With force, with cruel self-will—it is not even meant to be deceptive: Andrea knows why I do it—I turn my back on her. I feel my own cruelty like a knife, and as if to prove it, instantly cut myself. Andrea rushes Mercurochrome and band-aids, and I feel more guilty than ever: as if I had aimed the knife at her and had, by a stroke of mercy on the part of the gods, managed to miss her and cut myself instead. At the same time I am positively furious with myself for not being able to help her. It is as if, having stopped your car a moment for a small injured animal limping across the road, the injured creature then refuses to budge; now, having stopped, you are endlessly delayed, till finally you roar ahead blindly in a ruthless panic to be free at last—to be on your way. But where?

Andrea is silent as I have now begun shamelessly to listen to what Pinosh and Duncan are saying as they lower the bucket into the well; now they are lifting the spilling bucket. There is a rhythm, a unison, to their bodies as they do this. I wonder, briefly, if Jennifer's phrase thrown out at me in outrage does not have some truth in it. Yet with me Pinosh's ardor is impeccable. He performs with regular and judicious expertise and I respond expertly—a well-wound clock. It is all inalterably fixed, like a game we have decided to play till long after dark, till our parents, pitying us for our lack of internal discipline, call us away from this exhausting play. Or like a play which Pinosh has written, in which I recite my lines as if I had known them all my life. Pinosh asks: "You don't mind if I come in?" I am reading and would prefer not, but I say, "No, of course not." He sits down at the edge of my bed (we now have individual beds set up on concrete blocks). I keep my hands around the book, as though the book and I are inseparable; one flesh. Then begins the script. He acts out the parts that say I am irresistible. I act out the part that suggests he is overcoming my unwillingness. Meanwhile I am trying to hang onto the mood created by the summits of Macchu Picchu:

> everybody lost heart, anxiously waiting for death, the
> short death of every day:
> and the grinding bad luck of every day was
> like a black cup that they drank, with their hands shaking.

But it is all right, no danger of conflict: the mood will disappear in a moment or two, covered over by a rich sauce at a Roman feast—a feast at which, if one is not sufficiently hungry, one disappears under the table a moment to reappear with open gorge. THUS:

Well-seasoned coquetries on my part indicate to him that my reluctance, which we pretend is merely "feigned," can be overcome by his Charm. His Charm begins to work its magic (it is part of the modulation of the drama that we do not simply go-to-bed, else he does not get to play his role): such roles are enough to make one long for the honest and needy intentions of a dildo; at least it is silent and does not want to be assured that it is loved; that it has wit, charm, masculine energy, charisma; and that if the world had survived could have been a truly great Shakespearean actor.

Thus we continue. Neruda is left on the sidetable, and our existence is momentarily reaffirmed.

Precisely what attracts me in the conversation at the well is that there is no rehearsal for a larger part: they are quiet, serious, and I am hoping now that Andrea will never be able to find her medicine kit, that she will abandon me to the echoes of their speech. Their very silences are rich in complicity, and I ask myself why my own conversations with Pinosh are so foolish, so superficial. My fault, perhaps?

"Is there a meaning to existence, do you think?" Duncan is asking with absolute seriousness, his eyes fixed on Pinosh's face as if he were reading there the light of the future.

Pinosh is facing the sun; he squints slightly; he tries to smile. "Of course there is. The very *question* is a 'reason'—our intellectual curiosity . . ."

"You really think so? But what if, as now, all mankind is to be destroyed? What reason . . . what reason for their non-existence?"

"Ah, there you have me. I can explain the reason for life, I can't give any meaning to the destruction of it . . . Why would anyone want to destroy

> . . . this scepter'd isle
> This earth of majesty, this seat of Mars
> This other Eden, demi-paradise . . .

Even the angriest Jehovah would, it seems to me, have better sense than to do such a thing."

"Yet we're about to do it," Duncan insisted. "The world as we know it, perhaps the entire planet—"

"That's a bit much," said Pinosh weakly, as though he could tolerate a limited death—one for himself and perhaps even a few friends: but the death of the planet was beyond him. He didn't like it, he didn't like it one bit: he preferred another play, with a reconciliation scene at the end.

"I'll tell you what I think—" In his haste to turn toward Pinosh as he spoke, Duncan splashed the water over the sides of the bucket. "I think we're on the losing side." He held Pinosh's gaze a moment before announcing in a tone oddly without emphasis: "I think the Devil has won."

Pinosh bent his head as he lowered the bucket. At that moment I pitied him: a marvel of memory and of gorgeous array, he was, but he was neither historically nor intellectually equipped for Manicheanism. His apparent impulse was to laugh.

But Duncan is nearly trembling with seriousness. As Pinosh's arms reach out to pull the bucket to the rim of the well, Duncan reaches out his arms too, as if to help carry the bucket. For some reason, some fibrillation in the arms of the men as they both reach simultaneously for the bucket, the bucket spills in mid-air: water pours over, wetting Duncan from the throat to the waist. Duncan stands for a moment as if affixed to the well. Were it not for the look of dismay (and perhaps of fear and pity) which now appear in Pinosh's face, a look which hits Duncan so hard that after a moment his own face crumbles—were it not for this, one might believe they were going to stand there forever, like a pair of saints in the desert painted by Ribera, listening for far off mystic annunciations.

Duncan seems suddenly too weak to pour water. He turns away, rubbing his arms as with a real or feigned injury to his muscles, to his nerve. He lets himself drop under a live oak tree —no longer watching Pinosh, but plucking aimlessly at the sparse grass.

Andrea has returned with the medicine kit. I had ceased to notice that I was bleeding, but spots of blood fleck the makeshift apron which is wound round me like a swaddling band. My head reels: it is as if I have witnessed some ancient myth, some Ovidian tale of metamorphosis. But who is undergoing the transformation? Not Duncan surely, whose poor pale fire began to glow like the dark side of the moon from the moment he first saw my lover.

"Why you're still bleeding," exclaimed Andrea, and I sit down, my legs trembling as if it were I who have taken part in some ancient blood-rite.

THANKSGIVING DAY

Since the afternoon of that vision, there has been a sense of waiting, a certainty that some depth in Duncan or Pinosh or the rest of us will erupt, which will affect us all in the colony. The others sense it too and wait with a combination of anxiety and disbelief, as if they are about to be called as witnesses to their own execution, an execution which cannot happen to them personally however, it is only an accident which they will be forced to see . . .

It is with a similar combination of reality and detachment, I think, that Jennifer regards her own growing body. She has begun to wear Carillo's shirts, a proclamation of love and possession so open, so tender, that I envy her: I feel never again could any emotion so violent, so innocent as 'Love,' take possession of me. Perhaps it is because she is young and believes in her own emotions. When she and C. walk together he does not touch her or hold her hand; rather, it is as if he is listening to some other chorus in the woods, the sound of feet on the wind, the cry of birds. I see that I am picturing him as being in tune with Nature, not with her. My own jealousy shows through even if I pretend to record objectively for the sake of objectivity. It is altogether too true that when I see them walk together my own arm leans toward him: take *me*, take *me*, I can almost feel the surge of his blood against mine, yet it is with her that he is walking. So when I think of him I pretend to believe that he is not thinking of her but rather of the wind, the wail of birds, the voices of his lost comrades. Certainly false and self-indulgent on my part. Delusion upon delusion. It is only too painfully clear (painful, of course, only to myself—a foolish woman dying alone, as everyone does, though surrounded by "survivors") that he is experiencing a new kind of pride. The baby is his: perhaps the only object or person in the entire universe which he can feel to be absolutely his own: renounce *that* ownership, *compañero* Carillo!

On the other hand, Jennifer's bewilderment that her body is no longer in possession of itself but has been literally invaded by another presence would be comic if it were not so sad: such ignorance is appalling. It is as if all the words she had read or thought of—*mother, motherhood, motherlove*—had created a mist through which now blindly, as through a dense fog, she must make her way step by step, day by day, until the moment of truth: the child will be born, and it will either be an ordeal of simple-pain or of complex-pain. If the birth is too complicated for us ignorant midwives, she could die. So we listen, keenly cheerful, but Cassandras in our silences, while Jennifer prattles—utterly unaware, it seems, that babies hunger, sicken, die.

I came upon her yesterday doing the exercises from the book Andrea had lent her: *Natural Childbirth* (as though having a real doctor has become *un*natural!). Like some pious Moslem, she had brought out a rug to lay on the ground and sat on it with her knees apart, the soles of her feet touching each other. As Andrea read out exercise instructions from time to time, Carillo was building a trap. He says there are bobcats about, perhaps wandering mountain lions too: we should be prepared, he says. I joke that it's impossible, we must have killed off all the lions decades ago, they're none left except in the zoos, but Carillo soberly insists that it is not only possible but likely: the smell of food roasting on our outdoor pit (not a total success, but Duncan and Pinosh have declared themselves eminently satisfied with it) might well attract hungry prowlers—"animals," he corrects himself hastily. And I wonder if he knows more than he says.

Jennifer explains, more to herself than to us: "It's a matter of breathing. If you don't stiffen up, Nature takes its course; it's got to come out, after all. It's a matter of gravity or something, isn't it?"

Klara sighs. Carillo looks over at Klara with a worried frown; he wants to know the meaning of her sigh. For the first time I have a sense of knowing a secret he does not: I sense Klara's terror at what the girl has laid upon herself, but in Klara's ancient wisdom she remains silent, hopeful that the promise which has beguiled us for thousands of years will be fulfilled: that in the bliss of birth the pain is forgotten. But whatever it is which crosses her face has not been forgotten. I see it like an ancient agony: Orestes must destroy his mother; it is not Orestes' fault, but Sophocles'. . . .

"What will you call him?" asks Andrea.

"If he's a him, I'll call him Bartleby—Bart for short."

Andrea encourages her by politely inquiring: "An unusual name—how did you think of it?"

Jennifer slews her eyes around at Carillo: she is never unaware of his presence. "Oh. I just like the name. I knew somebody by the name once, and I like the name." She scrambles nimbly to her feet, bends her body into a sort of push-up position designed to strengthen, she says, her abdominal muscles. Her back humps up like a cat's, she breathes deeply, she lowers her body. Andrea gazes in fascination, as though she were watching a bird fly from one end of the sky to the other. Andrea pulls her own sweater down more snugly around her hips, anxious perhaps to conceal the line at which her body melds into a single mass. I ponder the absurdity of this life in which, on the brink of death, we putter with exercises to keep fit, we conceal the flesh which hungers, we fly into rages as to whether we should hear the news of the dying planet. "I have to do two sets of each," explains Jennifer to Carillo, who now sets down a small box. It is what Mark would have called a varmint-box, designed to catch small animals upon whom one did not wish to waste one's shot: squirrels, rabbits, chipmunks.

Noting the box, Jennifer exclaims breathlessly while her back rises and falls: "I'll never eat rabbit meat. Never, never, never."

Carillo smiles. "Andrea'll fix it so you won't even know what it is. Won't you, Andrea?"

Andrea beams at his attention. She describes a hasenpfeffer she has prepared in the past, so delicious that even Malcolm's colleagues did not know—but I am no longer listening. My mind turns away from these things with the weariness of a terminal patient being read the appetizing menu his body can no longer use.

Andrea laughs ingratiatingly. "But what if it's a girl, Jennifer? You can't count on getting what you want!" She would like this conversation to go on forever, one feels. She is enjoying a vicarious pleasure. Also, her questions make Jennifer happy, and she wishes to keep Jennifer happy: perhaps she is grateful that Jennifer is too preoccupied to be bothered with Malcolm. How is it that, like the characters in *Midsummer Night's Dream,* we are so transparent in our affections? Fearful of revealing my own, I have become silent. Now and then my eyes rest on Carillo's hands as he tests the trap: it springs perfectly. Like a small animal, I feel myself rush into it. . . .

It is strange that in the weeks since our arrival here, I have dreamt of Mark only once. I wonder, occasionally, with what activities Mark is distracting his soul; whether he regrets his decision, whether already he has found someone to comfort him . . . Is he, like Malcolm, continuing his work at the margins of annihilation? But his research required audiences, interviews, travel, reports, statistics, computers; he needed the courier systems of the world to find out what he needed to know. My mind begins forming a poem for Mark, speaking to him, explaining to him that in my need I have fallen in love with a stone, a myth, a man out of history who therefore can exist only after history is recorded. They will write of this man (I tell Mark) as they tell of the heroes of the Resistance, only nobody believes anymore in heroism, and there is nothing to resist: how can one lay siege to nuclear warheads, to guided missiles, to the cobalt bomb? How can one hold hostage the finger on the trigger aimed at the world: there will only be other fingers and other triggers—in Peking, in Moscow, in the Middle East: even India, land of Gandhi, will have her hour of destruction.

While I am silently composing my poem for Mark, suddenly Jennifer is screaming. At first I am annoyed, I imagine she is merely up to some teen-age antic, that they are screams of delighted protest at some new contortion Andrea has discovered for her in their book. Then I too see the apparition which somehow does not surprise me: it is Duncan and he is wearing a long black soutane and a corded belt. It is as if he has decided to invest himself with the ceremonies of priesthood, the outer sign, at least, of his inner "faith." But it is not the faith, we see now, of the Church Militant, but of a very new (or rather, very old) religion, which Duncan in his wild eschatology has decided to resurrect: in one hand, like Moses of old turning his staff into serpents to frighten the Pharoah, is a long snake, as thick as a fist; it is wound around his body and writhing across his shoulders as though it were a seahorse swimming through a wake of water and air. In a moment we are all either screaming or shouting. Carillo has leaped to his feet: *Have you gone mad?* Duncan looks at him coolly. "He's perfectly harmless. I've had him for weeks, don't you know? And he hasn't once got out of his cage."

But Jennifer in terror is still screaming. She *loathes* snakes, she shrieks, and loathes Duncan too, and loathes everyone in this place, and she wishes she had never come here: "You're all a bunch of freaks and weirdoes!" She disappears into the house and we hear very distinctly the sound of sobbing, not of despair but of fury. It is the rage to survive.

Klara

My father had picked the wrong time to go mad; the war was operating briskly, money was flowing from the coffins to the coffers as usual, and the population in Detroit between the time of our arrival at Ellis Island and the end of the World War (the *First,* as it was called!) had nearly doubled. Galina had abandoned all notions of becoming a doctor, lawyer, merchant or chief, and had quietly taken on first, temporary teaching in the public schools, then full-time teaching. She began to wear her clothes neatly, and spent at least a half hour brushing her hair every night. I took a job as a clerk at a big drug store downtown where I sold over-the-counter drugs and cosmetics and dressed in white like a nurse. I was hoping after graduation to free myself from the powders and nostrums of the drug store and find a position in a clean office, efficiently typing other people's letters in *English* (I had no idea at the time that such work could be anything less than rewarding).

Since Galina and I brought in virtually the only source of money, we were accorded a decision-making power in the household usually reserved for the men: if Mother wanted to buy something, it was us she consulted: could we afford it? At this time, ironically enough, if Galina had pursued her ambition to become a doctor or nearly anything else for that matter, there would have been no objections in the household (providing she continued to provide). But her attention had concentrated itself on a teacher of social studies whom she had met during her lunch hour, and their courtship took all her time—except when her former rebelliousness rose long enough to picket with me at Ford's or to contemplate an (unthinkable) teachers' strike to adjust wages to wartime inflation. (Galina's salary was eighty dollars a month, and *that* was higher than most other teachers: her friends questioned her motives and her very sanity when she went to protest meetings.) When, during the winter just before the end of the War, I joined Galina at a demonstration, handing out union leaflets, I would have howled in grief and rage had I known that so much talent was about to be swallowed up in the bearing of children and the scrubbing of clothes (it was to be years before Galina could afford one of the new electric washing machines which were to become an object of idolatry among soap opera listeners).

It was while we were standing in the sleet, our shoulders covered with a rubber cape to keep the leaflets dry, that I met Celestina Pelassi. After about a week of this physical endurance test outside the gates of the factory we became fast friends. Celestina's was one of the many rural families that had moved to Detroit in order to work for Ford, but her father had not had the luck to be hired by the great mogul and Celestina was about to drop out of high school to work in a cigar factory.

In spite of our own poverty I was shocked: Celestina seemed to me about to sacrifice what was still to us the highest privilege, what the Kleists had come to America for—their daughters' high school education (in Russia, neither Father nor Mother would have been admitted to the gymnasium). I asked Tina how much she would earn. She said she did not know for certain, she would be paid by the hour and it would all depend on how many hours she could work: if she could manage to put in sixty hours, her income would be "really good." Tina's quiet resignation to a fate that seemed to me nothing short of imprisonment (I had heard descriptions of the cigar lofts even then) was either the highest courage or the deepest ignorance. "But Tina," I wailed. "How will you stand it? Cooped up in a dark loft, wrapping cigars all day. Breathing air that twenty others have used and reused. Barely having time to wash your hands before eating your sandwich. Then, to come home in the dark and cook dinner for yourself and your brothers. Tina, you can't do this to yourself. There must be . . . something else." I was young, and my emotions in those days welled easily to my eyes; I was nearly crying at the specter I had called up of Tina's future.

I had thought my sympathy was its own excuse for eloquence. So, I was unprepared for the tears of rage and insult which now stood in Tina's eyes. I realized with a sinking heart that my outburst had been of no use to her and that in addition I had perhaps lost a new friend. (In those days Galina and I were slow to make friends: with our wrinkled cotton stockings and our long hair eternally escaping from a careless topknot, we were more often objects of ridicule than friendship.)

"It's easy for *you* to talk. With your education! But what can I do? And besides, whatever I do, it's only for a few years. . . ."

"What do you mean?"

She turned away from me in the cold, to hand a leaflet to a passing worker. The worker shifted his chilled neck in his collar just long enough to accept the leaflet, then with a glance, he threw it to the ground. I saw that Tina was choking back tears. I stood silent, miserable. From a distance I could see Galina at the other gate, pacing back and forth on the frozen ground to restore some warmth to her legs. We were like a ragged, broken army.

"Well, I'll be married, won't I?" Tina said at last, with a kind of defiance. "I wouldn't be doing it for long."

My odd look must have angered her further, because she said with annoyance: "Oh of course *you* don't have to get married! You'll have a high school diploma, and you'll get a job in an office and people will call you Miss Kleist, and you'll answer the telephone in this . . . *voice,* being secretary to the President and all that . . . And besides," she added with a malice I would not have expected, "there's no man good enough for you! Anybody can see, you Kleist sisters are waiting for God himself!"

I was much shaken at her words. Was this in fact the impression the Kleist sisters made on people, that we thought we were too good for the men and boys of our own culture? It was my first experience with the fantastic misconceptions that rumor without knowledge could create. For the absurd fact was that both Galina and I had been making every effort, within the limits of our small community, to get ourselves married. Galina had finally "succeeded," but toward what ultimate Good, the sight of the pale little school teacher she loved was enough to make me more than question. Marriage was the only way, we thought, that we could achieve the freedom we needed. And as for Mother—she dreamed of marriage for us the way, had we been sons, she would have dreamed of our becoming the first Jewish governor or the discoverer of a cure from some dread (Jewish) disease.

It was a matter of great importance to me that Tina and I

understand each other. When we had distributed all our leaflets, I begged her to come home with me. We rode home on the street car together and I brewed us some hot tea with lemon. In those days we still drank it from a glass and used lumps of sugar. I remember even now Tina's mild surprise that we did not keep granulated sugar in a bowl: these are the small items which mark the passing of a culture. . . . We talked for hours. . . .

Afterwards, when she had gone and I sat alone in the kitchen I thought long and hard about what Celestina had said, about herself, about myself, as women. What struck me was her absolute faith that someone would soon love her and marry her; that they would have four or five children, that they would live in a nice home and that they would not quarrel like my father and mother, but would live together at an assured level of happiness and comfort until they were old. To my frightened imagination it did not seem at all inevitable that someone would love me: indeed, so far no one had. Rather, it had been I and I alone who had battered my heart against unrealizable odds, trying desperately to attract the notice of the few yeshiva boys who lived in our neighborhood. They were no more aware of me than of a block of ice in winter. I was part of the landscape, nothing more. Sometimes perhaps I was merely eccentric in my flat-heeled shoes, sometimes frightening, as when I stood in front of the voting booths on Election Day, brandishing my suffragist sign—but attractive? marriageable? 'A daughter of Zion on mincing toes'? Never. Alone in the kitchen, mulling over Tina's housewifely wisdom, I recalled with shame how I pursued the impervious Gary Schutz.

Much has been written since my youth of the black man or woman's lust to enter the white man's world. But the world which to me was as soft as the velvet seats of the Czar's palace, or as mysterious as that of the English gentleman flanked by hunting dogs, was the world on the other side of our particular ghetto— the white Protestant middle class—a class as abstemious as the Jew in its drinking habits, whose children attended church in white stockings and black patent leathers, and whose parents, probably, owned most of Detroit. Theirs was an identity as lofty and secret as that of crown princes; we could not aspire to them, and Galina and I never attempted to cross that line of caste and class.

But we were exposed instead to another kind of game, a pseudo-egalitarianism of faith, in which we imagined that, since it was forbidden to jeopardize our heritage by assimilation, the one good thing we could do, the single act which automatically dissolved all class lines, was to marry one of our own. It never occurred to me, though I think now it must soon have imposed itself as an economic reality upon Galina who was so much shrewder than I, that Our Own wouldn't look twice at us—a couple of ragged sisters who only a few years ago combed their long hair for lice and whose father was kept under restraints in an institution: we might as well have been dope addicts and criminals for the heavy stigma our father's poverty and madness put upon us.

But I was still blissfully unaware of this. And since marriage was the name of the game, I cheerfully set my telescopic sight on Gary Schutz. If you are up to your ears in egalitarianism yourself, you forget sometimes that the rest of the world is still judging you by your ancestors.

I had met Gary in my senior year at high school; or rather I hadn't met him, he was a "found art object." I was cutting my way across the empty high school football field on my way to work (it was about 3:23—I measured every minute in those synchronized days) when this apparition in white rose to his feet from where he had been sitting among the empty bleachers.

Under my light spring coat I had already donned the white uniform which I wore at the drug store. School did not let out until 3:20, but I could still make it to work on time and punch their clock before 4:00 provided I did not take time to go downstairs to change clothes after my arrival. Since my last class at school was a study period, I was able to slip into the girls' rest room, button into my uniform, and be prepared to catch the bus as soon as the first bell rang through the building.

But now there was Gary, standing in the sunlight, wearing as I distinctly remember, a white tennis outfit and swinging his racket disconsolately. I was immediately happy to see that he was not happy: he had been waiting for his tennis partner, who was late. Perhaps she would not come at all. I was prepared to be Cupid's scab: I prayed as we stood there and chatted (he had no watch, he said anything on his wrist goofed up his game, and he had asked me the time) that his tennis partner would never come. Noticing my white shoes and uniform, he asked me if I were a nurse or something. And with that light-hearted, self-satirizing touch meant to hide the ignominy of being forced to earn a living while the world watched (a sort of modern-day Roman amphitheater, it is), I explained where I was going. I made it sound like the wonderful adventures of Oz instead of what it was: a grubby, tiresome job where all the perfumes gave me a headache, and my hands would be crisscrossed by the end of day with red scars of Kissproof, Tangee and Max Factor's: I was never again able to wear cologne after that stint at the drug store. But meanwhile, I stood there with Gary four or five minutes, keeping him amused with the details of my job: willing to play the clown.

He said, "Are you in a hurry? I mean, do you have to get there on time? I mean *of course* you have to get there on time, but what time do you have to get there?"

We both laughed, and I was instantly in love: you don't need much at that age. We talked for another five minutes or so, while he awaited his date; Laura was her name. It never occurred to me that he was using me to make his girlfriend jealous: I thought he really wanted to know how you sold cologne and Kissproof to the working girls. And I, although I would be docked an hour for being ten minutes late, and although it was sufficient to be late twice to be put "on notice" altogether, I stood in the sunshine, clutching my clothes in their brown paper bag and feeling pleased with myself that I had taken time to clean my shoes, which were as white as his. What I kept noticing was that his eyes were as soft and velvety, that his skin was as fresh and rested as if he had just gotten up from a nap.

Now why is it that this scene, after a lifetime, should still arouse this wild pain in my heart? Why is it I can still see Laura approaching, also in white tennis clothes: her arms and legs are bare, she is carrying nothing but a tennis racket which is swung across her neck like a laborer's pickaxe. She is not even looking at us as she approaches, but off toward the court. A certainty, like a poisoned cloak, flays my flesh that now that she has arrived I have served my purpose; *hurry away, your house is on fire and your children are gone* . . . His eyes begin to panic. Perhaps he has overdone his power play? Perhaps she, Laura, will think? . . . Whatever she may think is more important by a lifetime than what I think or feel, and quickly I make some excuse, hide the sight of her by pretending to look for my busfare. (I have already missed my bus and in order to avoid waiting twenty minutes right beside the tennis court for the next bus, I will walk four long blocks down to another bus stop.) But Gary is already waving goodbye to me; one shoe is pointed like a sundial toward Laura's figure, the other is digging into the ground as though somehow I have pinioned him by one toe. To save him any further anguish, it is I who begin to run as if I *must* catch my bus, and so I run, I rush with a burst of shame. But what has happened that I am suddenly reduced to this state? It is simple, I have begun to run along an infinite railroad track—Gary on one side, I on the other. Separated by a few railroad ties, we can communicate, converse, touch each other, run as hard as we can to the other end, even finish up simultaneously at the same railroad station: but we cannot run single file on the same track, one behind or in front of the other, because my father is in an insane asylum and his owns (I later discover) the very building in which I am employed.

Every Jewish parent, I had been told from infancy, wants his son or daughter to marry a Jew: we are instructed that such marriages will save the institution of marriage itself, will save the children, will save Israel from destruction. So with this rationalization (I think, to tell the truth, I would have done the same had Gary been an Eskimo), I pursued Gary Schutz. I did not even know that it was called "pursuit." I only knew by instinct that marriage was the goal and all Jewish men were goalkeepers. Therefore, I did insane humiliating things that I did not even know would be regarded as insane, because I thought anyone would behave as I did. In short, I knew none of the secrets of coquetry, and thought honesty, fervor, intelligence, even sexual passion, might earn for me the Earthly Paradise of being united with Gary. That he was dumb as a crow, endlessly cawing *com-mie! com-mie!* on political questions, did not affect my infatuation. You couldn't expect everything else and common sense too. So for months we carried on our banal and secret affair. Beneath our parents' very eyes we arranged for rendezvous, met on the school tennis court only to disappear into the woody acres behind the school, met at the wharf's edge in Waterworks Parks, met—inevitably—almost every afternoon in Gary's new automobile, where like thousands of others of our generation we contrived to dissolve our lust and shame and confusion in the confines of a new Ford. Why we were never arrested is still a mystery to me. I remember once a policeman approached Gary's car at a time when we were sitting half-undressed in the front seat. As calmly as a Count to his serfs, Gary pulled the leather pillow out from behind his head so as to cover his lap. I did not stir or speak, fearful our guilt would be revealed in my trembling voice. Such adventures, the excitement of sexual passion, of denial and escape drew us together in a wildly prohibited way. No child of the sixties could understand it: we shared the *mischief* of sex.

This went on all during the months prior to graduation; I lived in a feverish dream in which I went to the drug store totally exhausted, but somehow revived at the end of the long evening's work. The very sight of Gary waiting for me outside, impatiently glancing at his watch from time to time, instilled new energy in me. On one occasion, I remember, he was looking over several college catalogues: he wanted, he said, to see what they had to offer him.

Then suddenly Gary became swept up in the ritual of social life which surrounded graduation: he was elected to this and to that; then he was chosen, along with Laura, to play the leading part in the high school play *Our Town.* He soon found a dozen excellent excuses not to be waiting for me. It's an old story, really. Any person's memoirs could tell the rest: I began to wait for him in the hallways, in the street, anywhere I could catch a glimpse of him, yet with fear in my heart. It was an anticipation of the end —a need to test the sharpness of the axe, to know that when it fell the blade would cut through the bone, ending all feeling.

Thus one Spring day only a few days before graduation, I saw him coming down the long central staircase of the high school. I stopped, caught in the grips of a *déjà vu:* Laura was with him, and they were walking down the stairs slowly enough so that their bodies touched, and their feet reached the step below at the same time. I watched their feet, fascinated by this perfect rhythm.

Then I looked up, Laura was wearing a woolen cardigan of an unusual color, a mauve or fuchsia. Why do I remember that? Because unusual colors are hard to blend in with a wardrobe of any kind, and my first thought was: she bought that sweater to wear with *one* particular outfit. Moreover, it was a sweater that had everything to do with fashion, its warmth was irrelevant. As she and Gary came closer, I noticed on the tip of her bosom, like a modest nipple designed to stir attention and nourish dreams, Gary's class pin. In those days to be 'pinned' by a senior was as serious as a ritual betrothal.

I did not pretend not to see them; on the contrary, I walked toward them deliberately. At my approach Gary pressed the soft cushiony layer of flesh which one could see tightening the waist-line of Laura's skirt. Laura did not giggle at the sight of me, she was too well-bred for that, but they both paused about three steps above me while I stood stock still, awaiting some word that would shatter any illusion, make it *final.* But Gary was understandably speechless.

Laura gently touched the pin with (I noticed) White-Gloss fingertips. "Gary's pinned me," she said. "Isn't that sweet?" She turned toward us both a smile that was without malice, yet which took in perfectly who I was. I could not help thinking then that Gary was right. She was perfect, she was what he needed and therefore wanted, she had all the quiet elegance that would go with the vague ambitions he had described—the ambiguous per-fection of the right ornamental word at the proper moment. It was more than custom, it was a commonwealth of graces, each one acquired in a different realm, the very existence of which, colonies, feudalities, ambassadorships, were a mere blur on the map to me.

I do not recall what I said, I did not look at Gary; I felt I did not need to look at him, I felt I knew every arch and shift of his expressive face. It was Laura who was the object of my attention, because it was the first time I realized that one could pretend not to know what was obvious. . . .

Shortly after that my sister married Harold and I married Aaron Arnowitz. A reaction? A return to common sense? A tem-porary return to the fold which turns out not temporary after all but as permanent as Hell or Paradise? In my case, I was su-premely lucky. Aaron, an immigrant like myself, had come to America to seek his fortune; a wife was part of his fortune. With-out romantic clamor, and even though Aaron was, as it was called, a "free-thinker," he attended the services of the neighbor-hood synagogue just long enough to cast his eye around the sisterhood. He looked around for several months, talked to a few young ladies, and, as he told me later, chose me because the others had good looks, but I had *saichel.* "And," Aaron added, "I always remember the proverb: 'Take a wife, step down a little. Find a friend, step up a little.' " Not exactly a courtship in the style of Mary Pickford and Douglas Fairbanks, but to me, after all Gary's lies, evasions, protestations and class hypocrisies, it seemed as simple as a nursery rhyme: The-farmer-takes-a-wife, the-wife-takes-a-child, etc.

Within a year after we were married, as was in those days the natural course of events, both Galina and I were having our first child at Detroit Receiving.

All this was a burgeoning of Jewish nature as traditional as brisses, weddings, bar mitzvahs, and funerals. But what none of us foresaw anymore than did those financial geniuses of the twenties was that within a year after my mother had danced at my wedding, weeping with joy that at last what she had come to America for had been realized—*both* daughters married and saved from politics forever—the nation, indeed the entire world, was to be thrown into an economic disaster without parallel.

Aaron was a simple man with sensuous tastes; he was only a worker, but he loved fine food, clean linen, good wine for the holidays, bright wallpaper and lavish furnishings. All these he invested in our home and in our marriage as though happiness in America, along with economic security, were written into the marriage contract. So we began like the others, counting our possessions. Before what is known to history as The Crash, I too was lulled into believing in the American Dream. No more political causes: with Bashe at my breast (we called her Bashe to satisfy my mother; she herself later changed it to Babette), with Aaron steadily employed, for nearly an entire year my world revolved about nursing the baby and scrubbing the wooden floors till they gleamed like the marble halls of the Czarina. I even learned, for the first time (every day my pious mother gave thanks), to bake Jewish goodies and cook according to Aaron's Russian tastes. We did not know we were on an ice floe which was rapidly melting around us.

But it, of course, came quickly to pass. Aaron, along with about a hundred thousand others in Automobile City, was laid off. I forget the exact date but it was shortly before Christmas in '29. We were frightened, but we were cheerful: weren't we both young and strong, and hadn't the New Land been bountiful to us? So Aaron tossed Babette into the air as though she were a new species defying gravity, a child with secret wings which would keep her from falling, even should he himself (though never, never could it happen!) fail to catch her.

Then, the following spring, it was the sixth of March, I remember—we are doomed to remember the days of our ordeal even as the days of our joy—Aaron and I left Babette with my mother and went to show our solidarity with the other unemployed workers. We were standing in Cadillac Square. . . .

Klara looked up at the sky. They had been standing for nearly two hours, among thousands of people—how many thousands Klara had no idea. There was a cold mist in the air, neither rain nor snow, but simply a relentless assault on the senses, an acid bath trying to penetrate the skin. The speeches multiplied endlessly, the crowd grew ever more dense, so that she was obliged to lean against Aaron's back in order not to be pushed down to the ground. Speech upon speech rained from the loudspeakers: speeches against the automobile industry, against Ford and Mellon and Hoover and Father Coughlin, followed by speeches from people with foreign accents who spoke about Spain, about Italy. She heard the Italian word *fascisti* over and over. Klara pressed closer to Aaron, wanting him to protect her, thinking with a strange sense of surprise that he was only a few inches taller than she and that he probably could see the speakers little better than she could. She put her arms around him so that they would not be separated in the crowd.

People were cold, they were angry, some carried flags, some skirmished tentatively with each other in protest against the flags. Somebody began singing a song in Spanish which Klara did not understand, and almost at once the riot force arrived, it was as if the song had been the signal they were waiting for. Astonishingly, the police were quiet and did not curse them: silent, helmeted, with gleaming jackets to protect them from the cold, they moved like sleek armored fish through the sea of bodies: it was like *Potemkin* all over again, thought Klara, feeling herself grow faint. Aaron turned quickly in the crowd, gripping her arm. Now that she realized it was impossible for him to protect her, she was somehow astonished that he should try. But there he was, pushing fiercely against the police, trying to move Klara beyond the *cordon,* out of Cadillac Square, which was now totally surrounded by police, many on horseback. Nightsticks were suddenly flung into the air—batons in unison—there were dull thudding sounds, there were screams. A man—no, a boy—no bigger than Aaron, but younger, was being dragged away, pulled by the shirt, a white shirt, streaked with blood in uneven straggling strokes, like a child's first crayon scrawl. *Cover your head! Cover your head!* Aaron yelled as he pushed her precisely that foot away from the down-coming blow of the nightstick, which he himself received, and then he lay quiet: not like her father, behind whose sullen gaze as he had lain, shackled and mad, in the police car, there had been concealed the dry ice of rage; but quietly he lay, as though suddenly free of pain, anesthetized. Klara clawed at the policeman whose eyes glued over with guilt (guilt but not shame, not remorse, she thought) "I didn't hardly hit him. Damned melonhead . . ." But she could see that the policeman was frightened, and somehow that frightened her more than ever: Aaron lay still.

They had meant to arrest Aaron and file charges for assaulting an officer, but while he lay motionless in the hospital, the charges were mysteriously dropped. A civil liberties lawyer came to see Klara and said she should sue, nobody knew yet what the results would be . . .

Aaron lay silently, breathing shallowly, his mind a screen track on which nothing played, nothing but sleep and darkness. Klara sat by his bedside, only remembering Babette long enough to go down to a phone booth in the waiting room of the hospital and call a neighbor who was one of those fortunates who could afford a phone, who would try to find her mother, who would be more frightened by the telephone call than by Klara's anxious questions, "How is Babette, does she eat right? No, no change, no change, none at all. They don't know. Sometimes. You never know. The thing is, is the brain getting oxygen?"

Aaron, she spoke to him as he lay motionless, *is your brain getting oxygen? Take my lungs, my brain, Aaron. Don't leave me. Babette needs you. I'm terrified, Aaron, how can I care for Babette and Mama and me? Take a deep breath, Aaron, maybe it'll all suddenly come back to you, you'll remember how easy it is to bring blood to the right cells, to revive the brain* . . . Then suddenly she got angry with him, he would die, he would abandon her. *Think Aaron, don't like there like a goddamned mummy, like an Egyptian Pharoah. Aaron, get up!*

As the weeks went by, she despaired, she ceased to sit by his bedside. The law case dragged on, there was no money: it seemed to her that since the Kleists had first set their feet down in the Land of Plenty, where gold ran in the streets, the eternal question had been money. Now, with ferocity, she decided she must have money. Women were suddenly taking away the jobs of men, because the automobile industry, in order to cut corners and survive the Depression, would now pay women thirty-five cents an hour for jobs for which the men had received over a dollar an hour. Against all her own best principles, as if in sudden repudiation of the unionist's basic ethic and with savage self-contempt, Klara now accepted thirty-five cents an hour, feeling that she was stealing the very bread from the mouths of families with nine or ten children . . .

She would come home from her job more dead than alive, then she would make a listless call at the hospital. It was as if she did not believe Aaron would ever move again, nor did it matter (there were more ways to die than in a coma, she was discovering, as she put in a fifty-four hour work week). But she dared not look for less strenuous work—clerical or sales (by comparison her work at the drugstore now seemed utopian: imagine! a place where you wore white clothes and the only noise was the soft laughter of women trying on cologne and the jingle of cash registers). But at the drugstore the women were now working on straight commission and Klara knew that she could not sell enough, even if she worked ninety hours a week, to support three generations of women-without-men—grandmother, mother and daughter: a veritable dynasty of poverty, she thought bitterly.

One morning on her way to work (it was 6:30 and just getting light; it took her an hour to get out to the west side of the city), she met Celestina on the streetcar. Tina had changed in some mysterious way, Klara had difficulty identifying her as the same slender, defensive girl with whom she had distributed leaflets. Tina was wearing bib overalls, a red kerchief, and was carrying a lunch pail. She was headed for Ford's she said (Klara had avoided Ford's because of Ford's reputation for not hiring Jews).

"My husband works there too," Celestina informed her. "We have different shifts. He takes care of the kids at night when they're asleep anyway." She laughed. "He's lucky. I come home when they're getting out of school. Sometimes they're sick, and that's hell. But otherwise. . . ." She shrugged. "We do O.K."

Despair gripped Klara. Celestina and her husband had enough money to live on and shared their family responsibilities. Whereas, it had been she, Klara, who but a short time ago had been envied for her "Education," who now came home to her mother's complaints or to Babette asking questions Klara could not begin to answer: when was Daddy coming home from the hospital, and why could she not have tricycle, and why couldn't they go on a picnic, and go swimming at Belle Isle, and why couldn't they write Santa Claus like the kids next door who had received food, clothes, dolls and bicycles from this mysterious benefactor? Why not indeed? echoed Klara from the bottom of her heart, but could only turn away from the child and try to forget herself in her reading. At this time she was reading widely into the social theories of Proudhon and Shaw and Marx and Emma Goldman. That there were so many points of disagreement among so many clever people aiming at similar results was utterly depressing. It did seem to her they ought to be able to resolve their differences: that they could not appeared somehow a reflection on their collective intelligence. Nevertheless, Klara was on the verge of casting her intellectual ballot with a small group of socialists (even though they in turn disagreed among themselves) when she met Celestina.

"And the cigar factory?"

"Oh, that. Naturally they fired me when I got the women together. Imagine, they thought they could get away with it—they let over twenty of us go, but they wanted the same production yield. We told them we couldn't do it, it was impossible, we were already putting in sixty hours a week . . . They said we'd have to do it, or they'd find somebody who would do it for us. You can believe them, they'd have no trouble finding people. Have you seen Tent City? People living in those tents, they send their kids out every day just to steal what they can eat or to scavenge what they can get. Those people would be glad to have our jobs, at any pay scale. Who could blame them?

"So I got the women to organize . . ."

"You, Celestina!"

"Well, what's so surprising about that? My husband was very much interested. He had joined the Party. . . ." Tina lowered her voice. "Listen, come to our meetings. Don't sit back and let them do this to you. Do you realize?—over two million people in Michigan unemployed? . . . And the fat cats—do you think they're losing money in all this? No, they're making *millions, millions!* Klara, you wouldn't believe . . . I want you to meet my husband too. And come to our meeting." She scribbled an address on a scrap of paper.

Klara had gone to the meeting more out of loneliness than any true political conviction; she was developing a deep distrust of doctrinaire politics but felt, too, that her own reluctance to identify with any theory was exactly what was wrong with the Left.

They needed unity, and instead, wishy-washy "intellectuals" lik͟
herself were constantly destroying that unity to ask questions like
a child: *Why* must it follow that the working class will rise against
its oppressors? Why must all the Czars and Czarinas be executed?
Foolish, weakening questions, she felt them so herself, yet
couldn't stop asking. So, she had begun to attend the meetings
(her sister rarely went anywhere anymore except to meetings of
the local school board) basking in what she hoped was friendship
among people she believed were well-intentioned, even though
she so often disagreed with them. At least she was no longer so
much alone that talking to Babette was like breaking a vow of
silence. In spite of the economy, there was an atmosphere of
hope. . . .

Then suddenly Aaron recovered consciousness. She was not
there when it happened, there was a message from Dr. Pettinger
waiting for her at the check-out gate: "Your husband wishes to
speak to you." *Speak to you! Speak to you!* Never, Klara thought, had
she ever heard such beautiful words. She ran to the hospital still
dressed in her denim overalls and heavy work shoes. Upon entering the hospital, panic seized her. Would he recognize her this
way? Would her appearance throw him into some kind of shock?
She found her way to the women's rest room, carefully combed
and brushed her long hair, and although she could not get out
of her work clothes, she straightened out the collar of her blouse
so that she looked more . . . feminine. The word made her laugh:
for more than a year she had been feeling like some sort of
medieval priest doing penance in a hair shirt. Then she ran to
Aaron's hospital room. Outside the door she stopped, circling it
like a hunting dog. She had the absurd feeling that she should
knock. . . .

"Aaron," she whispered, and he at once turned his head.

His eyes filled with tears: "Klara."

Though she had waited months for him to speak, she cau-
tioned him gratefully: "Don't say anything, don't strain yourself.
You're all right now. Everything's all right now." Aaron gripped
her hand. He had lost nearly all the flesh of his body, and the
knuckles stood out, distinct and hard as sculptured ivory.

He was home, but everything was not all right. He knew everybody, understood everything, so long as he was "well." But when
the headaches came upon him, it was all black rage. Afterwards

he could not even remember why he was angry. And it took little to excite the headache, then the rage, then the darkness ... Sometimes it was Babette with her toy, sometimes it was someone at the bakery (he had taken a job where he cleaned the equipment nightly). One night it was because (as he said) she had no business going to these meetings with Celestina, Klara was not a Party member, she would only get them into trouble, she would lose her job. Their landlord hated Jews (Aaron reminded her) and would use politics as an excuse to evict them, maybe even get them deported. People *did* get deported: people had been deported during the Palmer raids, had she forgotten?

Klara had not realized during the long months of Aaron's illness how much she had come to rely on her own judgment. Now it was difficult to obey him, to heed his advice. With a shock she realized now that her promise to Celestina meant more to her than Aaron's displeasure: she had *promised* Tina that she would join with her and the thousands who were rallying in a protest march against Ford's employment policies. Klara was not even certain what the workers' demands were, but she felt that she supported Celestina and her husband 'to the death'—as she put it to Aaron. It was a foolish phrase, she instantly regretted it. Lately everything Aaron said seemed to force her to extreme utterances.

He watched her put on a beret. "You're going to be deported yet, you'll see. You think you're an Emma Goldman? Well, O.K. —don't forget what happened to her. Why must you wear that stupid red beret? You're not a Red, are you, Klara?"

She tried to make a joke of it. "It's for Tina. She wants the marchers to look three thousand strong. For myself, I'd rather carry a picture of Franklin Delano: he's better looking than the guy *she's* carrying, and Roosevelt's a millionaire besides ..." In spite of her jesting tone, Klara had an inexplicable faith in the new president, she expected miracles of him. ... Actually Klara would rather have stayed home but even her sister, momentarily breaking away from "babies, baking, and Harold," as she put it, had consented to join them.

Aaron refused to go. "If she works for that *anti-semitt,* what can she expect?" he observed sourly. As Klara kissed him goodbye, he looked at her strangely; his hands were damp as he held her own; he even ran after her in the street to ask her if she had enough money. Money for what? she found herself murmuring

to her sister as all three women climbed into Celestina's Model
T. It refused to start and Celestina, with a groan, got out to crank
the starter, while she and Galina prepared to assist with a pushing
motion from the rear. The crank flew with a violent wrench from
Celestina's hands. Tina tried again; the three women held their
breaths in agonized attention waiting for the engine to catch. . . .
Years later, when such scenes had become part of comic filmdom
on speeded up cameras, Klara had sat in a New York theater and
had seen a film of women with coats down to their ankles, with
fur around their collars and wearing cloche hats, all racing
through the streets in a bumping, jogging Model T: and the
audience had roared with laughter. But Klara had wept, wept
more lonely tears than ever before in her life: because by then
Celestina was dead of cancer, Galina had died in childbirth after
valiantly bringing one more great giant of a son into the world
who was to die in Korea, and Klara had sat alone in the theater
in New York, watching the silent antics of the funny women
dressed in furs: *so different from the way we really looked that day.*

The truth was that her sister's nose had been red with cold;
Celestina's hair had also been (absurdly) hennaed because, she
said, she wanted to look like a fiery redhead. And she, Klara, had
been already shivering, not with the March cold (why, she asked
herself, did so many demonstrations take place at that season
when *longen folk to goon on pilgrimages?*) but because she had realized with sudden terror why Aaron had not wished her to go on
the march today. It was because he himself was frightened. It now
occurred to Klara that since coming home from the hospital he
had not attended a single union meeting; that lately he had begun
talking of the possibility of the bakery's laying off bakers, drivers,
and *even clean-up men,* he had begun talking about going on relief. . . . How long would this new Aaron persist? For the first time
she faced up to the possibility that this new Aaron was now her
husband, that the concussion in Cadillac Square had hurdled
Aaron out of the present and into the Past forever, for only the
Past, having been survived, could be trusted. . . . She now saw
that his fearful considerations as she had left the house—the
distraught kisses, the offer of money—were part of a concern for
himself, not for her: what would happen to Aaron if *she* were
injured?

The thought was shattering, and during the march toward the
Ford factory, Klara thought of little else. It was true, wasn't it?

It was she who was earning the most money, who was still strong, who had cared for Babette during the long agonizing months when Aaron had lain more dead than alive; it was she who still attended meetings, had taken up a foreign language at night school, was still studying, planning for the future. Lately, she had been thinking of leaving Detroit and starting a new life for all of them in California.

During the walk toward the Ford building Klara became confused. It seemed to her suddenly that she was back with Aaron in Cadillac Square; there were so many similarities between the marches that long afterwards she would confuse the two events when she recounted them. Again, as before, there were speeches, but this time the police did not wait for any signal, but plowed in almost at once—the bright splashes of red berets in the wintry sunlight seemed to be enough to have incensed them. This time she was screaming when the shots rang out. . . . Scattered and confused by tear gas, the crowd began to run. It was like a crazy Maypole dance in which poles and dancers had become brutally entwined. Arrests were taking place everywhere. Klara saw women being arrested. Surely they three would be next? Then suddenly the three were separated from each other; Klara's tight grip on her companions had been broken by the crowd, it was now every woman for herself as they all began screaming and running. Celestina, who knew the area better than the Kleist sisters, was yelling at them to follow her, but she only made herself conspicuous by her yelling and gesticulation and was promptly arrested. Terrified at what she might face if she were arrested—deportation, interrogation, the brutality of "the tank" in which all those arrested would perhaps be thrown together in a common cell—Klara ran, ducked, climbed over grappling bodies. Finally she found an odd-looking vehicle to hunker down beside and hide behind till the panic ebbed. She never realized what sort of machine she had hidden behind till later in newspapers she thought she recognized what was soon to become a major contribution to our European allies, a new sort of armored tank.

Suddenly it was over. The police had made dozens of arrests, and had become dour and indifferent to the strange woman they saw now walking away from the riot-quelled area with an air of as much dignity and innocence as she could muster.

One demonstrator had been shot.

A few days later Klara joined the funeral procession for the man who had been killed. In silence she walked the four miles in the icy rain—following the body of the fallen victim. She felt a kind of death herself, without emotion—cold-eyed and furious with the world for this useless death. Then suddenly someone began slowly drumming the funeral dirge for the revolutionaries of *her* revolution, which she had witnessed as a mere child while history exploded around her. Only then did she begin sobbing and crying out like the others, staggering with grief in the wake of the coffin as though the man were her own flesh and blood. But what she was sobbing and crying out for was the injustice done during those years since 1905 to a child's image of the world: she had ceased to believe in revolution which wrought political convulsion and death and had begun to believe, as an alternative Cause, in Education.

Just as Aaron had predicted, she was promptly fired from her job for having taken part in the march. Klara begged Galina to try to get her into the school system as a teaching substitute. In order to qualify as soon as possible she took courses both at a small college out in Highland Park and at Wayne University. And when eventually she received her first teaching assignment, and threaded her way through the barbed wire and firing line of the first day, she felt as if she had crossed No Man's Land. At the end of her first month, exhausted but pleased with herself, she announced to Galina that she had found her métier.

"Métier, shmétier, you'll hate the little bastards before you're through."

Klara was shocked: she had thought her sister's work idealistic, a way of changing the world. She resisted Galina's tone of delusion; instead, she spent long hours that night over her Lesson Plan. "Today the ninth grade, tomorrow the world," said Klara blithely, and jotted down some ideas for teaching the vocabulary of *Ivanhoe.*

"It's a living," said Galina.

Klara tried hard to distinguish between her need to earn money and her students' need to learn. But it was not long before she understood her sister's bitterness: the moral responsibilities of their profession were endless, but she and Galina were paid as if they were caring, not for the minds and souls of the next generation which would solve economic crises, find a cure for cancer, end war, and discover a path to Mars, Venus, Pluto, the universe, but as if they were hosing down a sewer pipe. Geniuses, morons, the handicapped (both physically and emotionally) students hungry for a kind word, students as indifferent as stone, students whose parents were on relief and students whose parents were active in parent-teacher organizations, were all slushed through the sewer pipe by the furious impact of her Lesson Plan. There was no time to discuss the rise of dictatorships in Italy and Spain, of expansionism in Japan, of anti-Semitism in Germany, the bestowal of dictatorial powers on a *petit monstre* called Hitler . . . Instead they concentrated on the prejudices of the Norman invader toward their Anglo-Saxon subjects. So what else was new? . . . thought Klara bitterly. It appeared a kind of madness to be sane under such conditions: one disaster followed another. The banks had failed, then reopened, weak and unpredictable as a post-operative patient. Even teachers were not wanted anymore; she and Galina were fortunate to be hired once or twice a week. Jews were fleeing from Germany, Spain, Italy. . . . There was a boycott on Japanese goods, though this affected them scarcely at all: Klara rarely ever bought Babette any of the tiny porcelain trinkets labeled "Made in Japan." What was absolutely necessary for Babette's survival was clothes, and that was all they ever bought for gifts: mittens, scarves, overshoes. Years later Klara recalled with sorrow that in a city martyred by snow every winter, Babette had never had a sled.

Once Klara had consented to building a snowman with Babette. The late afternoon sun was light, almost flavorsome, as though it might have somewhere in it if one could but taste it, the flavor of vanilla or the tang of white wine. It did not seem possible, anyway, with that mellow light falling on the snow that they could come to any harm. But Babette had lost her gloves in the snow and, holding up her half-frozen hands, had begun weeping helplessly. Klara rubbed the child's hands, blowing her own warm breath on them to restore circulation; then she had kissed each little finger, still as pink and smooth as an untasted apple. Almost without thinking she had pulled off her own gloves and slipped them over Babette's hands, where they flopped merrily. . . . But the snowman had still to be kneaded and rolled, like round loaves of bread, and Babette could not do it alone, Klara had to do most of it. Within minutes Klara's hands were so numb she could not feel what direction the snowman's head was leading them. Her fingers were turning white, in panic she realized that she had a typical case of frostbite. Her first wild concern was— how would she teach her classes the next day? She rushed into the house, turned on the faucet and stood in agony while the tepid water dissolved the cold into increasing splinters of pain. . . . Aaron insisted she go to the hospital, where she waited hours for the emergency ward to check her in and check her out. At last they assured her that she would lose only a few fingernails . . . She was lucky, they said.

She never again took Babette out snowmanning; but she decided at that point that life might be simpler in a place where one's child did not run the risk of frostbite and gangrene. But how to move away? There were no jobs anywhere in the nation and in some cities there were not even any relief offices. At least in Detroit children could still line up for hot soup, and she was averaging two days work every week. She waited, biding her time.

The 'Time' came, and with it the Great Irony, as she always called it.

It came in the form of preparation for the great destruction which in turn wrought the Great Irony of reemployment. What the AAA, the NRA, the CWA, and the PWA could not do, the elimination of hundreds of thousands of Jews, the persecution of Catholic priests, the torture and imprisonment of dissenters in the Nazi Party, succeeded in bringing about: the miracle of employment. Suddenly, with increased aid being shipped to our future Allies, Aaron found a job in a clothing store on Second Boulevard, and looking very elegant himself—after years of rage and self-contempt—he began selling clothes to the young men who attended Wayne University. He began to sport a plaid black and white jacket, wear ties and two-toned shoes; he wore his hair neat, he became courteous to Klara and affectionate with Babette. At last his long illness was over, he was cured into self-respect by a job. Klara laughed bitterly and could not even enjoy their prosperity, her mind was on the coming holocaust.

On September 1, 1939 she sat down and like another poet who —unlike herself—was meant for international reknown, she wrote in careful, stilted English a memorial poem for the land of Shakespeare, Jonson, Donne, Swift, Macaulay, Dickens—and *Ivanhoe*. Without any facetious intent, clumsily using the only poetic form she knew (the sonnet), she wrote: *To Ivanhoe, With Love.*

Even now, in Duncan's colony, she had a copy of that poem, the only one she was ever to write: for which, Klara observed wryly to Michele, let us thank God. . . .

If you want to go to a new land, to start a new life, the important thing is to have a cousin there. It doesn't matter that he will be of little or no help—perhaps even a hindrance after your arrival. The main thing is that he should be able to write you luring letters, describing the streets which are (of course) paved with gold, the plentiful jobs available in the factories, the fine public schools, the economical cost of living, the wonderful housing arrangements he will prepare for you in advance, the beaches near the ocean, the tropical fruits. . . . All these lures of California, tale upon tale received from cousin Hirschel Kleist, and which were both true and untrue, finally persuaded her and Aaron that they could start a new life in California. Feeling secure with a few hundred dollars and a second-hand car, like hundreds of thousands before them they packed their new clothes (which were to turn out to be for the most part quite unsuitable for the new climate) and settled Babette in the back seat with a kitten and a litter basket. By the end of the second day they had twice lost the kitten on the highways, and later were to spend several hours looking for it in La Platte, only to abandon the kitten and drive on. Babette remained tearful and despondent about her kitten until they reached Wyoming, where she brightened up in the hope of seeing real Indians. The dramatic colors of the stone and earth across Wyoming filled them all with awe and reverence. In spite of Klara's trepidations, the trip was an Americanizing experience; she arrived in California a patriot, entranced by the vastness of a country she had for years been too busy surviving in to know or enjoy. And now for the first time she felt indeed that there was space here for the poor and heavy-laden. The crossing of the desert at night into California was an experience she was to tell tales of all her life; it remained the surreal epitome of her new life. There were moments when in restrospect the crossing into California seemed more daring than the Kleists' early trip from Russia years ago. On the ship, childish and ignorant, they had had only their fear of drowning and of infectious diseases, but here the endless steppes beckoned like so many promises leading them through the desert: but without the Law.

The sense of triumph and exhilaration when they entered the

land of the gold rush was to remain with them for months. Certainly, an enterprising family like themselves who had managed to cross the desert without mishap would be rewarded with all the good things of this world. Klara's cousin had promised it; even the Government seemed anxious to help fulfill Hirsch's promise, for the Los Angeles factories were now building fighter planes as fast as they could. Babette was excited and happy, intrigued by the strange dry earth, by the orange and eucalyptus trees. For several weeks Babette had the streets of Los Angeles confused with the Wild West and thought every man she saw wearing a sombrero was a cowboy, and every brown-skinned person an Indian. She thrived in the sunshine, she discovered papaya and avocado, and her blonde hair turned gold in the sunlight: it was as if the family chronicle of immigration had now been completed. Babette, like her parents before her, had adjusted to a new country, the land of milk and honey: there were now no more Paradises for them to seek.

California, they were told, was different not only geographically but politically. Even the people (the people claimed) were vastly different from those Easterners who preferred the old ways. But in spite of these differences, Klara discovered the war was the same ongoing war, a war which had begun with the killing of the Jews and seemed in danger of ending with the killing of the world. And with a strange new obsessive animation which resembled fear, Aaron began to demand of her: was *he* to let the rest of the world fight to make the world safe for the Jews? When Klara wept and wrung her hands and said he was insane, there was no need for him to go, there were millions of younger, stronger men, he demanded to know: who had more to lose than the Jews, if Hitler should win? On and on he went about the Jews: never had she seen Aaron so convinced that their fate was indissolubly entwined with the fate of Czechoslovakia, Poland, England, the world. If Russia fell to Germany he said, all the members of his family who had struggled to help send him to America, who wrote regularly of their longings and sufferings, would be wiped out like so many cattle. And even if this were not so, even if he had not a single relative left in all Europe and Russia, was it not their responsibility as Jews to share the dangers of the others? Were they to sit back in the sunlight of California plucking dates from the trees and making money from the bombs which would be dropped, some of them, upon their own people in an attempt to liberate them? Was that what we had learned to expect of ourselves in America? Finally, he said, strangely undercutting all his previous moral arguments, if he did not enlist, they would eventually draft him anyway, it was only a matter of time. If he went before he was called up, he said, he would do better, he would perhaps be eligible for officers' school, he would receive more pay, he would. . . . His arguments were endless. He talked so much that finally Klara understood what he was really saying—that he was terrified of the Army, that he was so frightened at the ideaof dying that in order to avert this final cowardice, the shame of refusing to save his own people, he had to run to the battle *at once,* before his slender stock of nerve and courage ran out . . .

And to all this Klara had no reply except to cling to him, crying that it was enough, she had suffered enough, she had paid her price for survival during the long months of his illness. But she knew it was not true, that it was only the beginning of it all.

Three months later they left Babette with cousin Hirsch and rode the bus to San Diego where Aaron was inducted into the Navy. Why he chose the Navy, Klara never afterwards understood, he knew no more of the water than a Jew in Russia knew of rifles: he could not distinguish between the oar and the gunwhale, and was barely able to tread water. But Aaron said the Navy was more dignified: as though death by drowning were cleaner and neater than death on the beaches of Normandy.

She saw Aaron only once in his uniform—looking faintly ridiculous with the white cap atop his already receding hairline *(poor Aaron: so many troubles, your hair was already turning grey and they never left you time to grow bald).* The little white cap reminded her oddly of those paper boats children make, and having no place to sail them, they capsize the boats and wear them on their heads where, of course, the fun of the game was in the inevitable slippage. Aaron's cap sat askew, not jaunty, but awkward and nervously white, rendering him conspicuous even in twilight. They walked along the streets of San Diego holding hands like young lovers, unable to speak the unspeakable, with Aaron assuring her the allotment would keep her and Babette comfortable; that the war was really almost over, England had been so brave, the Russians had been so brave, and besides he was safer at sea than he would be in the Army, and be sure and write to him in care of this address, which he handed her. Then suddenly he swooped her into his arms in the middle of the street and was sobbing wildly, like an innocent man being carried to the scaffold: he had done nothing, nothing, his sobbing said, to incur this sentence of death.

When he had gone, Klara rode back to Los Angeles on the bus; the windows were dirty and dusty, the air stale, she could scarcely see the faces of the pedestrians as they passed, not quickly but slowly, while the fumes from the exhaust drained the last breath of oxygen. The people on the other side of the window seemed part of some imperfectly designed charcoal drawing which had been smudged in the process; but then Klara noticed a strange phenomenon: it was high noon, the sun was blazing and a store suddenly opened its door to the street. From out of the door came women, no men at all: they had apparently been released for their lunch period (afterwards she realized that she had been passing a laundry). The women moved slowly into the street, single file, mournfully, their faces shaded by small scarves to shield them from the harsh sunlight; the scene was soundless— they paused, looked from left to right, they passed in front of Klara's waiting bus. Then the light changed and the bus charged away: looking back, Klara saw that there was not another soul in the streets, only this procession of widows.

There are people who are doomed to be sacrificed to history, to be buried in far-off places in mud flats and bamboo jungles— or not buried at all, but to lie forty fathoms deep, to end where they began—in the primordial sea. Aaron was one of these. It took eighteen months for them to notify her of his death, but by then she had already been in mourning for a year—Aaron's silence had told her more than the government: she knew Aaron would never have let her letters to him go unanswered. . . .

The government promised her money—Aaron's money— would be coming shortly; but there was the usual bureaucratic delay, and it was not long before her anxiety sent her looking for work. She now had the coveted teaching experience, and she thought it would be simple to get a position. Babette was old enough for school, and she would manage somehow. But the requirements had become more exacting—she lacked several courses which were now mandatory. She did not panic, because she still had some money left. But on her way home from the interview in which the school superintendent had made it clear there could be no exceptions to the state requirements, she noticed a sign in one of those eating places which are always a part of the local community, only a few blocks from where she lived: *Wanted Immediately. Experienced Waitress. Full-time.* Her interview with the superintendent had frightened her more than she realized; her sense of being a well-qualified American citizen endowed with all the necessary attributes of Education and Intelligence had been drained away. She stood for a few seconds on the hot dusty Los Angeles street, wondering *what if?* . . . And propelled by the innate insecurity of a steerage immigrant she walked into the restaurant to claim that she was an experienced waitress: did they have a job?

She thought she was fooling her employer. Later, she realized he had simply known that he could continue to pay her fifteen dollars a week long after she had grown so experienced that she was worth at least forty. The job which was to have been temporary prolonged itself by a natural law of economics. She became adept at the work, and later graduated to carpeted dining rooms and crystal chandeliers where sometimes they paid her twenty-five cents an hour and sometimes nothing at all (the people who ate and drank were expected according to their gastronomic satisfactions or lascivious intentions to pay what the management refused to pay: her salary).

She was at first so relieved to find ready money for her expenditures that she did not ask herself what the owner of The Helios found so desirable in her—a clumsy worker who knew the names of none of the local beers or drinks, and did not know a word of Spanish: half the menu was unreadable to her. She did not even understand that she was an "Anglo," and that she was therefore a sexual asset and therefore an economic asset. She was merely very pleased that she could immediately pay for Babette's new shoes, for the antibiotics the child needed for ear infections, for a tricycle, a dust-free bedroom (air-conditioning had become a necessity for Babette's newly-developed allergy), and for the baby-sitting she needed in order to attend classes at the university three evenings a week. She stubbornly whittled away at a few credits toward the validation of her teaching certification, even though when she later became involved in the struggle for the unionization of restaurant employees she lost interest in the certificate. In fact, she was never to use it: she became so caught up in the abuse of employees in the restaurant business that she was never afterwards able to enjoy a dinner in a restaurant without first asking of the waiter or waitress "Is this a good place to work?"—a question which usually so disconcerted everyone that she was regarded as a crank by those who rightly looked upon restaurants as places of relaxation where one was rewarded for having waited upon the will and pleasure of others by being waited upon in one's turn.

The Helios was one of those restaurants quickly recognized by anyone who has ever been in one as a "typical Greek joint." The owner, Pappas, was concerned with making enough money to return to the islands of his youth, and all notions of equity, luxury or quality were as casually eliminated from his moral vision as though they had been so many cockroaches in the kitchen: just sweep them away, and don't let the customers know we have them. He was not an immoral man, he cared for his wife and children, and he had risen from poverty in the way he understood: hard work, thrift and exploitation at minimal wages. How else were the poor to rise in the world but by imitating the ways of the rich? In his youth he had many times lunched on bread and olives, more than once without olives. He had slept on a pallet, he had had meat only once a week. Whereas she, Klara—he told her—had the right to eat from the daily menu (all except steaks and chops, he added hurriedly, which he rarely indulged in himself), and he paid her in cash (she needn't even declare her fifteen dollars as taxable income). And he had not complained, had he, when she'd broken cups and saucers while learning how to stack them six at a time on one hand . . . (Yes, that was true, thought Klara nodding: he had merely shaken his head with infinite sadness, like a man watching acts of derangement from the other side of an asylum gate.) Pappas went on to explain: he needed money, so did she. They were aspirants in the same system, not enemies; someday, he prodded her, perhaps Klara would own her own restaurant. It behooved her to learn all she could, and he was willing to let her start at the bottom. She could even smoke here if she wanted to (Klara didn't want to).

Afterwards, Klara used to muse about her first employer; he had not even been *l'homme moyenne sensuel;* with a kind of gratitude she reflected that he had not so much as laid a hand on her furtively as he passed her in the lane behind the narrow counter on the way to his cash register. What more benign employer could one want in a world of demons and disasters? But Klara had read too many books, her head was full of trade unionism. She confessed to herself that she was a traitor to Pappas' trust in her: she studied her situation like a labyrinth from which she must free herself.

Without the aid of computers and calculators, she measured the space from the first booth which faced the Los Angeles street to the outermost bastions of the kitchen where the soup sat simmering like lava all night: it was the length of a New York City block. From 4:30 in the afternoon until 1:30 in the morning she walked this concrete slab: how many times? she asked herself. She stared at her legs in the mirror (there was a mirror in the bathroom because Pappas did not like slip hems to be showing and he also liked the women to tie a big starched bow in the back with their apron strings, a bow quaintly dipping just above the hips), and she marveled how those skinny legs could carry not only herself but pounds of plates, vegetables, beef, beer, cake, fowl and fish all night long. Plus the weight of her patrons' sexual fantasies, for not only was she occupied with the care and feeding of her patrons, who were mostly men, but with fending off the eternal sexual inferences of everything she served: the look of the very beer bottles suggested phallic impulses to her customers. The curl of a loin chop suggested vulva, a bowl of pudding with a cherry suggested . . . ah, anything with cherries at all brought inevitable laughter. She soon learned how to deal with this like an oil slick—it simply lay on the surface of the conversation. They could dip themselves into it like oil-drenched waterfowl if they wished, she herself went skimming underneath, doing her work, listening to the music which blared its eternal mono-poem of love and wartime fidelity. In her pocket she carried a paperback of Plato's *Dialogues* (they were "doing" The Great Books in her English class): she had discovered that Pappas didn't like her to read, not even on her own half-hour lunch time, but that he didn't mind if the author was Greek—a matter of ethnic pride.

There was seldom any tipping at The Helios since the men were mainly working-class Mexicans with a sprinkling of Pappas' Greek friends, and it did not take much arithmetic for Klara to figure out that in this period of wartime prosperity she was receiving less pay than a migrant working picking peaches. There were two other "girls" working at The Helios, and Klara finally persuaded them to demand an increase in wages; and when Pappas refused, the other women who were very plucky joined with her in one of those "sit-down" strikes which were all the fashion during the war. And she learned a great deal.

She learned, for instance, that Pappas was very *hurt.* It was his feelings, he said, not the money. He had taken her on when he had known she couldn't hold a cup of coffee without spilling it (did she remember that?). And he had treated her like his own family: when she was sick, she was allowed to take a day off, and he never questioned her truthfulness. Another employer, he pointed out, would have been suspicious that she was looking for another place on those days (Klara smiled ruefully: strange, it had never occurred to her to do that, she had always been too tired to burn up a day's energy looking for a new place). But Pappas was nearly weeping, she saw, and it astonished her that he was genuinely fond of her, that as he himself said, he had treated her like a daughter, he had wanted her to learn *every*thing about the business, from the ground up, he wasn't jealous of her, he wasn't trying to hold her back. He had had no idea she was unhappy; why didn't she come to him privately and tell him, they could have settled this between them. What did she want, a raise in pay? He would have given her one, she needn't have told the others, the others were just tramps, looking for a man, really. He thought that Ginny Mae was picking up money on the side, you know?

Klara was stunned by this combination of outrage and injured paternalism. But she and the other women held their ground and continued their "sit-down" on the sidewalk where Pappas had— not overgently—ejected them. Pappas was more angry with Klara than with the other women, and never spoke to her again, not even when, months later, she and Hirsch dropped in with Babette for a sandwich. In fact, when Hirsch brushed Klara's hair back from her eyes in what Klara herself thought a purely cousinly way, she thought that Pappas was going to call the police and have her thrown out. He glared at Hirsch as though he thought Hirsch her lover or her pimp and not her cousin at all.

And, in fact, the world was full of surprises. Cousin Hirsch began to take on more and more responsibility for her, to run her errands, to worry about her health, bring her eggs and meat bought with his own ration coupons, and huge navel oranges. And he wooed Babette as ingratiatingly as a courtier, as though she were a Queen in disguise. He would hold her high in the air, then let her fall to his lap, kissing her with a soft sucking sound while he repeated. "You like Uncle Hirsch, don't you? Yes, you like Uncle Hirsch? Here. . . ." handing her a candy bar he'd se-creted in his pocket. Babette, with a stern, unconvinced look would unwrap the candy, taste it, and then only if she really liked it would smile at him, loosening the long leash of his love, letting him go. . . . Then for the next hour or more, Hirsch would beam at Babette, who might be lingering over her candy: "It's good, isn't it? I like them myself. I've always liked chocolate covered caramels. . . ." Mother and daughter would smile conspiratorially at these idiocies: such manic demonstrations of affection were contagious.

It was absurd: first cousins were meant to avoid each other; sexuality was suspect; it was frowned upon historically by the wise women of the race. Hemophiliacs and feeble-mindedness resulted when first cousins married: no need yet for the discovery of the genetic code for these wise old women to know what had gone amiss. There was a punishment lying in wait for those who abused the law, it was not natural. So Klara had always been told. And now here was Hirsch, tenderly taking the dinner plates from her, offering to wash them (a Jewish male offering to wash the dinner plates was something Klara's mother would have been astonished to see); lavishing attentions on Babette . . . Uncle Hirsch took her to the zoo, Uncle Hirsch bought her her first two-wheel bike and spent one entire Sunday afternoon keeping the wobbling wheels from falling to one side. When they went to the movies, Uncle Hirsch always bought popcorn. And when the three of them went swimming together, Uncle Hirsch held Babette with unshakeable patience until, squealing and triumphant, she could stay afloat herself. "Watch me, Uncle Hirsch! Watch me! Mummy, watch me!"

All this for Babette; but Klara knew that she was being courted. Such unselfishness must have a primitive inspiration: the survival of the lonely. At a time when most able-bodied men were fighting the Axis powers, Hirsch was nevertheless the loneliest bachelor in California. And Klara, separated from her origins by a continent, and from the rest of the world by Aaron's death, was the loneliest of widows: it was as if people distrusted her because she was a tragic case, which might be catching.

"And what about you, Klara?" he called from the pool. "Can you swim? You should learn to swim. Everybody should . . ." At the look on her face, he stopped, his legs still in the water. The top of his tank suit cut out in half-moons on either side was still dry, in spite of Babette's splashing: he had simply held her out in front of him like a wriggling fish.

He waded over to Klara where she sat at the poolside, her legs dangling over the side, happy to see Babette cared for, her own body knowing instinctively where all this care led to.

"You mustn't brood about him, may his soul rest in peace. You're young, still, and Babette is in good health, knock on wood. . . ." He looked around for wood, but found only concrete and tile; so, deliberately, in order to draw a smile from her, he knocked on his own head. "Come on, I'll teach you," he said.

Klara let herself down by her arms, sliding into the cool water. The sun was dazzling. "Babette," he instructed. "You stay in the shallow part—see this line? Absolutely no farther. If you go an inch farther, I'll—" he tried to look threatening. Babette glanced at her mother; she enjoyed this show of authority, not fearing Uncle Hirsch's threat at all. She smiled benevolently, as if giving Hirsch permission to play with her mother a while, then tossed her waterball into the air and threw herself on top of it.

Klara and Hirsch waded a few feet from the child, just deep enough so that as Hirsch held her up, Klara's fingertips could touch bottom. Sometimes he let go briefly, and she seemed to sink; then his hands pressed under her abdomen, supporting her till she could float again lightly. But a perfect balance was difficult to achieve: he tried another position, his arms around her shoulders, his back to Babette. Slowly his hand slid through the water to Klara's breast, and rested there: she could feel his excitement through their suits. "What do you think, Klara," he said, his voice thready with excitement. "Could you learn this? Could you learn to swim, Klara? Now the other side. On your back. Spread your arms." He positioned himself at first at her toes . . . She lay quiescent, floating, the sun blinding her, forcing her to close her eyes. "That's right, relax. Let the water hold you. You can trust the water if you relax. Just lay there . . ." He moved now between her legs, his hands resting lightly on her thighs. She knew what she wanted him to do, but this was not the place. She let herself sink into the water, her feet touching bottom. Immediately he caught her as if she had been in danger of drowning, his arms clutching her tightly, his body pushing up fiercely toward her. "Are you all right, Klara, are you all right?"

That night they became lovers, and within the year they were married.

In spite of herself, the old wives' tales had succeeded in arousing Klara's fears, and although they had scoffed at Superstition, when Klara became pregnant she worried all through the nine months. Then when the baby was born with spinal bifida, she wept hysterically and blamed herself and Hirsch, crying out that it was their curse, he had taken his uncle's daughter to bed, it was incest. . . . When she recovered from her grief, she was fearful of pregnancy and tried to avoid Hirsch: what had drawn them together now held them apart. They had been passionate, they had enjoyed each other's bodies like starved creatures in a jungle, clinging, pushing, sucking, hugging, devouring, as though eager to dissolve in each other's bodies. But they could not evade the dangerous trap, no perfect contraceptive had yet been invented, and when again Klara became pregnant, she worried for five bitter months that the child would again be a genetic curse. Then, one night in the middle of a heavy rainstorm, she had a miscarriage. The pain was unbearable, she suffered like a mangled body in a war trench, wanting only to die. When this deadly birth had been endured, they began to avoid each other, distrusting the lust which had brought them together, the madly enticing invitations of the flesh to breed and destroy. She was afraid, so afraid, she became frigid . . . and the tender, loving Hirsch who had wanted only to be a passionate husband and good father became bitter, he returned to his loneliness: instead of love he pursued money.

First Hirsch bought what he called "a little income property" on the South side of Los Angeles. Then he bought a small drug store and hired a pharmacist to run it. Soon he was selling health supplies, hearing-aids, weight-reducing machines right out of the drug store. Klara, remembering her days behind the cosmetic counter in Detroit, wondered dazedly what has happening to them: but it was only the story of America, and she was in it. She began to understand that her husband was an entrepreneur. In the same way that he had lured her into lust by his charm and charisma, he now lured businessmen into dreams. He took them out to lunch, he pried their wives with martinis and hot glances which promised secret love affairs. And he began to buy and sell property with dazzling speed. While Klara was working with the trade unions—she would say bitterly when they quarrelled over it—*deliberately undermining people like him,* he was out hiring painters, contractors, plasterers, roofers, masons, to repair his dwellings and raising people's rent. "And so what? Don't you live better every time Mrs. Jones' rent goes up a dollar?" Klara began to see that their quarrels were not domestic, they were international. They were on opposing sides of the economic barricades; yet Klara as his wife profited, profited. Ah yes, she could go into a store and buy a smart suit that nobody would know the price of, it was so smooth and beautiful, it could cost two hundred secret dollars if a penny. Who needed to know how well off they were? Hirsch chided her. She could go on doing her so-called work; let the girls strike if they wanted to: the employer's job, he said, was to fight strikes; her job—a kind of hospital volunteerism, he added with emphasis—was to try to get higher wages. "You want to go to the West Indies and cut sugar cane? So go," said Hirsch. "Who's stopping you? . . . I'll buy you a first-class ticket with Pan-American . . ." He was buying stock in commercial airlines. The irony dealt her self-esteem an (she thought) irrecoverable blow.

One day while passing a building which was being remodeled, she saw Hirsch standing outside. He was gesturing, pointing to the roof; he stood for a moment with his head bowed while he listened to a man wearing a bright green steel helmet explain something to him. Hirsch took out a notebook, scribbled some figures. The man shook his head: "No way," he said. Hirsch revised his figures. The two men looked suddenly gratified, as if each had won a victory; they moved good-naturedly toward the hallway of the building. With conscious deference the man in the helmet held the door open for Hirsch while his employer passed through. At that moment Hirsch spotted Klara watching them. . . . He sped across the street, to where they were excavating a new building. . . .

"What are you doing here?" he demanded. "This is no place for a woman."

"I was on my way to—" But why should she apologize? She flushed with the insult. "What are *you* doing here?" she countered. "Who's that man?" she pointed in the direction of the man in the helmet who had discreetly disappeared.

"Who? Him? What do you mean? He works for me. This is my building. . . ."

"Your *building?* What are you saying? We own this building?"

"Of course, idiot. You think it's a circus? I'm here busting my guts all the time. You think I've got nothing to do but play games with the unions? . . ." He laughed bitterly. "No, you'd better go home before you get hurt here. They're going to pull some of it down, then put up some new apartments. It's not a game," he repeated.

No, it's not a game, it's a war, she agreed silently.

Much shaken, she walked the twenty blocks to Babette's school, forgetting that this was the day Babette had a ballet lesson and would be driven home by her teacher. Buildings, ballet lessons: the daughter of Isaac Kleist would seem to have gone far in America. But her conscience was ill at ease. She saw that she could not uproot this society, she had become a part of it.

For years this hypocrisy troubled her; sometimes when she was making her most passionate statement on the inherent conflict between labor and management, a pang of guilt would shoot through her: what was she preaching but her own destruction? If her listeners were in fact to seize the means of production, her own way of life would be rubble and ruin. To the guillotine with Klara the oppressor! But somehow the illogic of her position never troubled the people who asked her to come and speak . . . No one ever said to her face: But Klara, you are wealthy, your husband has become a rich man, are you really ready to go to Albania and fight the revolution? Apparently the answers to such questions were so patently absurd that no one thought to ask them. Yet they were the heart of the matter. And because the answer to these questions was *no,* that few or none would want to cut sugar cane in Cuba or eat millet in Albania after becoming a real estate developer in California, after buying into International Airlines Inc., there would be no revolution in her lifetime. . . .

Sadly she put away her Proudhon, her Emma Goldman, her *Rise of Capitalism.* She worked harder than ever to achieve the rights of the working woman because she knew now there was no danger, no danger at all, that no matter how much she fought against Hirsch & Company, there would always be enough to do —there was no danger whatsoever that she, Klara Kleist, would bring about the dictatorship of the proletariat. Thus—she laughed bitterly—she could have it both ways: she could be an indignant moralist fighting for the working class; and she could live in a house in La Jolla and each one of them could drive his own car on the expressways: Hirsch and Babette and herself. . . .

And yet I did a lot of good, I did. I worked hard. I fought for trade unionism in the Southwest, especially among Chicanos. I contributed thousands to Israel, to help build a nation. I brought up Babette to be civilized and *eidel,* a *mensch;* she never blew up any banks nor injured a single person. Doesn't some glory, then, redound to me? Yes, God, I am adding up my assets and debits for eternity. What did Klara Kleist do? you will ask me. Well, she *tried.* . . . But the weight of wealth and the burden of being a woman were too much. Can a woman survive alone? It's a good question, God. Suppose you had made woman first? Would she have needed Adam? Or would she have connived with the serpent and eaten apples joyously forever?

So Galina and I lost the revolution: perhaps we were not sufficiently oppressed. Because we prospered in America we forgot the dream, forgot that every time we bought a silver samovar, somebody in Africa died of starvation. We were beguiled into forgetting. It was like Jesus taught his earliest followers: to say *yea* or *nay,* all else was evil. And having not the heart to say either, we lost the revolution. Because it was not forced upon us, because we were neither hungry nor cold nor beaten but rather comfortable and prosperous and middling-happy. Had we been born in Argentina, perhaps, or Chile, we should doubtless have continued our struggle, Galina and I. But we were blessed *(blessées)* by America.

And now even America is slipping into the sea. Even America will run out of oil, minerals, bauxite, copper, pure water, and it will all come to a halt. Zero Population will not help, baskets of wheat to India will not help, even the Revolution will not help. Because an Idea is not enough to stop the accelerating end . . . God be with us on this night of peril. Amen.

And is that all, you greedy Martians must now be asking? Is that all? Is that all an old woman has to say about her life—that it was too bad, it should have been different, but what the devil, the spirit is willing but the flesh is weak? No, no, you Martians, that wasn't it at all. I have read through what I have written, and it was not that way at all. To begin with, I see I did not tell you about my first love. Yes, yes, I know. I told you about Gary Schutz, but that was a mere mockery of vanity and adolescence, and I told you about my marriages, how they were put together almost by accident or by some Hand blindly shaping things in the night. But there is one thing I have not told you about: how I loved Simon. . . .

For that is the strange thing about an old woman; that I am not thinking as I sit here watching Duncan dance with serpents of my early days of struggle in America, or of the years of blessing in California, or of our trips to Israel or our summers in Acapulco, nor even of Hirsch's eternal busyness and his random affairs with his clients' wives . . . No, no, that is not what an old woman thinks of. That is all too painful, like looking over an endless bank statement, showing all the checks you have sent out over a lifetime: with what care you planned and purchased, with what honesty you paid, with what terror you lay in the hospitals of life: but you survived all that and the Records show that you paid all your bills.

But what is not on the record is what now plays like music across my mind as I sit looking at Jennifer, already great with child at an age when . . . well, yes, I was a bit younger than she when my teacher and I walked out toward the Black Sea that spring morning. I had just been accepted for the *gymnasium,* my joy was overwhelming, the morning sky was blue and there were small white clouds, puffed as cherubim in the sky. The sound of the sea came up to us like leaves rustling over the breakwater.

Although he was already a teacher, Simon was only a few years older than I. We had been talking about my future, the way teachers always do. They feel it is their professional duty, they must express their faith in the intelligence of the young, encourage them . . . And so Simon was saying that I had the ability to do anything. "*Anything,* Klara. You must get an education and do everything." My powers, and what I was to do with them, were vague, universal, perfect. His faith in me, a mere girl, rose like red wine to my brain. I leaped from stone to stone on the breakwater, the wind brushed my skin. I did not know then that Simon was sickly, frail, fearful, that within the year our entire family would have embarked for America and that I would never see him again. I stood ecstatically facing the Black Sea and then I began to run up the embankment. "Stop!" he called, "You'll fall . . ." But I raced to the top, where he followed me, and there on a stone where we stood, he kissed me. It was my first kiss.

You smile? But it was very daring at that time to be kissed by a man, one's teacher. . . . you don't understand the risk of it. It

could have caused a scandal, his dismissal, my shame for life . . .
And I loved him.

That's all? you ask. Only a kiss? And you Martians? How do
you breed? Surely you must be like us, if you understand what
you have just read. What I am saying is that nothing came of it,
and that's why I remember it always. All the rest I understand;
but this enchantment I will never understand, and because it is
only enchantment, it need not ever change.

No more, no more. This life has been too beautiful, too poig-
nant, too mystifying, too painful, too beautiful. Another life
would be more than we were meant to bear.

Morning.

I sometimes wonder

THE MIDDLE

Michele

Outdoors. A warm spring evening. We are seated around the campfire. It is strange, but we are no longer fearful of Duncan's "madness." What does it mean to be "mad" anyway in a world where They are figuring out the best way to blow up a billion human beings. Like persons denied freedom of assembly, gathering together two at a time to avoid any suggestion of conspiracy, we all decided that there was nothing to do but tolerate Duncan's obsession. There seemed little harm in it, he seemed rather like a lonely Quaker exiled into Pennsylvania: what numerical force could he rally to Satan? So we have tacitly agreed to let him play with the Devil, and if his Devil should turn out to be real, we will have made a safe bet of it (Pascal's wager transmogrified).

Like some primitive tribe, then, we have allowed him to summon us whenever he wished to perfom his "ceremonies." What else have we to do with our time? Reading by the unaccustomed oil lamps, as the wick burns down one is reminded unceasingly of the final flickering light: *repent ye the end isnigh!* So it is better to be amused. Tonight we have had Pinosh's fantastic perfomance of the final scene from Faustus, complete with Devil, who has suddenly become so ubiquitous . . . (Michele: staunch that mockery; you're as guilty as Duncan in this—positively titillated by it all, enjoying your Last Days as though they were a version of Titticut's Follies).

Pinosh's puppets screamed: Mephistopheles flew away with Faustus' soul. *O lente, lente, currite, noctis equi,* cried the puppet, and I thought Duncan would swoon with pleasure.

When Faustus had disappeared, it seemed a good time for the Devil to show up, in all his triumphs. Duncan came "on stage," confirming what we had just witnessed: that the Devil was stronger than Faustus or anybody. . . . He wound the huge snake around his shoulders, enveloped himself in it as in a suit of mail, pleaded with it, cajoled it, and finally prayed to it. I could hear Andrea (and even Malcolm) gasp at the spectacle of "Modern Man" reenacting the ancient struggle. Only Duncan, unlike Faust, did not struggle to keep his soul: he had become one with his master. I recall once reading a biography of a British poet who had defected to the Nazis, becoming one of their leading propagandists. When, after the war, he was tried for treason, he was asked why he had betrayed his own country: "I wanted to be on the winning side," he said.

We sat quietly watching, repressing our fears that "something" would happen—perhaps it was only our Jungian memory. Although Duncan insists that his snakes have had their venom removed, we are not certain we can always believe him. Malcolm says he does not have sufficient expertise in "snakery" to recognize "safety gadgets," adding: "I know one thing, I'll kill everyone of them if I get the chance." Fortunately, Duncan did not hear this remark, or there would have been another fight. If one among us were to be killed, we would have to have a trial for our first capital crime: who among us would be jurors, who Judge?

Duncan now weaved and bowed and laid incense on his serpentine "altar." Carillo turned to Andrea and asked where Klara was. Klara usually attends any communal activities, even when she is tired—which she is, frequently. We have tried to limit her physical work, but she is always insisting on working in the vegetable garden or collecting firewood—work entirely too strenuous for her. Even the care and feeding of the goats has been deliberately rotated so that Klara is excluded. Thus every seventh day one of us is responsible for the goats. "A Goats' Sabbath," Duncan calls it.

Andrea said she had seen Klara going into the room which we have designated as the Study or the Library, really a place with a few chairs, books and a hammock strung between the two windows. The hammock is very comfortable and it has become a colony joke that those who go in to "study" usually mean they will enjoy a nap in the hammock. But it is unlike Klara to disguise her naps; we all understand that she has needs which we do not: she tires more easily, she needs more privacy,·and recently we have "forbidden" her to cook because when she burns herself, the burn takes weeks to heal. Against her wishes, then, we have "assigned" her the tasks of keeping the study clean and dusting the few books in it. Also, when the weather is good, of walking Tikki in the woods nearby.

Duncan, who had not heard Carillo's question, continued to perform his "obscene" obsequies. I feel myself obliged to put *obscene* in quotes: we are all too sophisticated here not to understand that obscenity is in the eye of the beholder. Except for Jennifer, any one of us would be prepared to defend Duncan's Religion on the basis of that sentimental masterpiece, the Constitution: concepts of Life, Liberty and the Pursuit of Happiness still float around us like circus ballons. Yet I have this impure notion that it is as much the imminent holocaust which has destroyed the meaning of "obscenity," "religion," and "morality" as any concept of intellectual freedom.

Carillo has decided to go and bring Klara to the campfire. "Yes, tell her to come join our celebration," adds Malcolm. "Tell her to come meet the Devil Himself."

Duncan hunched himself like a cat, speaking directly to us for the first time, as though he were coming out of a trance: "The idea of the Devil is proof that He exists. . . ."

"Oh wow!" exclaimed Jennifer. "Philosophy 201. That's what we need! Followed by Everywoman's Course in Home Ec, and What-the-Graduating-Senior-Needs-to-Know."

"*I* believe in the Devil," announced Andrea suddenly. "But not your—" "There's only one Devil," interrupted Duncan, "even as there's only one God."

"Oh shit," said Malcolm.

Jennifer bloused out the khaki shirt she was wearing; for a moment she stiffened as though with pain, then slowly she stretched out both legs in front of her: "He moved," she said with astonishment.

"Who? The Devil?"

"No. *Him.* Bartleby."

We were somehow silenced by this information; the air became charged with expectation, as though at any moment we could disappear, become anything or nothing. Our lives, we knew, were in eternal flux: perhaps we would vanish and reappear in another form?

Tikki, who had been in the house with Klara, now rushed toward the campfire, barking in fury and terror at the snake which lay draped around Duncan's shoulder like some gleaming caparison of skin and mail. Each time the snake flicked its tongue the dog's barking seemed to increase a decibel. "For Christ's sake," said Malcolm, "Put your goddamned little devil away." "Thou hast said it," observed Duncan, gratified by his language. Then Pinosh, to our surprise, with perfectly credible solemnity, walked up to the snake on its "altar," muttering: " 'Fair is foul, and foul is fair: Hover through the fog and filthy air'." Then he thrust a long stringy object which was probably a shoelace (I *refuse* to believe it was a field mouse) toward the beast, who swallowed it at once. Jennifer retched, begging *please, please,* and covered her stomach protectively as though she feared this strange sight might mar Bartleby's senses.

Suddenly Tikki ceased his furious and futile attack on Duncan's god, and began howling. He dug his paws into the ground as though an invisible bullet had stopped him. It was then we saw Carillo walking straight as a ramrod, carrying Klara.

Her hands (amazingly small) were still curled into inflexible balls of pain, her rigid body still clutched at her heart: Carillo had not moved her into any false position of repose. Now he lay the dead body before us like a votive offering while he stood over her protectively, as though he would keep water and air and sunlight from corrupting her innocence. Jennifer began sobbing, Tikki began again to howl, and in a gesture which somehow surprised us all, Andrea flung herself upon Klara's cold lips, kissing them. *Klara, Klara, my friend,* she said weeping. And then, as if this were the talismanic word which had broken the spell of our civilized grief, we all burst into tears.

Andrea it was whose keening lamentation made us all ashamed of our unfeeling hearts. Why Andrea? On the brink of eternity, those we think we know continue to astonish us. . . .

The next morning when we had recovered from the shock of accepting the first death among us, there was a brief discussion as to whether the burial were a matter for the "outside" authorities, in which case, we would have to break the basic rule of our colony which was to remain an intact, independent group, surviving even the deaths of our friends.

Carillo said: "It won't be the last death. We should bury her at once. She'd come to regard us as her brothers and sisters. She wouldn't have wanted to leave us . . . to be taken to a strange place."

Carillo went to the house, brought out spades and laid them on the ground. He did not assign them to us, we were simply to do as he did if we wished. Without a murmur, each one of us took up a spade. But Andrea, after several attempts, finally threw her spade aside and sat sobbing on the ground.

Jennifer interrupted her work suddenly: "Wait! I'll get her coat. And the little dictionary, the one that belonged to her sister. . . ."

Andrea's sobs became louder. I patted her on the shoulder, not to comfort her: what I pleaded for was a lessening of her grief. We will all go to pieces, I thought, if we cannot bear the death of a woman who has lived a long life, full of love and use. We will turn into gibbering victims, wailing with the justice of our own end. My spurious comfort had no effect on Andrea; she continued to sob, throwing her apron over her head to hide the mottled mess of grief she had made of her face.

Jennifer returned with Klara's coat and with the little dictionary her family had bought somewhere after their arrival. There were many pages missing. But the first page, mended over and over again with transparent tape, was still intact. Involuntarily, my eyes took in the words, as though they were a secret code: *aardvark, aardwolf, Aaron.* . . . What faith in the New World seemed to lie in the hills and valleys of each syllable.

It was Jennifer who held Klara's small delicate body long enough to wrap the coat around her shoulders; then, lining the sides of an empty ammunition box with leaves, we laid Klara Kleist to rest.

The earth was very hard and full of tree roots; it seemed we would never finish our task. Jennifer would pause frequently, take a deep breath and appear to tremble from head to toe. Carillo removed the spade from her hands and pointed to a place where she should sit; obedient as a frightened child, she went and sat beside Andrea, who embraced her.

Pinosh brought out a large, illustrated book—Heritage Press or one of those editions intended for the Future—and began reading something which sounded familiar. With a slight shock I recognized one of Ahab's apostrophes to the White Whale. But I said nothing. In our present world Ahab's doomed and dooming incantations seemed wiser than Isaiah and all the prophets.

It was a very shallow grave: no need to dig far to find Death's trough, it was a clearly-marked place we would all find while the earth turned. I decided I would not weep anymore.

We covered the grave with a few flowers we found nearby, then we rolled stones toward the mound and carefully constructed a marker (for what purpose? I wondered; but no one questioned its usefulness). Then Pinosh surprised us again with an action none of us could have anticipated, least of all I who, although he was my lover, knew nothing about him except that he seemed determined, like Mercutio, to play his role to the end. He began singing, and he had one of the most beautiful tenor voices I have ever heard. Our court jester, our goat with Shakespeare's crown, was singing *Crossing the Bar.* For a moment I thought he meant some parody of our sentiment, that he was tweaking our noses while we stood in the very ditch of Death. But no, in a clear, unfaltering tenor he rendered Klara her last rites. And what our grief had not done to us, the beauty of his voice achieved. We wept.

When the burial was over, we felt joined together in a way we had never been before. It was as if by this death we had recorded for history the fact that we were indeed Eden's first family, facing together the loss of those we loved: filled with a guiltless, astonished gratitude for our own survival, however fragile.

As we walked back to the house, by some instinct we arranged ourselves in a protective cordon around Jennifer as if to shield her swollen body from the bruises and scratches of the underbrush: when she stumbled, I felt myself stiffen, prepared to break her fall.

Jennifer

I don't care *what* they say, it's *my* baby, and I'll have it my way. Bunch of *zombies!* I've borrowed Andrea's book, and I'm doing the exercises, and Andrea says she knows how to cut the cord, and so why should I leave? He wants me to go to El Paso to have the baby, he says I'm being carried away. . . . He says we're living in a dream world, that there's too much going on out there to let the clock wind down. Maybe so. But is 'out there' worth doing? I'm getting so I like it here. I mean the jack rabbits big as my shadow leap across the stream when I'm out there washing our shirts (if he didn't *like* the Army, why does he keep all these chinos and khakis? Martyrdom?). They're like kangaroos the way they jump. Or wallabies. The rabbits I mean. Gee I wish sometimes I'd gone to Australia, only it would've been too bad to have missed *him.*

Dear Diary, you've heard so many love stories. You remember the night I told you about Aeneas? Well, I really thought that was *it,* the way he rolled his head across the back of the theater seat, and stretched his legs out in front of him. *Cool!* I thought, this guy really has *charisma.* And when he took me out to The Snow Palace to dance, wow! We cross-circuited, we did, sparks flying everywhere. Yet after a couple of hours, my lips felt sort of tired and stale, and I felt, you know, *bored.* I can't explain it. Aeneas was telling me about his (older) brother's boat, and how I looked terrific in a bathing suit, and how he was going to get me to go down to Florida with him, that his brother was at a college in Florida, not far from Ft. Lauderdale, that I ought to go down just to look it over, it had a great campus, etc. etc. I don't know, it was like I could see clear to the bottom of Fort Lauderdale, every rock and floating fish. Only I didn't really want to be in it. Then for

Christmas Aeneas sent me some fins and a snorkel, with a note: "Goin' Fishin!?" It was already a sort of tiresome joke, a used-up code. And I was thinking, what's the big deal? Why doesn't he just come out and say he's planning this big scene with plenty of pot and liquor and sex and let me make up my own mind whether I want to orgy with him. But no, he has to go on and on about this college his brother is going to as if *that* was the main thing, as if we were all going to hop down to Ft. Lauderdale to cop ourselves a week-end education. Hypocrites make me *sick.* So while he was going on and on with this snow job, I pulled in my teensy-weensy toes as if the water had got too cold for me, and like, hugged my knees in that way I learned from skin flicks and travel (Kodakchrome) movies about girls in bikinis at the Bahamas, and I whispered, *real* sexy: "Oh Aeneas, you're the end!"

In more ways than one, he was. That was The End, dear Diary. That little episode really turned me off men for a while. Then I met Sean who was really an O.K. guy, kind of mute and serious and I was wondering, should I encourage this monolith? when dreams of nuclear confrontations started rampaging around in my brain. Would it all end like our history teacher was telling us, in a bang and a whimper? For better or for worser (for richer or for poorer, I guess it is now) I signed up with Duncan and the old folks went off to Australia. I hope they get stuck in a kangaroo pocket and can't get out, I do, I do. Letting her only child go off into the wilderness to die maybe. *Of course* I wanted to go, even though I told them I hated them both and that they could go eight thousand miles away to Hell and back for all I cared; but I didn't expect them to *believe* me, especially not *her,* she ought to *know better.* Well, I don't even want to hear from them, I hope they get lost in the outback, gored by an anteater, attacked by Aborigines . . .

Besides, if I *had* gone with them, I wouldn't have Bartleby. . . . And if I didn't have this baby, *he* would—

Her belly was swollen fantastically, one would not have thought the skin could bear so much. Stretch marks had already appeared, in spite of Andrea's book. She had laved the belly with oil every day (over Malcolm's protest that oil was needed for cooking not cosmetics). Now she lay for hours watching the invisible life beneath flutter just below the skin, like the wind flaring the edge of water.

"You—Bartleby," she whispered. "Who are you?"

One day Carillo had come into the study while she lay in the hammock. He drew up a wooden stool and sat watching her in silence.

"Do you want to feel him?" she asked. "Put your hand right there. No, there. That's a *foot!* What big feet—he'll be a giant. . . ."

Instead of being pleased at this, a frown crossed his face: "You ought to have prenatal care. What does anybody here know about these things?"

"These things are *natural.* They don't need care. Everybody has had babies before, just look at all the people. The planet is full of 'em."

He looked away. "Nobody's ever had your baby before."

"Yours too," she said sullenly.

"Nothing is mine," he asserted. "Nothing belongs to me, not even my child. He . . . or she will belong to the People."

"Oh fuck the people. I'm the one having this baby, and he may be a club-footed idiot who won't give a damn about revolutions. He may turn out to be a queer like that Dirty Duncan."

He sighed. "Don't call him that. Don't call people queers, zombies, weirdoes. It's not . . . humane."

She did it mainly to keep him preaching at her; she enjoyed arousing him to any kind of fervor. He was so controlled, so low-keyed that even when he made love to her she could feel his heart beating *Love is/Love is not, Love is/Love is not: each action creates a reaction; therefore let every act be calm, deliberate, catalytic. . . .* So she said spitefully, *catalytically:* "He is. He's a queer and everybody knows it."

He studied her face, then put his hand on her stomach, as if in a vow: "He's a human being." He had dropped the subject.

But she ran after his mind like a lathe, trying to rasp him down to the inner core to where the sap ran: she wanted to see his xylem and phloem, she thought, like they taught you in biology about trees. "I think he's out of his head, that's what I think. Parading around here with snakes like some kind of sorcerer or something. Well, he's not going to lay any of his black magic on *me.* I don't believe in that religious shit." Her voice, she realized, was quavering. "Do you think . . . all those scary 'ceremonies'. . . do you think they really could hurt a baby? I mean, I've heard that they can hear sounds, and that if the mother gets really scared that the foetus *feels* it, do you think that? . . ."

He looked at her somberly. "When your time comes you're going to a hospital."

"Oh yes, Mr. Smarty. Who are you to boss me around? Somebody appoint *you* Commissar of the End of the World?" Tears blurred her eyes.

"I am the father of . . . I am Bartleby's father," he said; and covered her with a freshly-washed sheet, still roughly hieroglyphed with wrinkles, like a hand that has been too long in the water.

Carillo

After Buell fled to Mexico, Carillo was rejected for adoption in open court and shipped off to the State Reformatory. Here he discovered that even a hungry, ridiculed, ignorant but also innocent Minor is better off than an Adult without human rights. Because he was a few years older than most of the kids at the Reformatory, he considered himself an Adult: and as such he endured not only his own humiliation and suffering, but that of the others. Had he been St. George himself, he could not have more romantically pursued his role as Protector of the small and the weak. Later, he pondered the question: why had he, though he himself had been as powerless as a worm, become their protector? There was no answer. He had fought for them in fierce, brutal struggles, pulling away half-crazed assailants from ten-year-olds who looked to him like the starving doe he had seen at a time of killing frost.

So the authorities, with something resembling boredom-with-malice, felt obliged to isolate Carillo in a cubicle without blanket, window, light or sound, a place of silence.

The Hole, as it was called, had been ingeniously sound-proofed. This at first had seemed to him an odd extravagance on the part of the State, but he soon realized that the silence of the Hole served two functions: first, it blotted out his own screams when they beat him; and second, the silence itself became the ultimate torture. It brought him to his knees, begging God to send him some Sound so that he could orient himself to the Nothing: only Sound could prove to him that he was not wholly lost and spinning somewhere in the black hole of the universe.

But he was totally powerless. He could not bring Sound into his cell, he could bring nothing to himself, not even death: they had stripped him of everything, even of the means of ending all. He could not, later, remember how long he had been in The Hole alone, when at last they thrust another inmate into his cell—a huge guy, obviously new to the Reformatory, who tore the silence with his violent screams as he tossed on the bunk beneath Carillo's, like a man in chains. His violence only intensified Carillo's isolation. In the twilight of their cell, they barely spoke to each other. Days and nights began to merge; Carillo lost his sense of time. Then one day, after what he thought must have been weeks, he discovered an amazing metaphysical explanation for all of his suffering: it was part of an intricate system of ransoms, like that of the Jewish God on his father's side. According to this teleological system, there must be periodic hostages of whom Carillo was one: obviously God was going to sacrifice him, Carillo, and let The Rest go. Like his Jewish Antecedent, he was expected to acquiesce in the sacrifice: more, since there was no Nero, no Pilate, no Sanhedrin, nor even a trustworthily perfidious Iscariot, he, Carillo, would have to carry out the whole transaction alone.

Fortunately Carrie had taught him how it was done, only poor Carrie had not had time to figure out the philosophical aspects of her sacrifice. So one night, having found a sharpened blade, he quietly slashed his wrists and waited for the final darkness (not silent, he hoped). But by a curious irony, the man in the bunk beneath him, upon waking to realize what daft person was disturbing his sleep with the seepage of blood, yanked Carillo from his bunk, kicking and cursing him for a crazy idiot who did nothing but cause trouble. And of course he called the guards.

They were obliged to send him to the emergency room to be sewn up, and while he sat, dizzy with pain and loss of blood, the nurse—not one of the regular institutional nurses—unexpectedly left him alone in the room. She wanted to get him some codeine, she said, which would get Carillo through the night. *Who wants to get through the night?* Carillo remembered thinking. Then with a flood of excitement he raised his head at a familiar *Sound:* that of a vehicle, a truck maybe, driving on a gravelled surface. . . . Not a large truck, but maybe a fair-sized panel; maybe a delivery truck. A flood of strength suddenly coursed through him; he leaped to the drapes behind which lay revealed a floor-to-ceiling window facing a courtyard—a courtyard complete with entrance ramp, delivery crates: and a truck. He took it all in in nervous gasps. In his excitement he thought he would burst open the stitched slashes at his wrists. . . .

He had several minutes to find his way to the truck; the picture window gave no exit. He flew to a door—not the one the nurse had used—he knew he must brave it out, casually *walk* through the door, as if, having been treated, he had now been quietly dismissed. The door opened on what appeared to be still another office. Like a blind man, he cleaved to the railing along the stairwell. If he fainted now, there would never be another chance. Two more years of being thrown in and out of The Hole and he would be a vegetable; and perhaps blind as a mole.

The bread truck was unlocked; most of the bread had been carried into the surrounding complex of buildings. Inside there were wooden shelves onto which baskets were to be slid, and niches, so that the bread could be installed like light bulbs into their small fitted places. Carillo climbed in and flattened himself on the upper shelf, against the roof. He began to pray. Presently the rear door flew open, the driver flung in an empty loading basket and slammed the doors to, without locking them: who needed to protect a few loaves of bread?

Within twenty minutes they were out on the wide Texas highway. Any direction would have suited Carillo, but what he needed above all was a rest stop so that he could change his clothes. When, finally, the driver stopped and got out of the truck, Carillo began a countdown, giving the driver about twenty seconds to open the rear panel. If he didn't do that, it was likely they were at some sort of rest stop. When after about thirty seconds, the driver did not appear, Carillo crawled out of his wedge of space and tottered like an old man to the bathroom.

There he sat in the toilet for perhaps half an hour, just breathing heavily. Then he stripped himself down to undershirt and jeans, trying to make his clothes look less like a uniform (jeans were in style, and the so-called democratization of fashion gave hippies, reformatory kids and college graduates an Equal Opportunity at disguise). Then cautiously he stepped out and looked around the place, which turned out to be a small-town bus stop. He looked for signs, but there were none in sight. Impossible to figure out in which direction they had been driving. Then he checked out the fare to Alamogordo, trying to look as if he were more interested in Arrival and Departure times than in the price of the fare: it was too much money. Impossible to get together the money unless he stole a wallet or beat up somebody, something he had vowed never to do.

He was standing in despair, looking at the map on the wall which showed them to be only about an hour's ride from New Mexico when suddenly a fat man came in, weighing three hundred pounds if he weighed an ounce, Carillo swore. The man was anguished and sweating; he had injured himself while trying to change a tire: the jack had collapsed and the rear end of the car had banged him up. He needed somebody to take over the driving, someone who could maybe change a tire. He looked angrily at Carillo as if he envied him his young strength, his muscular body and his disciplined appetites. Trying to look as charming as a kid up for adoption, Carillo offered his services and the guy grudgingly accepted, as if he were doing Carillo a great favor. To Carillo's relief, fat-man decided against having Carillo change the tire—perhaps he feared losing his driver to still another accident —instead they rode the bad tire into a gas station where it was easily replaced with a new one (Carillo saw fat-man open a wallet full of twenties).

Then they headed North and they were out of Texas with the speed of a new Chrysler backed by a full wallet. Fat-man said his next stop would be Albuquerque. Did he, Carillo, want to go that far? *Yeah, sure,* Carillo said, but first he wanted to call his mother and let her know that he was safe and on his way back to Albuquerque after a streak of bad luck (Carillo had invented what he thought was a credible story of having been robbed in Houston and he was now supposedly hitchhiking home by a marvelous coincidence to Albuquerque). Could he, Carillo, borrow some money from fat-man till they got to Albuquerque? His mother would pay fat-man back, Carillo said. With an odd look of cynical amusement the guy gave Carillo two bucks "for his services." At the next stop, Carillo rushed to the cafeteria counter and downed two hamburgers and a milk shake, his first food in a forgotten time span; for the past hour he had been so hungry he had begun to see flashes of food in his mind's eye, like the stars you are supposed to see when they hit you on the head with a blackjack. And the hunger had made him understand something perhaps for the first time: why a man might kill, kill, kill for bread.

When he returned to the car, fat-man, eyeing him with a mixture of concern and suspicion, announced that his right hand was feeling better—he'd drive the car himself now. As he opened the glove compartment to reach for maps, Carillo spotted a .22 lying peacefully beneath the paper maps. *He's suddenly gotten afraid of me,* thought Carillo, with a grim smile.

Upon their arrival in Albuquerque his benefactor, who had grown more relaxed and also strangely fond of Carillo (*now that he knows I'm not gonna kill him, now that he's let me know he's the one with the gun*), asked him what he was going to do now. Carillo only later realized that the man, who was not so dumb as he was wide, had not believed a word of Carillo's story about being robbed in Houston. Fat-man looked him hard in the eye: "You look like hell, you know that, don't you?" Carillo adjusted the radio in the car, tuned it to another station. He pretended to look surprised. "You look like a junkie or a pusher, if you want to know the truth. And if you're lookin' to get a job, I'm tellin' *you* you're more likely to end up gettin' your picture took by the police in a line-up."

Carillo tried bravado: "Just drop me off at Brooks Brothers and I'll spruce up some."

"No joke it isn't. Nobody can get him a job without clothes," fat-man insisted. "Clothes make the man, everybody knows that." There was a long audible sigh, as though fat-man were tearing his flesh: later, Carillo understood it was his Religion, literally ripping at him, pulling him through the eye of the needle: it was painful, it was a blessing, therefore, it must be Good. Grunting as he moved his huge buttocks to reach for his wallet, he said: "Blessed be him that gives and him that receives. And if you're ever in California, give me a buzz, I'll put you to work." He handed Carillo a ten-dollar bill and a business card: San Joaquin Produce & Tomato Company. "It's just a loan: you can send it back to me when you hit the jackpot in Las Vegas." It was one of those jokes meant to be interpreted any way you liked. Carillo's first instinct was to ask to go along right then and there: hire himself out at once to the San Joaquin Tomato Company. But he didn't want to push his luck. The ten dollar bill was almost untouched, spotlessly hygienic money right out of the bank. There was something talismanic about it. Carillo felt he was freaking out: he wanted to kiss the big echoing chamber of blubber right on his paunchy jowls. But he knew the San Joaquin Produce & Tomato Company was not seeking kisses from Carillo—he was ransoming himself from Purgatory. So Carillo shook hands very somberly, very carefully, allowing himself one wild, wistful wonder if it were possible maybe fat-man was his father, that unknown 'Daddy' of mythological powers. Then, he locked the door and with a debonair salute waved his benefactor (*father?*) on to California.

He repaid the ten dollars in as many weeks, one at a time. He thought of it as an investment, he didn't want to destroy Produce & Tomato Company's charitable streak. Like the quality of mercy it was twice-blessed, and so far he, Carillo, had been blessed by it but once. He had another blessing coming, maybe. If he ever got out to California.

Meanwhile, the new money as a Capital Investment was a great success. He went into an army surplus store, and came out with a zipped-up windbreaker to cover half his nakedness and a pair of chinos to cover the other half. He stepped out onto the streets of Albuquerque feeling quite princely.

The glare from the sun was white and clean and bright as a razor blade on his retinas; he decided to invest a quarter in some plastic sunglasses. Then, before going to apply for work, he practiced ten or fifteen minutes casually removing them in response to the prospective boss's asking: "Do you have some identification, Mr. Vaca?"

Identification, hell! What they wanted was a strong back and a closed mouth. He had no trouble at all finding work. It was a time of affluence, construction was booming: every bomb going to Vietnam created jobs. Carillo used to think, we're a one-crop economy: war is our sugar harvest. Later his mathematics were to falter under the weight of calculating how many people must die everyday to keep the factories churning out B-52's, F-111's napalm, fragmentation bombs and helicopters . . . But for the moment he calculated none of this. He knew only that, with a strong back and barely comprehensible English, his employers thought him a bargain for construction work at a dollar an hour: he could work like two men (he knew) since he was not (legally) a man and his eagerness to prove that he really was made him valuable. He lacked a few months yet to his seventeenth birthday—a simple detail, but one which was to affect his future in a way he could never have predicted.

For several weeks he was too pleased with his escape, too self-indulgent in the New Mexico sunshine to notice the people around him: then he began to count heads. Not unsurprisingly, just as in the insect world, one could quickly make out the drones from the queen bees; the most casual glance revealed to him the social fabric: those with straight shining black hair, with faces like

Indians, hoed the land and harvested the vegetables; the rest went to school, ran the banks, owned the stores, and rode horses like the women in D.H. Lawrence . . . It was a perfect dichotomy.

To supplement his earnings, Carillo began working on weekends for a gas station on the outskirts of town. During his lunch hour he would walk down the road toward a barrio where the migrant workers and other Mexican-Americans who had dropped out of the struggle for upward mobility lived side by side. Here they shared their common language and customs even though the native-born Mexican regarded with distrust the illegal migrants who, they felt, had brought their own wages down so that they all were forced to live at this level. . . .

Carillo was sitting at the side of the road eating his sandwich (he remembered wishing he had brought a cloth to wipe his hands on) and drinking coffee out of a thermos when he realized he was being observed by a Chicana who sat not far away, nursing her child. The sight of the young woman serenely offering her body as though her needs were nothing and the needs of the infant were all, inspired in Carillo something like pain or religious reverence (he at once dismissed the "pain" as sentimentality, but while it remained with him, it was a powerful feeling). He had to shake himself free of it in order to approach the woman, saying, "*Café, por favor?*" He realized, of course, that his Spanish was crazy, you didn't say *por favor* when you were offering something but rather when you were asking for something. Yet she somehow understood that he was asking her to share his cup.

It was a strangely intimate trusting act: a perfect stranger accepting his offering, not even turning the cup around to place her mouth were his had not been.

While she sipped Carillo's coffee, the baby woke, the milk bubbled to his mouth and they laughed at his little puckered face now exposed to the sun. The infant was as dark as a hazel nut, and Carillo suddenly became aware of how different he looked to the woman and her child. With his blond hair and grey eyes —even though his face was streaked with the sweat and grime of the car windows he'd been washing all day—he must still have all the characteristics of a *gringo*. He wanted to reject that, say *no, no, don't like me if you think I'm* . . . But he said only:

"My name is Carillo."

She answered in Spanish: "Mine is Elena Espada."

"And *his* name?"

"León. *El león,*" she explained, smiling.

Carillo took the tiny fist and shook it gently. "Well, Señor León Espada, how do you do?"

She looked troubled; she glanced at him as if she expected some predictable response as she said. "No. Not Espada. My father says, 'not *his* name.' No name for León, he is only . . . The Lion. León's father—" She shrugged, her eyes dulled over; she looked off into the distance, gathered her shawl around her. She rose to go.

"Wait . . . " he said. "Wait, There's more coffee."

She sat down again. Her eyes, he thought, were the color of a dark river. Her emotions moved on their surface in a play of light.

He was to learn to understand her almost solely by the expression in her eyes, for they had neither of them the time nor the talent to teach any other language. The next day—a Sunday, on which day he had half a day to himself—he found her waiting for him. Without a word he took the baby in one arm and her hand in his. They walked homeward to the Espada 'cabin' which her father had built on the edge of the city—an outer region of wooden shacks as primitive as those he was later to find in the slums of Lima or the coastal garbage dumps of Montevideo. Here now, in the very heart of his own country lay such another country, carefully blinding itself to the existence of such foreign *barrios.*

But Carillo did not think of all this at once. Only gradually it came to him, in sudden shafts of illumination. As the Espada family sat him down at their table and served him warm cola and *huacamole,* he felt himself riven by these lightning bolts of comprehension.

The Espadas were at once shy and distrustful; it was no longer a question of Elena's honor—the child in her arms was testimony to the failure of *machismo* to protect the honor of Espada's daughter under any circumstances. It was only the instinctive distrust of the flesh and bone which recognizes in blond hair and light skin its historical enemy and knows not what evil may come thereof. . . . But Elena's little brother knew as yet nothing of distrust; he was warm-hearted and friendly. He was delighted to have a comrade who permitted him to tag along when they wandered over the dumps, kicking cans and wiping their sandals whenever they missed their footing and slipped on bags of refuse the city had abandoned to over one hundred degrees of sunlight: gradually Carillo got used to the smell. But he naturally preferred to take Elena into the city where they would walk around the courthouse like an Anglo couple and sit briefly on one of the benches. Carillo wondered how they might make love (if she were willing); there was no privacy for them; she carried the baby wherever she went, even when she went harvesting in the fields with her parents. But Carillo was not even certain he wanted her, he had seen so much violence, so much rape and brutality between men and women as they learned quickly how to revenge themselves for past atrocities. . . . He was not certain he wished to inflict this upon either of them. Theirs was an idyll in which he was the handsome *gringo,* with grey eyes and a white shirt open at the throat. He found himself proud of the soft blond hair which had begun to curl on his chest and at the same time ashamed of his pride: he had done nothing to deserve it, and now here he was suddenly handsome, clean and *white:* a desirable. It was a situation of such charm that he wanted it to go on forever, he did not dare shatter it by a vulgar expression, a demanding caress. Elena's hand would touch his knee, his thigh, his hair lightly, lightly, then fall away again. She respected him too much to fall on his mouth, demanding kisses; and he feared that she would think . . . well . . . that he was the same as that other bastard who had taken her love and her body and as soon as he'd had his fill, gone on to another woman or wife or whore: León's father who, like Carillo's, had simply spilled his seed and vanished.

One day he had gone with the Espadas, ostensibly to help them bring in the fruit crop. The trucker simply picked him up in the morning along with the others, no questions asked; there was a chronic shortage of pickers now that the Vietnam war was on in earnest. Carillo had gone along solely because he was lonely without Elena and the baby. He even missed her skinny little brother, Pedro, with his protruding little rabbit teeth which made him look as if he were being clever and mischievous even when, for whatever childish reasons, he was close to tears. Halfheartedly Carillo trailed after them while they picked zucchini and melons, yellow, round and fluted, the size of a babe in the womb. Carillo had thought himself a well-seasoned worker; he had a young body, a strong back, and he had not been softened up by luxuries. But this was killing work. By noon his knees were sore and swollen, his fingers were numb. The sun felt like a hot griddle on his back, the skin on his arms was waffling into welts of light and dark, burned to dark toast where it had been exposed. The cat's cradle of stitches in his wrists began to seethe against his flesh, as though testing their strength, ready to break. He watched with amazement as Elena, hardly more than a girl, picked fruit like a clever and very hungry animal—carefully separating the green from the yellow, the cracked and bruised from the whole and the well—it was incredible. Each melon weighed a pound at least, yet she lifted these weights all day long as though they were cotton balls, careful not to let them fall: bruised fruit brought lower prices and severe criticism. At noon when they dropped into a furrow to eat their lunch, Elena nursed León, and drank a lot of coffee. She'd be sorry for that, she said with a rueful smile, pointing to a far-off ditch where she was allowed to relieve herself as often as she needed to. It meant a shorter crop of fruit since it took her at least ten minutes to walk there each time, and ten minutes to return, but what would León do if she didn't take in the fluids to make the milk? she asked.

What would he do indeed? Carillo was silent with awe, thinking of all the kids in the home whose parents had not had any milk in their breasts or any cash in their pocketbooks and so the orphanage had been fruitful and multiplied. . . . He hardly dared ask Elena how much she earned for all this. Besides, he didn't need to ask. Who would live like the Espadas at the edge of a dump if they could live in a real house with hot water and indoor plumbing (the Espadas had neither)? Carillo brooded about it for weeks on end, wondering what a man could do.

He thought of something: when the city elections were about to take place again, Carillo noticed that one of the candidates had a Latin-American name. Good! it was time to make the guy aware that his people were being given less than the unmuzzled ox which treadeth the corn.

The people running for office were clearly separated according to blood line: the people who owned cattle or oil; the people who owned only the land; and the people who virtually owned the people who worked the land. The Chicano population wanted their man in, but they also wanted him aware of what was going on: perhaps he didn't know, they said, how his people were being treated; he'd made some money over the years as a kind of middle-man, and maybe he'd forgotten himself. He needed reminding, his neighbors said. So Carillo and a few of the stronger pickers organized a walk around the courthouse with placards supporting Martínez but reminding him that people of his race were working for less than half the national minimum wage. He and Elena spent several joyful hours putting together placards, nailing them to strips of orange crating: signs that Elena could not read . . . MIGRANTS DESERVE A MINIMUM WAGE! and with a touch of irony: MARTINEZ: REMEMBER THE ALAMO! SUPPORT YOUR OWN PEOPLE. He even printed one sign with a chorus from "Joe Hill" but there were not enough people in the march who could read English, and they didn't know the song anyway. He decided he was not much of a poster-maker. But there was one song the marchers did know, and as spontaneously as if it had become the national anthem of the sixties, they began to sing *We Shall Overcome* in quavering unison. They must have learned it on television, watching black people get their heads busted for 'Freedom Now,' thought Carillo.

It was a perfect day for a march around the courthouse, a day which in the country of Elena's parents would have been a day of courtship: boys and girls walking arm in arm around the plaza under the admiring but watchful eyes of their chaperons. The sun came down on them, soft and amber as chamois, rubbing their skins to a glow. People were handing bottles of soft drinks around, reminding the children not to drop the empties around the courthouse. Mar-tín-ez! Mar-tín-ez! sang the crowd. Soon they worked it into a rhythmic chant. *Mar-tín-ez! Los trabajadores necesitan el pan. El pan, Mar-tín-ez!*

Each time they circled the courthouse Carillo waved his banner in a friendly way at the spectators—the courthouse lawyers, judges and defendants who had gathered at the windows to watch. They leaned out of the windows, their hands folded as though in prayer; but their faces clearly showed that they considered the performance in the streets an outrage interrupting their civil procedures. . . . Several policemen appeared at the windows and the windows were shut against the sounds of the street. The crowd now grew startlingly fast. Traffic was becoming jammed. From a corner of his eye Carillo spotted several police cars arriving. He thought he could recognize the police in spite of their unmarked cars by the way the two plainsclothesmen sat together, a welded bulwark in the front seat, their faces wearing masks of cold rage reined in, momentarily, by the law.

To make way for the sudden press of people, Carillo dropped out of the line circling the courthouse and took his place directly behind Elena who was holding León close to her body, his head over her left shoulder. León was having the time of his life; each time Carillo waved his banner, León would bob his head up over his mother's shoulder, give a great toothless smile, and snuggle down against Elena's throat. He obviously loved the noisy fanfare —the singing, the darting, laughing bodies which moved about him like pilot fish. Around and around the bodies went, like a carousel with himself perched above it all: gurgling, bouncing, his smile dripping saliva like honey. Sometimes Pedro would pretend to leap at him fiercely, and León would squeal with delight: it was a game with infinite variations. The carousel was now picking up speed as the crowd repeated their chorus: *Mar-tín-ez! Mar-tín-ez.* . . . Somebody had brought a harmonica.

Or was it a siren? Suddenly to one flank of their marching column Carillo could hear a new sound of pounding feet, of nightsticks tapped against the curb, and from out of the parked cars flowed dozens of police nearly all in plainclothes, wielding sticks, ordering the crowd to disperse. There were groans of protests. Then a shot was fired, no one knew from where. . . . Then Elena was screaming. . . . More shots were fired. . . .

Elena lay in the plaza of the courthouse. León was howling with terror: his carousel had become his nightmare, his mother lying motionless in the street. León's screams were full of wrenching seizures of grief, but it was all a silent film in Carillo's head, Carillo could hear nothing but Elena murmuring *Take care of him, Take care of him. I love you,* Carillo was saying, but she murmured only *Take care of him. I love you,* Carillo repeated (God, can't You make her understand me?). And for once the power Who had always ignored his petitions looked down and pitied him: Elena's eyes became dark pools of love. She touched her finger to Carillo's mouth, not to stop his words but to seal her love. *Care,* she said. But whether it was his name she had begun to speak or some last request, he was never to know.

Can a dead body absorb love? He rained love upon her, but she would not resurrect herself for him. She had never learned his language and she died without speaking a word of love.

They must have, finally, wrenched him away. He found himself again in a cell. Like himself, they regarded him as guilty, or at least responsible. He agreed utterly, silent as death himself. No punishment was too great. He sat in his cell, neither caring nor feeling; he was drugged with Death, the great Solacer. He need only wait, and It would come to him as it came like a patient silent warrior to all he loved. He did not think of anything, his mind was simply a round silent track on which he rode endlessly the same carousel: the baby bouncing with joy, the shot, the press of people, Elena's face bruised and bleeding from her fall, the life ebbing from the spine. Human fruit violently harvested.

Now and then he would begin to feel just enough vitality returning to him to curse himself aloud, even as he believed himself to be fatally cursed. Whoever loved him was crushed, whomever he loved was destroyed; he was the Moloch of destruction, the Dark power which ruled the universe had elected him as its agent: all his Good turned to tragedy. He felt he would never trust any sodden virtue in himself again, any contagion of altruism: it was only a lure used by diabolic agents to destroy the innocent.

This time he never once thought of taking his own life. He had seen suddenly what an absurdity, what an eggshell he was, doomed like the others to quick-coming death. No need to exert himself, it would come without his least effort—in the night, with a whisper, a bomb or a garrote, a fall through an empty stairwell or beneath a skidding car. What he had learned was, not the value of life, but its worthlessness. There was nothing left for him either to protect or destroy.

Thus when he was indicted on triple charges (manslaughter, inciting a riot and assaulting an officer) he stood numbly in front of the judge imagining that he, Carillo, was nodding his head in agreement: *Yes, yes, I am guilty. Yes, you are right: she's gone; that's murder, not manslaughter. . . .* He thought this time he would be, and should be, sent away forever.

But to his surprise the Judge seemed strangely convivial, his eyes beamed at Carillo, cheerful and prankish as though he and Carillo were sharing some masculine initiation in which he, the Judge, was merely the elder and cleverer of the two—a sort of Lord Chesterfield advising his son. But this *must* be his imagination, Carillo thought dismally; it was getting so he endowed every Establishment-type he met with secret paternalism. Now the Judge was haranguing him like a father, hortatory and conniving: if it was pussy he wanted (Carillo knew the Judge could not have used that word; still, what word *had* he used? Later Carillo could not remember but the sense was clear), the Judge said, there were

plenty of good times to be had overseas with the Oriental girls
... No, he was not saying that, Carillo thought with astonishment. He is not saying it. But the Judge's eyes were saying it. His
face had become flushed, his eyes glazed, somehow under his
cloak, old longings stirred, Carillo could feel him heist the weight
of his balls, heavy with reputation, lust and self-denial (*how is that
I can read his mind?* wondered Carillo). And now the Judge was
repeating. "You'll get all you want. . . out of life there—I know
all about it. I was young too in my day, you know. . . . "

But the most important thing (at the moment at least) that the
Judge was saying was that there was no need to despair (Carillo
decided he must look despairing rather than deeply distrustful as
he stood there, all ninety-seven pounds of him slumped on one
foot, his eyes glued to the Judge's, trying to see through to the
brain coiled in sections like pit vipers). Carillo need not despair
because Texas didn't want him back. The very mention of his
origins jolted Carillo into deepest suspicion. That they knew
where he had come from meant that they had made a warrant
check on him, therefore they knew where he'd sprung himself
from, and now, if the Texas Reformatory no longer wanted him:
who did? He had already seen enough of the jails in New Mexico
to know that they were no better than the ones he'd left. But the
Judge perhaps was only having his little joke, for he continued:
"The fact that Texas doesn't *want* you doesn't mean I won't have
to send you. I've no choice about that. . . . " Long pause. *What is
he building up to?* Carillo's emotions hovered between suspicion
and muted rage. "I mean to say, I don't have a choice. But *you*
do. I'm going to treat you like a man. I'm going to give you the
chance to make something of yourself. And to learn something
about your country too—what it means to be born free . . . " It
was no parody, Carillo understood: it was straight and ministe-
rial; the Judge meant every word of it. But what were the terms
of this opportunity? Carillo stood straighter now, trembling from
the ordeal of showing no emotion. He heard the word overseas.
He heard Vietnam. . . . So that was it. It was as if his foredoomed
spirit had always known they would bring him to this, oblige him
to kill his way to freedom.

"Otherwise, a one to three year sentence. You'd better take up
the offer. I guarantee you'll learn lots better things in Vietnam
than you would sitting in the State Prison on a one to three.
You're too old for the Reformatory, too young for prison: just

grown enough for soldiering and for getting women into trouble
... " He chuckled. What seventeen-year old could resist such an
offer? the chuckles seemed to ask; a chance to fuck every Vietnamese girl from Saigon to the China Sea. The variety of Carillo's
opportunities hung in the air like the smell of Lysol in a brothel
... The judge winked at Carillo. .... *In a minute he will pat me on
the shoulder and call me 'boy'* thought Carillo, but the Judge did no
such thing. He had relaxed his eternal vigilance as far as the
tedium of the day permitted him. The next case was already on
—the problem of a woman living in a trailer, being visited by her
lover. As Carillo was led from the courtroom he heard the question being asked: was this woman fit to be a mother?

For some reason, when they had returned him, temporarily, to
his cell he began laughing, then sobbing. Then, throwing himself
on the floor of his cell, he beat the floor with his fists so hard that
for days later, even during basic training in Louisiana, his trigger
finger was bruised and swollen.

Saigon. *No hurry to send them to the jungle, they'll get there soon
enough. Let them roam the streets first to see how these people live, absorb
their inabsorbable culture, inhale the stench of their neglected children. They
will go back thankful forever that they were not born Vietnamese, that their
children will be brought up in a clean country where women and girls are
taught to keep their bathrooms clean and to take the right pill for falling
asleep and never, never, to have any odor at all except the preordained
fragrance of the aerosol can. . . . Give them enough freedom to see that the
Vietnamese have none at all and wouldn't know what to do with it if they
had it. Would they? Would they?*
Carillo and his buddies roamed the streets, preparing for their
prolonged killing. And the way to prepare a man for killing was,
first of all, to make him disgusted with his own life, and secondly,
to make him disgusted with the lives of others. . . .

To Carillo it was the ultimate unfolding of a recurring nightmare: it was as if he had seen the beginning of it all years ago with
the orphaned girls crying "Daddy! Daddy! Take *me*. Take *me*. "
Only now the girls—their small breasts extended for charity like
the tin cups of the blind, and often scarred from shrapnel fragments—cried *Joe, joe. Take me, joe. Fuckee plenny backside.* Or *joe-joe,
you like a suck?*

As if they had decided to masquerade during their stay in
Saigon as some other than themselves, Carillo's two companions

adopted nicknames. The oldest of them called himself The Dildo; his claim was that all the slant-eyed girls were begging him for it, they weren't even taking his money anymore. . . . It was a world so grotesque that they could believe anything. It was impossible to exaggerate. So when Dildo proclaimed himself Emperor of the Cross-way Cunt, they laughed and applauded, and everyone pretended to believe him. It appeased for a moment their fear of those lianoid jungles full of bamboo shoots poisoned with excrement, jungles with treacherous booby-traps, with hand grenades that sprang from the innocent bodies of breastless girls. Carillo's other companion was a tough runty fellow who had astonished Carillo the first time he'd seen him in the shower: his legs were like small curved turds floating in space: how had he passed the physical? Still, he was tough. He had a mind like a bulldog's vise, he could yell curses fierce enough to make a dustbowl of the Asian continent, and he excelled in having his prick sucked. He liked it with infinite variations. He would carefully instruct the Saigon women as to the intricacies of his demands. *Women, not girls,* he explained to Carillo with contempt, *girls' mouths are too small and they don't know how to slick up their tongues.* So he had named himself Kum-Up-To, because he said, *when they're kneeling down at you you got to show em how to come up to you, else they miss your balls.* And he showed how the slight pressure on the balls added to his pleasure.

Carillo was simply The Prick—a title which, they assured him, was not meant as an insult but merely an ambiguous term which could be rendered honorific by prolific use: like the guys in their unit called The Gun and The Fist. So Carillo had made half-hearted attempts to live up to his name. But after one or two ordeals with girls too skinny to fondle and so hungry for the rice his coins would buy that it made him retch, he had begun to spin fake stories of instant bordello to match those of Kum-Up-To and Dildo. His pals were sometimes suspicious, his anecdotes frequently lacked the proper smack and gusto, but they let it ride. He was perhaps also saved by his reputation for being a mean, feisty fighter when enraged (itwas only a myth, but one which Carillo encouraged as another toehold on survival). Survival, he had discovered, was made up of all sorts of factitious elements.Above all, his survival was dependent on their laughter. Laughter wild, cynical,raucous, libertine and pitiless. For the real point of the game was to give Death the finger, to sneer at His image, flaunting one's mythic virility as a good luck charm: if you let on you were scared, you were a goner. . . . Like lion tamers, they were never to let the Beast know that all they had in their hands was a cracking whip, a chair and the Devil's own laugh.

So they sat around the Happy Bar and the barracks, swapping tales of happiness. Sometimes Dildo wrote little postcards never meant to be sent

Dear Mom: I am well and getting healthier every day. I can now do thirty push-ups a day. Do you have any pushing you want me to do? . . .

Dear Mom: You remember I told you about Advanced Individual Training? That was training for the demolitions infantry. That means you go out and bust up everything in sight.

Dear Mom. . . .

Dildo would read his little compositions aloud, and the men would be seized with paroxysms of laughter, tears of happy delirium in their eyes: Death could never catch them, they were too happy, too fearless, too virile, too alive. Their bright feathers and war paint would terrify the souls of the enemy. Still, sometimes a silence would fall on them, their time was running out. The festival of lust was nearly over and their well-seasoned bodies were in demand, not for venery and pricksongs, but for the real thing: for napalm and shrapnel and anti-personnel bombs and rockets and herbicides and helicopter crashes, and Viet Cong grenades and SAM missiles and heroin addiction and venereal disease. . . . No, no, their eyes said, they were not ready for that. They bought more beer . . .

Carillo finally learned how to employ these strategic silences. At such times, he could say with an air of boredom: "Well, guess I'll go get me a bit of *re*laxation. . . ." It could mean anything, was accepted by them to mean anything; and for the rest of the day he was free to court privacy like an idolater. He would leave his companions disguising their brooding hatred and fear and loneliness in the Happy Bar and would return to the streets.

One such afternoon he had bought a terrific camera. Even though he could have got it cheaper at the PX, he had preferred the quick exchange in the street, and for once he had not been cheated: the camera had the infallible eye of Mephistopheles watching from the wings—waiting the moment to snatch men's souls. It took pictures that even he didn't know he could take, it was like an extra hand or leg or some robot's brain recording what he came to call The Nighttime Saigon. For he had discovered an important truth: that there were two Saigons: the one which was reported to the States over the 6:30 news, the one which journalists and cameramen had boiled, distilled and purified to prevent the American people from retching over their dinners; and the other Saigon, the nighttime Saigon.

After a warning from a buddy that he wasn't to take that kind of picture, that the Army wouldn't like it at all, Carillo learned to conceal his photographs like an illicit passion. What he had discovered was so astonishing that he knew at once that it must, like heroin, be contraband; so, like the scag smuggler, he hid his negatives until he learned to ship them back to the States in the body bag of a friend.

When, after his return to the States, he came across photographs of the war in Leftist journals (and in some theological ones) he was surprised to discover a simple truth of journalism: that atrocity must be understated. Journalism, he began to see, was compelled to be a form of fiction: for the truth was unbelievable. *His* camera, however, would tell the whole truth—at least to himself—and he focussed his camera on Saigon like a needle piercing the pus. Of course no one would be able to look at his pictures. Readers of *Time* and *Newsweek* would have screamed and hurled the magazine from them like a contagion of Asian cholera. So he did not even try to circulate his photographs in the States. For in a society where it was considered a demonstration of hardihood for American students to take cold water showers in the youth hostels of southern France, how could it be believed that there could be a city within the city in which over a hundred thousand people not only had no showers but no shelter: no place to eat, sleep, live, make love, philosophize, and die but in the streets. Even he, inured to the minimal shelter of 'the hole' in a Texas Reformatory, could not have imagined it. It was not until one night, concealing his camera like a murder weapon while he stole through the streets of Saigon, that he saw the nomads of the city of night superimpose their image upon the daytime city. It was then, as the last rays of light removed themselves from the sky, like a tent roof folding itself and all its carnival illusions away, that from out of the darkness appeared the mat families. It was like watching the occupation of the moon by some extraterrestrial life; or rather, he thought, as he shifted his camera to another angle, it was like watching the strange silent emergence of flowers in the desert with film reels revealing within a few moments what had taken weeks and months to blossom. Tens of thousands of small bodies were now laying down the houses which like tortoises they had carried on their backs during the day. Carillo's camera recorded them as they bloomed swiftly in the night. Here was a dark toddler scarcely able to walk, perishing for want of sleep, waiting for the Time of the Mats (for it was "forbidden" to sleep on the sidewalks during the day). Singling out the child's family, Carillo slowed his camera. Quickly, while the older brother and sister waited, the mother laid the child down on the mat and covered it with a rag or shawl and instructed it to sleep, to sleep well and long. Because, the astonished camera recorded, the child was to tend his own sleeping on the sidewalks of Saigon. But where would the mother of this family go? Where the sister? the brother? Carillo's heart beat like that of a discovered spy as he watched and waited and clicked: he felt he had known this family almost all his life. Soon each one separated, with a touch, a call, a word: and the official night of employment had begun, the begging, the pushing, the offering of services.

But drawn by the spectacle of the sleeping child, Carillo and his camera remained behind, a parody of maternal care. The child, sleeping soundly under the solicitous eye of Carillo's camera, never noticed him, never awakened during the night to the sounds of passing feet. Indeed, Carillo noticed, it was true of all the infants sleeping on their mats: exhausted from being kept moving from daybreak to nightfall, they slept like the dead, scarcely stirring to resist the attendant demons which now descended on them: first came the flies made insolent and greedy by this unresisting flesh; then an invasion of invisible bloodsuckers: a drone of mosquitoes. And finally, when the darkness was complete, the rats. . . .

In sight of Carillo's astonished camera, the mat child slept, stirring only now and then in sullen stoical misery when the mosquitoes bit too close to his eyelids. . . . Then, while the camera watched, a long hirsute black rat moved in upon the soft flesh of the forearm. It was more than Carillo could stomach. With a roar of outrage, he seized the first thing he could find, a leafless twig, not more than a switch, and flailing furiously at the rat, he managed to drive it away, though without killing it. The child whimpered uneasily, but slept.

That night, unable to sleep, Carillo lay on his bunk trembling as with fever; his friends thought he was delirious. But he was merely haunted by a simmering question, not yet articulated. And as he lay in the barracks the camera of his inner mind continued to click over and over the same photograph; the bleeding forearm, the muted cry of the infant, the cunning look of the rat which had learned that sleeping mat-children moved but did not resist—that there was no need to wait for carrion; the living flesh was sweet, and wails of protest were nothing to fear. Soon the cunning Saigon rat would learn to surround their prey like wolves.

Carillo now sat upright in his bunk, his senses reeling from the surfacing question: what would happen to the child, the one whom he had saved tonight, if the mother were, say, to be struck down by a bicycle and were unable to return to the mat? Or if the father (if there was father) were detained for questioning? Since, physically, the Vietnamese of the south were identical to the Viet Cong of the north, Carillo could readily understand that there was no way the government could be certain a mat-man was not a spy except by questioning him; or sometimes, detaining him in a tiger cage . . . The sweat rose on his forehead as these unanswerable questions surfaced. It was hours before he slept again and he awoke at a moment near dawn having had a rare dream of Estelle; he had tears in his eyes. *I'm sorry, Estelle. I'm sorry, sorry.* . . . he murmured aloud.

The following night he returned to the same spot, to his chosen family. Since he had saved their baby from mutilation on the evening before, he now felt he belonged to the small family and they to him. He saw them as they now approached that spot which (perhaps by some international squatters' rights) had become "theirs." As unobtrusively as he could, he began taking dozens of pictures, first of the infant's mother, then of the sister and brother, and now—yes, here was their father: yet the man did not embrace the woman. No, he must be an uncle, thought Carillo, till he realized that when one is surviving by a thread, on a mat hardly broader than a Moslem prayer rug, one has no time or energy for connubial embraces. But no, this man was indeed not the father. From the little Vietnamese Carillo could understand, he was explaining that he was going away soon, that he would not be back. Where was the man going in his civilian clothes? Could he be a deserter? Carillo wondered. Carillo could not understand

all they were saying. The woman did not weep, but merely nodded solemnly. At one point there was a spontaneous silence
among the street noises, and the woman looked up at him: the
American soldier with a camera. Then she ignored him; indeed,
seemed scarcely aware of him. She was giving and receiving instructions for the night's survival of their family, and she had no
time for curiosity. Carillo sensed that if he had called her to him,
had shown her money, with the passive obedience of the
doomed, she would have come to him at once, knelt down, done
his bidding, taken his money, and returned at once to the sleeping infant. Now she nodded farewell to the male survivor of her
family—uncle? brother? pimp?—and again laid a thin cloth over
the baby. She handed a basket to her daughter, laying into it a
bit of food and a cloth, and signalled her on her way; moments
later the son, his own mat on his back until he should find a more
propitious moment to rest, followed his sister. Then the woman,
soft and deliberate as though she was going to perform a murder
instead of an act of survival, made her way to an alley of Saigon.
If she noted Carillo following, she gave no sign. She did not hawk
her wares, but stood quietly waiting till money was flashed or—
this time—(Carillo's camera noted with the clarity of a Dutch
interior) cigarettes. "Only two" he heard a soldier bargain while
Carillo stood in silent despair, like a betrayed lover, his camera
hanging heavy, remote to one side, painful as a wound. He waited
to see how long the woman would be gone. It seemed hours. . . .
Finally Carillo returned to the sleeping child.

The previous night he had driven away the rat. Tonight he saw
that he had not been a moment too soon: on the forearm lay
exposed an open wound, not festering yet, but luring flies. Carillo's eyes blurring with some internal vision, like a Buddhist monk
about to burn himself alive, he sat down on the sidewalk, awaiting
his enemy. He must have sat for several hours nearly drugged
with revulsion, with hate. Finally the thing emerged from some
foul hole, its gimlet eyes cunning, observant, its tail long, leath-
ery, supple, giving it balance, intelligence, almost prehensility: it
lay in the street, a black shadow within a black shadow, like a
sundial made meaningless by the powers of darkness. Its teeth
were neatly serrated, with near-human incisors. To Carillo's fe-
vered brain, it seemed to smile in challenge, a convulsive, fang-
toothed smile such as cartoonists show on madmen. . . .

It flicked its tail, it started, stopped; it sniffed, it pointed its
beaky nose at Carillo. It loped like a friendly puppy to the side

of the child, and perhaps, smelling the open wound, attacked the soft curve of the forearm, With a howl of rage Carillo leaped up, a heavy stick in hand, and split the rat open at the first blow. But it lived on, dragging its rodent guts to a black hole where it suddenly vanished. Like a madman Carillo banged at the hole, cursing and pounding till an old man hobbled out to see what Carillo wanted. Unable to explain, Carillo hurried away.

Toward morning he checked by again to see if the infant were still asleep. But there was nothing on the sidewalk: the mat family had disappeared, there was nothing to indicate that any human being had ever sheltered itself on that stone. Only, where Carillo had smashed the rat there was a splotchy star of entrails, oddly bright and garish, like plasticene.

Later during the war he heard that those mat-infants who died of pneumonia or accidental causes during the night—those whose parents for some reason did not return in time to claim the body—were thrown into the common dump outside Saigon, where the rats hummed like bees.

After such nights it was almost a relief to be sent to the jungle where the enemy, they assured him, was real though invisible. But even there he was an anomaly—a kinkajou among grey sleek and hungry timber wolves, desperate for survival. His combat unit considered Carillo dangerously naive, stupid: he seemed not to have the natural instincts of self-preservation. First of all, they complained, he waited too long to see what would happen before he acted: he needed to learn the value of the preemptive strike. And he asked too many questions. The consensus among them was that Carillo must be dissuaded from these tragic errors, and abruptly he was assigned to follow and learn from Jibaro—the best teacher in the unit.

But it was not till long afterwards that Carillo realized it was no accident of command that he had been assigned to accompany Jibaro. Jibaro was supremely suited to that art of killing from which Carillo instinctively shrank. When first Carillo heard Jibaro's name called out (the only name he was afterwards able to remember for him), *Jibaro!* he had felt a wave of friendliness: a Mexican-American name, it had seemed to him, and he felt a vague lifting of anguish. Perhaps they would understand each other as *compañeros.*

But Carillo's hopes were soon shattered as reports of Jibaro's prowess were cited around camp: Jibraro scored *First* in his tally of rapes and *First* in their unit for "touching meat." He had the highest number of Viet Cong kills to his credit, and he intended to keep his reputation high.

It was Jibaro who tried to teach Carillo that he must disregard all stories by villagers as lies and collaboration with the enemy. He was to shoot first, aiming at the heart, and ask questions afterwards.

Jibaro's open opinion of Carillo was that he was hopeless, he asked dumb-ass questions. They were not—Jibaro said—even the smart alecky, envious questions such as the other men had asked who pretended not to believe Jibaro's account of his kills. The others, laughing, used to ask Jibaro—doubting Thomases that they were—how could they be sure that each ear he had sliced from the heads of his Viet Cong soldier or villager represented one entire human kill? All ears looked alike, the right ear scarcely distinguishable from the left, they scoffed—delighted at the look of rage which appeared in Jibaro's pale eye. His combat comrades had refused to congratulate him. They wanted further proof. . . .

Accepting the challenge, Jibaro, like those Indians who had believed that the souls of their conquered foe resided in the hair, had begun returning with the *animae* of the Viet Cong securely entrapped in their scalps. These he wore in streaming tassels from his pistol belt. But Jibaro himself was dissatisfied with this arrangement. The enemy's hair, ravaged by endemic skin disease, or shortened by crew cuts, was often too scanty for decorative purposes: it made his task difficult and even implausible. Even to himself his best efforts sometimes lacked artistry.

So he had carried his art to its ultimate form. One afternoon after chow, most of the unit had stretched out to relax and watch Jibaro construct his artifact. Jibaro claimed to have learned the art while working in a charity hospital where there were many unclaimed bodies: an illegal traffic in shrunken heads had blossomed at the hospital almost spontaneously when it was discovered that they could be sold to curiosity-seekers as the genuine article, heads supposedly shrunken by descendants of the headhunters of Ecuador, whose perfect skill could reduce a skull to the size of a small monkey's head.

But now Jibaro aspired to perfection, he tried to make all his artifacts uniform; his heads, whether adult, child, or foetus, and regardless of sex, were given the same treatment with identical results. Those who could watch, watched; those who could not, went silently back to the barracks. There was no one to complain to, even if one wanted to, because Jibaro not only had the tacit sanction of his superior officers, but when he was soon able to send one of his perfected heads to the son of a famous general, the officer had it framed on a trophy board: such commendation was sufficent to safeguard Jibaro from all criticism whether from either Above or Below.

Carillo said to himself that he would not watch: but he watched, nevertheless. It was a time-consuming task, requiring patience and ingenuity, but Jibaro, well-practiced in his work, did not take much time for the initial proceedings. Later, he would spend hours, smoking and polishing the head to a high coppery glow.

First, with a well-sharpened knife, Jibaro sliced the decapitated head down the back: a precise incision, requiring the stable hand and fine vision of a hunter and perfect marksman.

Then Jibaro peeled the skull off and boiled it for what seemed hours in a small open vat around which from time to time the combat soldiers would gather and peer down into its contents, joking about Jibaro as wizard: it was certainly a kind of black magic, they quipped, maybe Jibaro could melt down or shrink away the entire Vietnamese population in a great boiling witches' brew. . . .

When the skull had been boiled down to a desirable size— preferably about the size of Jibaro's fist, Jibaro, in the ancient way of Stone Age headsmen, heated three carefully chosen stones, and with the skill and rhythm of a housewife making bread, he kneaded them to and fro within the hollow skull, smoothing and shrinking it. If, by this process, the head were still not sufficiently shrunken for trophy purposes, or perhaps were still too large to be slung conveniently at his pistol belt, Jibaro would patiently fill the hollow skin with hot sand again and again. When at last the head was sufficiently shrunken from the heat so that it was small enough to toss in the palm of his hand, like a pear or papaya, Jibaro declared it was done. At least thus far: for the final steps were what created the perfect specimen. Settling down to work with a can of beer to whet his spittle, Jibaro created a perfect son of Adam, a head *immaculato* smoked to a perfect shade of amber, the surface alternatively moistened and polished with his own saliva and plenty of brasso. And at last, resembling some lost, powerless god forbidden to speak, the homunculus' lips would be delicately sewn together in eternal silent sorrow, the black brows would be neatly brushed, and the image was ready to testify to Jibaro's long hours of dedication.

This was the man who was assigned to be Carillo's "buddy," to teach Carillo how to "waste" his enemy. And a few days later, the perfect head now hanging from Jibaro's new pistol belt— slightly modified by himself with strengthened loops so as to comfortably carry any incremental trophies—they set out together to attack a village.

Jibaro was as skilled a huntsman as he was an artisan. The main problem with killing the enemy was locating them, he said: men in the villages would flee before your arrival abandoning their women and children. And while you were burning their huts or fucking their women, they were planning an attack. But he had contrived an infallible means of luring the enemy into sight—by using the fool-proof method of the hunt—by using the young as bait to entrap the parent. Having explained this simple system Jibaro laid waste several huts. He had learned to alternate carnage with carnival and took time out to enjoy the fruit of his destruction: he would no more miss an opportunity for rape than he would have disobeyed an order, he said, signalling to Carillo that he could follow him and do likewise upon the woman he had seized and partially bound. Jibaro liked a woman's mouth taped, because he said, he like to look down into the woman's eyes, he was not like those necrophiliacs who knocked the women out first so that they never woke up again. He, Jibaro, liked to meet the fury and terror and pleading in their eyes. He only killed them afterwards.

When he had had his little pleasure (systematic as Jibaro was, it took an astonishingly short time to rape and kill) he now lined up the bait, as he called it. "You're going to see something that you'll never in your life see on the TV," Jibaro swore. And it was true, no script-writer could have invented it: one by one, their wailing cries looping around the countryside like decoys, the children's throats were slashed and left by the road to keen and croon their death throes to their absent males. . . . Their cries of distress shook the jungles, and from out of the very trees, it seemed, the invisible Viet Cong came to fight for their young.

But Carillo's first lesson in the art of decoy-and-destroy was not yet over. The dying children had succeeded in entrapping a

Viet Cong who emerged suddenly from ambush: Jibaro now whirled his gun on the attacking enemy and killed him as quickly and efficiently as if he had been shooting a rattlesnake: the Viet Cong died in minutes, screaming. But the action—like chain letters—had created its own reaction, and at the sound of the screaming death of his companion, another Viet Cong was stirred from hiding. If Carillo was ever to be initiated into this fraternity of men, it must be now. "There he is: kill the motherfucker!" shouted Jibaro. It was the first time Carillo had ever seen Jibaro nervous: apparently he was not sure Carillo would have the common sense or nerve to waste this Viet Cong soldier who stood now, his gun aimed at them. And Carillo was certain that Jibaro would kill them *both*—the VC soldier and himself—if somehow he, Carillo, was unable to pull the trigger. With a tremendous effort, like a man in a nightmare pushing the bedpost into the wall, he raised his gun, but the trembling of his hand made it droop to an angle, endangering his own body. "The *heart,* you dumb motherfucking bastard, aim for the heart! Don't jerk the trigger, goddam dumb rookies ... *Squeeze it!*" Like a simultaneous explosion, Jibaro's command seemed at last to break the paralysis of his finger, and Carillo's shot went through the air. He could not believe he had done it, it must have been the reverberating force of Jibaro's voice which had moved the trigger. But now the grass moved in faint fanlike breaths, like the sound of the sea from a great distance, and the wounded soldier was turning a strangely graceful backward parabola, falling toward the whispering sound of the grass. Carillo could not believe that he had fatally shot the man who was still staring at him, not in anger but in surprise: as if they had been going up together in a slow, silent, perfectly synchronized elevator in a gracious building renowned for its cleanliness, decency and functional architecture, and now one of them would be carried dead from the elevator. The people who awaited the dying man would never receive his message ... Now, turning and rolling as Carillo had seen so many times when the running back is grasping the football as if his life depended on it, the VC rolled into a womblike position, holding in his entrails, blocking the assault of death: surely no victory this, only to hold onto to one's bowels, no thought anymore of winning the game ... only to survive. But blood was leaking like gummy licorice from his mouth; he tried to swallow his own blood, tried to cough it away, tried to hold the widening hole wherein lay the secret vitals of man—those vitals which no one saw and which were not protected and no one felt shame for so long as they were firmly packed in the exquisite skin the color of sunlight on the mesa. . . . But now it was as if he saw how deluded he had been, he was nothing but a stocking stuffed for a season with shit and blood, and all this was oozing swiftly away from him with his life. It was as if he were holding all his inner vitals in his arms, a peace offering to Carillo who had not moved. Jibaro was congratulating Carillo, calling his clumsy gunshot an inspiration; it would prolong the man's death, and his cries of pain would be recycled. His screams would bring another VC to rescue him, and Jibaro would take care of the next one.

Hunkering down in the grass, they watched Carillo's first kill die. At first the man screamed with the rasping nerve-scraping grind of gears and rust and screeching machinery in a fiery furnace blast. Then there was a pause, a silence, as though he were mentally turning a page, tautening his strings: a musician preparing to transpose his score into another key. And then he began —in an odd piping voice, like a small hesitant bird which hops first on one foot, then the other, then takes a few steps, then peers at you, then pecks at the crumb, then with a flutter of wings takes triumphant flight into the blue sky, its small sustaining crumb clasped in its bill—he began to murmur, to babble, to carry on a sustained colloquy with his wife, his children. He spoke of love and love and love . . . then he spoke to Carillo, at which point the tears burst from Carillo's eyes in a flood and Jibaro cracked him across the cheek as though he had done something filthy . . . After nearly an hour in which Carillo and Jibaro sat only listening, listening, as though to a priest chanting some high unearthly mass, uniting sky and earth, man and man, and bird with heaven, the enemy died.

When he was motionless, Jibaro turned him over with his boot, face up: the anonymity of the face was stunning. Before, he had been an individual with a past, and a keening personal song of mourning: now he was no more distinguishable from the oceans of dead than a seed blown in the wind. Jibaro, without ferocity, casually divested the body of its exchangeable goods: some money, a ring. Apparently because it was Carillo's kill, not his own, Jibaro did not decapitate the corpse, although Carillo rather expected him to do so anyway: but Jibaro was an observer of protocol. "You want an ear or anything?" he asked of Carillo, and

when Carillo quickly shook his head, with sullen politeness Jibaro
abandoned the corpse.

But suddenly a shot rang out: they were being ambushed.
Crackling gunfire came directly at them. The decoying outcries
of the dying man had baited another Viet Cong. Jibaro and
Carillo flung themselves down in the grass. The new enemy was
clever, resourceful, he tried many positions, his gun smoked and
moved away quickly. "Fuck it, maybe there's more than one,"
said Jibaro, glancing with fury and astonishment at Carillo who
lay quietly as if dead, not firing his gun. "Goddamn you, *shoot.* Kill
the bastard," hissed Jibaro while above their heads whirred bullets which were no mockery, no target practice, but aimed with
venomous intent at themselves, the pillagers, the wreckers who
had searched and destroyed and wasted: the smell of the burning
hut hung in the air. . . .

At last, silence. Oddly—now he owed his life to Jibaro's excellent marksmanship. Jibaro had brought the last soldier down
screaming, the blood gushing from his head to his arms into his
palms, like stigmata. "We can't stick around to use this one for
bait. I can't stay here with a goddam cowardly motherfucker like
you. Just what the fuck did you mean, not firing at that Charlie?
I said *fire* and you just lay there like a bitch with a litter. I could
have you courtmartialled, you know that? Now, sit up, take aim.
Waste that motherfucker you see screaming his tail off out there,
you hear me? *Waste* him!"

Silently Carillo stood up and looked across the grass at the
agonizing enemy, so similar to the man who had died at Carillo's
hand, so different in his mode of dying. This man could only gasp
as he retched blood, gripping his head in his hands, his spattered
life delicately speckling the grass like some hybrid jungle flower.

Carillo handed over his gun to Jibaro.

"You'll have to shoot me first," he said.

Carillo was marched back to their unit under Jibaro's supervi-
sion and was at once thrown into the stockade where he spent
most of the rest of his "tour of duty." He left the war a different
man, an educated man, a man whose mind had fattened for nearly
thirteen months on smuggled books. He emerged what he
became, a guerrilla leader, a soldier of the Third World, an
officer of the People's Army, a revolutionary.

Michele

Growing tomatoes, cucumbers, green onions. I like the tomatoes and green onions best. I like the cleft chin of the tomato, with its curved cheek flushing first pale green, then vermilion, then cinnabar-red. I like its green stem, concave as an umbilicus. Near my small pile of tomatoes I place a sprawling sheaf of scallions. I imagine how they would look under water: a red coral reef of tomatoes, the scallions like the streaming hair of mermaids, swimming toward the sunlit surface—spherical white feet pushing from the oozy bottom: up, up, into the *real* world.

From such surreal indulgences, I am wrenched by the sound of sobbing, of heavy footsteps: bitter reminders of why we are idyllically gathered here, rehearsing the death of the planet. It is then, suddenly, that I am in love with life. Even the grubby worms in the earth comfort me: they are alive; anything is better than my apocalyptic vision of a deserted star, fouled by wind and dust, naked as the moon. Let us go back to the Flood, let us be Cave-dwellers, but at least let all this grow again, I say to Someone, Anyone but He is not listening.

In the midst of my despair—Andrea is sobbing. Her grief is real, immediate. Malcolm has been gone for a week, and she is certain that he has abandoned her. She wants to follow him, *anywhere,* she says, but she has no idea where to go. Carillo and Pinosh have combed the underbrush for him, fearing he may have wandered off and had some fatal accident. Duncan has refused to search for him. "Good riddance," he says hotly. So far, no trace of him. Nor did he leave any note for Andrea.

Andrea argues with a certain pride that Malcolm would not do anything so stupid as to wander away. Moreover, he wore a suit and took a suitcase with things he would have needed: she enu-

merates them with a strange combination of pleasure and despair. She is pleased that she knows his needs so well; she is in
despair that his needs reflect no need of her . . . pipe, books,
shorts, shaving gear, the slides he had collected from his mush-
room experiments over the past six months, and all his photo-
graphic equipment. This last is what makes Andrea feel he would
not return. The equipment was valuable, but it was also heavy.
He would have had to carry all this nearly four miles to the
nearest highway where he might flag down a car or bus. The fact
that he had chosen to do so is, to her, definitive. She has been
crying for days. When she is not in her room sobbing, she is as
now, standing at the kitchen window looking out to where we
once stood together watching Duncan try to draw love like water
from a well out of the arms of my lover. At that time I prayed she
would cease her unending monologue. Now she says nothing,
and I wish she would speak to me. I hold the scallions up for her
to see, shaking them vigorously so that the fresh earth spatters
round me like rain. Andrea tries to smile at my efforts, but too
late I realize there is some chagrin in her smile: perhaps she is
thinking that we were to have shared this work. But she has no
energy for communal effort, she has given herself up entirely to
grief. I try to shake off a feeling that instead of one day bravely
dying together in an apocalypse we are dying one by one, picked
off by our emotions. There are now only six of us, and we are far
from sufficient unto ourselves.

Indeed it is unnerving to realize how much we depended on
Malcolm: although none of us truly "loved" him, he was necessary to our well-being. He helped us build, he grew nourishing
food which needed no canning or preserving. None of the rest
of us knows anything about growing mushrooms. For that matter, we know nothing of the ecology of caves. As for myself, I
sometimes believe that I would rather die in the sun than subsist
in the caves. But even the self-deceiving image-maker (poet) in
me admits that that is not true. So I have determined to check out
Malcolm's work, to see if perhaps his work can be continued by
the rest of us. With an heroic effort I beckon to Andrea to accompany me (usually she will do so without asking *where?* since there
are so few possibilities anyway). But this time she shakes her
head, raises her fingers thoughtfully to her mouth, as though I
have interrupted her in a meditation. I bring the vegetables in to
her, ostensibly to ask her to wash them and store them away, but

to repeat my request: "I'm going to see what Malcolm's been doing all these months. In the cave, I mean. You want to come?"

Her eyes widened with apprehension as though I were about to confirm her worst suspicions. I have made things worse instead of better, dammit. With an awkward, embarrassed shrug—of sympathy, of cynicism, of rage with my own ineptitude—I trudge off to the cave, wondering what tools I should have brought with me: Noah, abandoned in the Flood without a plank or spar.

Overcoming my repugnance, I enter Malcolm's cave. It is protected against predatory animals by a sort of fiber fence which he has woven across its entrance. (Did I expect a tiger skin?) I am pleased at this ingeniousness and it allays my anxiety somewhat: what has been begun with such caution must necessarily continue to develop its own security system. After all, I assure myself, Malcolm spent entire days here, working.

There is enough light from the mouth of the cave so that I can see for about eight feet. The usual knobby appendages, the *stalactites* and *stalagmites* of my childhood days, when I played with such words on the crossword page (which were up? we children used to ask, and which were down? as a mnemonic device we used to sing *mites are mired down*). But now these I see are in earnest: no crossword strategy. I light the emergency lantern which Malcolm has left on a flattened rock, the match trembles in my hand.

As if the light has sharpened my other senses, I now hear a few piping cries, rather like that of a child whimpering in his sleep. I understand that they must be bats, and my heart freezes. I am more frightened at the idea of bats than of a bear or a true raging Cyclops. Then Reason assures that they could not be rabies-carrying bats else Malcolm would long ago have perished of disease, along with the rest of us. Still, the eerie sound fills me with dread; I mean to go no further, for fear I will actually see the fluttering nervous creatures sleeping upside down in their ceilinged couch. At twilight, a swaying bat or two has about it a poetic languor; one is lulled into a sense of security by the campfire, the scientific jargon of sonar fields, visibility, radar and the simple fact that there is no reason to fear them, these are not vampire bats; they are harmless except by their power to freeze your blood as though in Jungian memory. I raise the lantern and direct my flashlight at Malcolm's "garden." Mushrooms grow like larvae along the floor bottom, there is the smell of offal, guano.

I gag. We eat shit, I think. We eat shit and thrive on it; that is our civilization. We have come no further than the decomposition of matter, stuffed digestive tracts leading to the fertilizer heap. . . .

I had in part wanted to see the cave and Malcolm's 'garden' to prove Malcolm's frequent claim that we could, if necessary, live in it. But I now know that I for one could not. Although I am barely twenty feet into the cave, a claustrophobia seizes me. I glance over my shoulder at the daylight: suppose it should turn dark even while I stand here? It is a poetic nightmare, the poet in me taunts: a tunnel, piles of guano, and bats hovering like some multiplied and distorted version of Poe's raven, all croaking *Nevermore.*

I have managed to calm myself with this parody of my terror. But the sweat of my palms is real; the flashlight is limp in my hand.

I notice for the first time that Malcolm has put a small table to one side of the cave on which he has left a spiral notebook. I imagine Malcolm here in this stygian light, like one of Dante's doomed, collecting dozens of notebooks all filled with his scientific data. I open this one, but it has not yet been used, only a date is scrawled in the upper right-hand corner, as though he had intended perhaps to return and make some notation for that day. There is also a metal box in which perhaps he kept a few corruptible items from the flaky vault—a ceiling which, though it appeared as solid as the Sierras, could nevertheless one day split and crumble, covering all. . . . And suddenly I could envision our final end: the six of us cowering in the depths of this cave, huddled together, waiting for the silence.

No, I said, and turned off the flashlight. *No,* I said again, and extinguished the lantern. Then I stood in the darkness. The bats piped their warning messages; trees of stone swayed their great roots before my eyes: soon my feet would be entwined in these liana and I too would grow into their roots. I managed, in spite of my claustrophobic fear, not to faint. I began to assure myself that I was conducting a small private experiment in what is called Sensory Deprivation. I felt indeed deprived, deprived of all the people who had ever lived, of human civilization itself. When my eyelids flickered for a second, all I could see was the red light of my own consciousness: when that consciousness ebbed there would not even be that tiny light. I knew that for me this colony had failed. If my death was necessary, I wanted to die with the rest

of the planet, not exist on fungi, drinking blood when we ran out
of water, fighting for space with the bats who understood the
darkness better than I: regressing, not to the morality of Cave-
men, but the morality of flies. Like Duncan, I felt for the first time
that we who had been created in the image of God had been
euchred. Unfortunately for Milton, there was no longer any way
to justify the ways of God to Man.

I walked from the cave into the sunlight. Like Lazarus, I had
already experienced my own death. Yet there was something
liberating about it, as if every moment were now a sort of gift. Or
as if I had witnessed a battle over my own internment and now-
exalted and bemused—every thought was proof that I was still on
the winning side. Any anguish was preferable to that dark: it was
what Dostoevski had meant when he said that standing poised on
a wire over an abyss for all eternity was preferable to Death. . . .
I don't know how long I sat outside the cave, looking at the earth,
touching the weeds, feeling my separate thoughts as if an Idea
were something totally physical and could run through one's
mind like water over stones.

When I returned to the camp, Andrea seemed calmer and was
preparing dinner. Duncan was nervously pacing back and forth
in the kitchen. Jennifer sat sewing, her feet propped up on a
stool. I felt as if I had indeed been away a long time. Suddenly
Jennifer looked enormous, it seemed she could not possibly contain the child a moment longer. . . . I tried to remember how long
ago Carillo had joined us. What a transformation had taken place
in that agile swimmer's body since her pregnancy. Even her face
was changed: the skin was mottled and dry as though the child
were slowly absorbing everything from within the mother's frail
husk of skin: soon the butterfly would emerge, and the dry skin
of Jennifer's childhood would blow away. . . .

It was unusual to see Duncan not employed at one of his
projects: for the past few weeks he had been building a new snake
house which he claimed would be impregnable (or inescapable).
Only, he said, the snake house would need an adjacent structure,
for breeding mice. . . . Perhaps I was still shaky from my experience in the cave; I began to feel that there was, in fact, some
metaphysical force prompting these men to ransack the nether
world, building their survival on fundament and serpents, like
medieval wizards.

"Where have you been?" he demanded.

I stared. "Why? What business is it of yours?"

"Everything that takes place here is my business. I'm responsible for you all. I brought you here. I'm responsible for your physical safety."

"And for our souls too, don't forget that," Jennifer put in with total irony.

"And for your souls too," he said, still looking at me.

"I've been over to the cave to see if—"

"That's Malcolm's territory. You shouldn't have . . ."

"What do you mean 'shouldn't'? I'll go where I please. There's nothing sacred there: no snakes, only bats . . ." Any irony is wasted on him, I thought.

"How do you know that? It'd be easy for a snake to get past that little string gate Malcolm put up. You'd better stay to hell out of there. Ignorant women. . . ." he muttered.

Aah! I thought. *Now we're into misogyny, are we?* I tried to think of something utterly devastating to say, but found myself sympathizing with him. Could he help it if he had discovered he did not like women? Could I help it if I did not like the dark? Phobia for phobia, his had more relevance: and he could do something about it.

"It's getting dark," said Andrea uneasily. "Isn't it a rule—?"

She looked at me apologetically, doubtless feeling that I would think she was ingratiating herself with the Man-in-Command by being so conscientious about the rules: *the rule* was that, no matter where we happened to be working, we were to return to our camp by nightfall (fear-of-the-dark, written into our very social contract).

"Have you rung the bell?" I asked. Glancing around I noticed that neither Carillo nor Pinosh had returned yet. The table was not yet set: that was Pinosh's job. He also liked to help Andrea scrub the vegetables and prepare the salad. He claimed vegetables were *intimate.* He had always, he said, liked the seeds of green peppers, the inner whorls of artichokes, the secret folds of the hearts of celery: the shape of a cauliflower could evoke from him a pastoral poem. I used to admire his rhetorical panache, but after a while I began to see it as only another role—Pinosh playing Pinosh as he would like to be seen: the flamboyant, witty codpiece, the King's jester facing the scaffold in his Master's wig and an heroic couplet.

I disliked the idea of asking Duncan where my lover was, so I observed instead: "Where's Carillo? He said he would show us how to skin a rabbit."

"He's gone to look for Pinosh." Duncan averted his gaze from mine and began fumbling with the forks which had been dropped in a heap on the table. He peered among the tines as though he were practicing some ancient augury.

"Don't worry. Carillo will find him." Jennifer's confidence was absolute. "They're probably having a dip together. It's the best time of the evening for a swim. . . ."

I couldn't resist piquing Duncan by saying ambiguously: "They're probably having a *great* swim together!" *There: how do you like it? Maybe Carillo will steal Pinosh away from YOU; then we can play musical lovers, each one with a chance to make Pinocchio a real boy . . .*

I am over-reacting, I thought. Duncan is not going to seduce Pinosh, it is all my hyperactive imagination. Still—I felt a sort of anguish to realize I had reached this low point of suspicion. I longed for the days when I was sunken into a perfectly ordinary abyss, when being in love with Mark meant catering to his whims like a slave. Now my emotions are splintered: I sleep with Pinosh, I dream of Carillo, I hunger for what now seems Security with Mark—if only the security of a *geisha.*

Duncan stared at Jennifer, at her great swollen body, as though he were trying to make some association between her pregnancy and whatever was going on in his head.

"I'm going to look for him."

"For whom?" I said.

"For Pinosh. It's not like him to be late like this. He knows . . . we depend on him."

"Yes, to scrub the vegetables."

He began to stuff a few things in his pockets: bandages, Mercurochrome. Quickly he folded a heavy blanket and laid it saddlewise across his arm. Was all this part of an act, I wondered, or did he really believe something had happened? When he went to his room to get a gun, I became convinced that his fear was real. Duncan hated guns; his repeated criticism of Carillo was that he knew more about guns than he did anything else. "You break the beans because you handle them like bullets," he would complain to Carillo. "They're *fragile*—they're for eating, not killing. . . ." Carillo would listen to such complaints in silence, his face white with pain.

Duncan didn't ask me to go with him, but I wasn't standing on protocol. I had already begun to pull off the boots I'd worn to the cave, but when I saw Duncan's intention, I pulled them on again.

"What are you thinking?" I demanded breathlessly as I ran after him.

"I'm thinking that something's wrong. As leader of this colony—"

"Yes, yes, I know that. But where would he have gone?"

"I think Jennifer's guess that he's gone for a swim is a good one. I think I should have made a rule that no one was to go swimming by himself."

I didn't bother to correct him, to say 'we' should have made a rule; it was a relief to hear him sounding rational, however authoritarian.

"Wouldn't Carillo have reported back?"

"I think Carillo went to the woods. He would have figured Pinosh could hear the dinner bell from the stream. *I'm* figuring the same. That he did hear the dinner bell. Then, for some reason he didn't . . . couldn't come in. . . ."

"Oh." I noticed with involuntary admiration that he had brought a long flashlight and was playing the light along the ground, looking for fresh footprints.

"There," I pointed. "There *was* someone this way, headed for the stream."

"Those are not his footprints."

He knows exactly what imprint Pinosh's foot would make. As I used to know Mark's footprint in the shower. . . . Suddenly I slowed down, a sense of defeat filled me, I felt I was struggling against an invisible force about which I knew nothing. Duncan's face was a map of anxiety. "There now," he said. *"That's* Pinosh's print. He was wearing shoes, you see. I try to remind everybody all the time: never go barefoot. Even the ants are so vicious they can bite you up pretty bad. . . ." He stopped short. "Damn! I *knew* it. . . ."

I could see nothing in the thickening dusk. Duncan's voice was fierce with rage and love. "Dammit, I told him to be careful." He ran like a madman toward Pinosh's naked body which lay beside a stone in the stream. Pinosh was still conscious but his eyes were glazed.

". . . bitten," he said to Duncan, pointing to his legs. He seemed hardly to notice I was there.

"I knew it, I knew it," Duncan repeated in despair. "Damned fool, you!" Then he wasted no more breath. Before I had time to wonder what to do, he had bent down, had slashed at Pinosh's right leg with a snake knife. Then, like a lover drawing kisses, he sucked the poisonous venom into his own mouth. He spat it to the ground. He repeated his action.

I stood numb with shock. And with shame at my ignorance. Had it been I alone who had come upon Pinosh, I would not have known what to do. I would have had to run back for help, wasting time: *we have not been taught how to survive: only how to drive cars, wear our hair, and read poetry.*

The left leg had been bitten first and was now badly swollen. Duncan seemed uncertain whether he should risk slashing the other leg. "How long? ..." he asked of Pinosh.

Pinosh turned his head away at the sight of the knife, poised to cut again. "I'm not sure. The sun was ... westward. Mid-afternoon, anyway. It was very hot."

"Did you get a look at him? Did he rattle?"

"No rattle. It was a coral, I think. I didn't hear a thing. Suddenly I felt it lash out. ... I was sitting on this rock here."

Duncan lifted Pinosh toward the blanket which was spread out beside him. He stumbled as he bore Pinosh's weight, my lover's bare legs resting on the sandy ground. Then for a moment— while trying to regain his own balance—Duncan rested one knee upon the earth, with the full weight of Pinosh's body against himself. Like a pietà, I thought.

It was I who was sent back to the camp to fetch a litter. Carillo was there, and Andrea insisted on returning with him and me to the stream. Then Duncan and Carillo carried the litter back to the camp, and Andrea and I followed sorrowfully behind, as if in an ancient funeral procession.

It was already totally dark by the time we returned to the house; Andrea's supper lay cold and untouched; no one thought of eating. We were concerned with the fact that it had grown dark, that it was late, and that it was four miles to the nearest highway. Even to reach this highway one had to make his way cautiously through trees and underbrush. Though the woods were sparse, it was easy to become confused, especially at night, and wander around looking for the dirt road that led to the main highway. And the two men would be carrying a litter. I did not dare ask them how they meant to get Pinosh to the hospital in the city; I simply knew they would do it—Duncan would walk all night if necessary, and Carillo would adopt some strategy. We would have to rely on their personal combination of love, intelligence and courage. In the long run, the human element.

Duncan hung a lantern alongside the litter. Each man shoved a flashlight into his pocket. They buckled their boots carefully. I knew they would refuse, but I offered to come along. Perhaps they would need a third person to help carry the litter. "In an emergency . . . ," I added.

"There'll be no more emergencies," said Carillo. "This is what we'll do: if we can't get a ride, we'll ring in a fire alarm. The fire department will take us straight to the hospital. They'll also have some medical equipment—"

"There's a ranch—" I said.

"I know. But it's another four or five miles beyond the highway."

"—anything that'll bring us there quicker," said Duncan. "Would the police—?"

"Well, the highway patrol might see us, and they'd stop for us maybe. That'd be good. Or we could try to flag down a trucker. We'll do what we can . . ."

Carillo had not looked at Jennifer all this time. She stood nervously clutching her sewing, her eyes wide with fear.

"You take care now," he said.

We could see that she did not want to ask the question, but it came, expelled from her involuntarily, like a breath: "How long? . . ."

"How can I tell you that?" he said sadly. He added: "You want to come with me a second? I want to . . . And would you fix us a thermos of water, please?" he added to Andrea and me.

Pinosh lay in silence; I had never seen him so lifeless. Duncan felt his forehead, took his pulse; his lips were a clenched enigma. He waited in silent tension for the jug of water, for Jennifer to release Carillo's hand . . .

Within minutes, it seemed, they were ready to go. I thought Jennifer would run after them, beg to go with them, but she must have known it would be impossible: she could only add to their burdens.

"Wait," said Pinosh suddenly, and called me to him. I knelt down beside his litter like a child waiting for a blessing. He put his hand out in a comradely way, managing a wan smile. He gripped my hand as tightly as he could, then released it and allowed himself to sink back on the litter. "I wanted to say thanks. I wanted you to know, you know—it was not a play, not a performance . . ."

Tears of gratitude came to my eyes. I did not make any assurances aloud; I thought, like a prayer: *Pinosh, darling you're going to be all right.* I bent my head to hear what he was saying:

"... not so deep as a well, nor so wide as a church-door; but 'tis enough, 'twill serve. . . ."

He closed his eyes, a faint smile lurked at his lips.

When the men had gone, Andrea and Jennifer and I attacked the darkness, we lit every lamp. Then by tacit assent we sat in the kitchen together, slowly swallowing our cold supper as though it were sodden straw. Suddenly instead of a colony we were the lone survivors of a wreck, flung on a faraway island . . . And we had much work to do, suddenly doubled by the loss of half our people. "The work will keep us from worrying," I said aloud, without believing it. Because the amount of work to be done was part of our worry, and with Jennifer so heavily pregnant, that left Andrea and me to do most of it. Andrea and I tried to joke about it: you feed the goats, chop the firewood, milk the nannies, gather the berries and vegetables and I'll stay here and deliver the baby. . . . But it was no joke, we were scared. Suddenly, too, we were frightened not only of our heavy responsibilities but of the possibility of intruders. We had not thought of asking Duncan to leave his gun; besides, none of us would have known how to shoot it. Jennifer, it was true, could now shoot a rifle. But the thought of Jennifer clumsily wielding a rifle in the midst of a crisis —it was enough to make the sweat burst out all over me.

Andrea remarked that if an intruder came in, we would *rape* him, and this idea was so absurd that we all laughed in a kind of terrified hysteria.

"Oh Jesus!" exclaimed Jennifer. "I'm going to take a bath." Evidently she hoped to relieve her anxiety by becoming absorbed in the ritual of bathing. Because taking-a-bath meant to us first heating the water a bucket at a time on the oilstove; then, carrying it to the galvanized tub which simply sat in the bathroom but had no draining system. . . . Nevertheless Andrea and I both encouraged her to do so. We would have encouraged her to do anything that would take her mind off her real fear: that Carillo, having found an honorable excuse for vanishing into the city, would— like Malcolm—simply disappear. Possibly he would make contact with his former comrades and remain with them: what need did he have of Jennifer? What need could he have of a woman and child? These were our unspoken thoughts.

We had managed to fill the tub with about six inches of luke-warm water and were just settling down for the night, praying to lose ourselves in sleep, however fitful and full of bad dreams, when we heard a crash of the water bucket rolling around on the floor.

We heard Jennifer crying out, not loudly but in a kind of muted terror and awe: *Oh, oh oh.*

With a bound Andrea and I reached the bathroom, almost at once. The door was wide open, there was a trace of moisture on the mirror, and Jennifer, dressed in her pajamas, stood stark still in the middle of the floor. She was holding herself in what would have struck me as the prenatal position (her hands clutching her crotch, her pajamas bottoms wet) except that it was just the reverse—Jennifer was not being born but giving birth.

"Isn't it too soon?" wailed Andrea.

Jennifer

Jennifer shook her head. Not too soon. Since when did babies know when they were supposed to arrive? And Bartleby had been kicking and pounding for weeks now, trying to reach his father's voice which admonished him, sometimes, in the dark: "Bartleby, *sleep* now. And let your mother sleep." And sometimes, the baby would obey, as if calmed by this familiar voice. She had grown to love the baby more because lately her body had aroused more tenderness in Carillo than she could have dreamed of. It was as if, when sex had become so awkward as to become laughably grotesque, when they had by tacit consent agreed that lust was great, but the burden of this responsibility was greater, and that her womb was no longer a box to be burdened with jars, jolts, quivers and gyrations, it was as if at this moment he had begun (truly?) to love her. Perhaps she should be jealous of this baby, she had thought whimsically, he loved the baby more than he did her. But she was not unhappy about it, so long as it kept him from returning to his comrades . . . from forgetting her altogether. As she listened to him she sometimes felt so dumb and young and ignorant she wondered how he could stand her (still *he* didn't even know how to swim! she had thought once with hysterical laughter). She tried to resist her desperate intensity, her greed for him. She wanted him always with her, she wanted his hands to touch her, she wanted his voice saying, "Foolish girl, you know nothing about pain, what do you know, foolish girl? . . ." It had not sounded like an epithet, but an endearment. She had tried to resist by poking fun at his small ignorances, by laughing at his accent, neither educated nor crisp, not even very deep nor very masculine, but metronomic, full of pauses, ideas shuffled and reshuffled before deciding to speak. . . . But all she had succeeded in doing was proving to herself that she thought of him all the time except when she was thinking about the baby. Now she need not think of the baby any more, he was coming, he was arriving now in a flood of waters, like Moses, on a wave of water.

Only: even if it was not too soon, as Andrea now wailed, it was not the right time: his father had gone with the sick man, a man nearly in a coma from this awful wilderness. And would he come back? *Bye baby bunting, daddy's gone a-hunting.* But it was no lullabye she heard, it was a painful awakening. With the first rush of the water—she looked down in terror at her legs, feeling faint: was there blood too?—she felt a pain shoot through her back and abdomen like a quiver of light.

Under other conditions she might have growled affectionately: "Damn you, Bartleby, just wait till you get here, I'll get you for this, *petit monstre!*" Or something, anything, that would help her over that great hump of fear. But she could see, by the look on Andrea's face (as if she needed a reflection besides that of herself in the mirror now opaque with steam) that she, Jennifer, was terrified. And Andrea's face also mirrored Michele's, and the three of them stood for a moment, united in terror.

Andrea said, her voice tremulous and brisk: "Relax. Remember we've been through all this already. The first thing is not to get scared. . . ."

But we haven't been through it, Jennifer wanted to protest. We haven't been through a thing that was real. This is real. This is my insides falling out and there's no one to put them back in. Above all, no Carillo to help me, to cling to. At once, all her pain became emotional: she wanted Carillo back, she wanted him this instant; she wanted him to help her through this terror; she was suddenly furious with him that he had left her like this, alone, had abandoned her to a couple of women who neither of them had ever had a baby and knew only what they'd read in books. She began whimpering, realizing that he could not be back in time, nothing could bring him back, not even the birth or death of the baby could bring him back until the hours had passed and the brink had been crossed over alone. Her whimpers turned to dry sobs which shook her from head to foot, which increased her pains, which frightened her even more, because she knew she was not supposed to be heaving uncontrollable sobs, but should be taking carefully scheduled, long breaths which would relax every nerve in her body, would open her womb . . . would ease Bartleby out, and bring her maternal bliss.

JENNIFER

None, none of this happened. She screamed with pain, she bit Andrea's hand, she crawled on the floor like an animal, she ripped her sheets apart and squatted down, watching the slow trickle of fluid coming down her thighs, screaming God, God, God, *why doesn't he come? When the pains subsided for a while she thought they might not come back; for a moment she irrationally hoped the child would die and just automatically slide out, like dead fruit. Anything, even the death of the child, to be rid of the pain. Then she felt guilty and ashamed, as if she had betrayed Carillo, and now for certain he would never love her. So she tried to be brave and bring him the child she knew that he loved more than he loved her, more than he would ever love her; so she managed to remain silent for a while, not screaming, biting her lips, the sweat of the struggle on her like mortality, she was bursting with it: the child would certainly emerge from her navel, shooting upward like a great, diving swimmer plunging into space, then gracefully downward. This image comforted her; she had only to wait and someone would come and, like Caesar, Bartleby would be ripped from her womb without any effort on her part. She would have drugs, operating tables, anesthetists, spotless nurses in white caps and doctors like on television: always with their sterile surgical masks. Only not to do it all oneself. Only let us wait quietly, Bartleby and me, and there will be a rescue party. . . . now there* was *a rescue party, she could see it, feel it, she didn't want to wake up to it though, because if she did, the pain would be on her again and she didn't want to have anything to do with it, it was not part of* her, *it was an enemy which lurked in the exterior and when she opened her eyes it would seize her like a wolf which had only been waiting for this signal. So she kept her eyes closed, evading the enemy, pretending to herself that she was asleep, and pretending also to Andrea and to Michele, no not Michele. Michele had gone out sobbing,* a coward Michele, you should be lying here, if you think it's so bad to watch, *she thought in a flash,* why is Andrea strong and Michele unable even to watch? *But she had no answers because the big question was not Andrea nor Michele but why was she herself unable to watch: she wanted only oblivion, she wanted only Carillo. She felt suddenly that if he would only return she would be able to stand anything, that if he would hold her and and say what do you know of pain, foolish girl? she would show him, show him, show him. . . .*

Now came something she would never tell him, never talk about, it was too humiliating, she didn't even want him there then, she prayed he wouldn't come back at that moment. She tried to explain to Andrea she needed a pan, to get a pan, but her voice was so strangled with shame that Andrea did not understand her. O God, God, to think that all this is reduced to the unbearable need to move one's bowels, she felt she would burst, the only comparable thing was once when a child but then Maman had broken down and said no, I can't do it either, they'll have to figure out another way and had thrown the hot water bottle from her into the bathtub and wept for Jennifer. And later the doctor had prescribed a stool softener which was easier, it worked, so why had she and Maman gone through all that hell? Why indeed? A wave of love and affection for her mother suddenly grew with the pain. So Maman had gone through this to bring Jennifer into the world and had loved her in spite of it, had forgiven her all that pain and she, Jennifer, had hated her just for going away with him *and "forgetting" Jennifer, as if anyone could ever forget anyone brought into the world in this way. But maybe Maman had not forgiven . . . maybe that was why . . . but she . . .*

She thought she was screaming with pain, but actually the pain took all her energies and she lay now exhausted, counting her breaths, one, two, the spasms were so close they were all together, the one thing she needed, her basic primitive need was not yet appeased, and finally, weakly, she said,

"Please, please . . . I need . . . a bedpan. . . ."

With these pitiful words came the great act of birth, for suddenly with the rush of relief came also the little blue and red head that was not Bartleby but turned out to be—Margot, but the rushing relief of emptying what she thought were her bowels was always afterwards confused with the relief of emptiness, of seeing something emerge, purple, red, blue, and covered with a layer as of spittle and Andrea cut the cord, and instead of the great relief and bliss as Jennifer with a cry of pain released what she thought was a burst of shit and blood her keening cry was filled with the despairing thought that if Carillo came now and saw her doing it he would be utterly disgusted and never make love to her again.

But he was not to see her till she had been washed, and Margot was also washed, and the two of them were arranged on the bed like a triptych Madonna and Child—Margot trussed up in swaddling bands to heal the belly where her life had already begun by being wounded, and Jennifer wound round and round with clothes to absorb the bright-red ominous bleeding which did not resemble any afterbirth Andrea had ever read about in her books of natural childbirth.

Michele

He returned at six in the morning, he had walked from the last bus stop, which is about ten miles from here. His boots were covered with dust, there was a new beard growing on his face: it was as if he had been away to a long war, and in the meantime Jennifer had given birth, he had a daughter, and we two women, like ancient practitioners of The Old Religion, explained our witchcraft. He knew at once by our faces that we had been through a long vigil; Andrea's skirts were still flecked with blood. The house was in total disorder as we had been too exhausted from our vicarious suffering to do anything more than sit in our chairs, meaning to keep watch, but dozing off in spite of ourselves: we were too frightened even to divide up our vigil into shared sleep. It was as if we felt, each of us, that only our undivided attention kept Jennifer from harm.

Jennifer had dozed off when Carillo returned. Andrea and I wanted to give them the privacy they needed after such an ordeal, but we were so shaken out of our natural selves that we simply forgot to leave them. We did not even remember not to stare. . . . The transfiguration in Jennifer was amazing. The terrified howling animal we had witnessed now lay quietly, tears running down her cheeks onto the pillow. No bliss: no, I would say there was no bliss: but there was enormous relief. He embraced her where she lay. Her lips quivered; they were cracked and dry and she must have smelled terrible. We had not had time to clean her adequately, and we were fearful, anyway, that our best efforts at sterile conditions were perilous.

We felt that we ought to say what is said under such conditions (but when, since the days of the Oregon Trail, had there been such conditions?), that he had a beautiful daughter. But he asked briefly if the child were O.K., meaning, we felt, only the most basic question: was she alive and not in any way deformed? So we said *yes;* we did not add that its hold on life seemed very fragile, that its cry had been very weak indeed, and that she was so small that it hardly seemed possible such a tiny creature would survive a trip to the hospital. Margot had as yet received no nourishment from her mother, of course; and we had been able to give her only a little boiled water.

"Jennifer has no milk yet, of course," Andrea explained.

He seemed unconcerned about this. His gripping preoccupation was with removing Jennifer from the camp. It was not that he was indifferent to the child; it was rather as if Margot were a reward which he had not time to enjoy, a pleasure which he could not allow himself until he was certain the mother would survive. Although Jennifer was no longer in pain, she was still bleeding and in spite of all Andrea's efforts, she had not succeeded in ejecting the entire afterbirth.

"There'll be a van here today. Some friends of mine have agreed to drive here—they'll bring an R.N. with them too." He did not add that the nurse would know more than all of us put together about how to protect Jennifer from infection. He did not need to say it—both Andrea and I were painfully aware of our shortcomings. *I was not prepared for this,* I wanted to say absurdly, to apologize for my useless life in which I had been trained to save nothing from disaster except a few lines of not-even-immortal poetry.

He asked us to get her things ready. Then he motioned to me to follow him to the study. I feared that he had some dreadful news about Malcolm to tell me, not yet meant for Andrea to hear. . . .

Andrea slumped into her chair; now that the ordeal was over she seemed indifferent, almost hostile to both Jennifer and the baby: it was as if she could forgive Jennifer the "gifts" she would receive—the baby girl, Carillo's love, a future in which, instead of Armageddon she might after all find some joy—so long as Jennifer was ransoming her future bliss with great pain. But now she sank back, watching with suspicion—and perhaps envy—as Carillo and I closed the bedroom door.

"This camp must be vacated," Carillo said at once.

I remained silent. Finally I hazarded what I knew would be Andrea's first question: "You saw Malcolm?"

He looked startled. "No, I did not. Why should I see him? He chose to leave, that was his decision."

"But if he comes back . . ."

"Andrea cannot remain here *alone.*"

I looked at him questioningly.

He hesitated. "I hope you will forgive me for interfering. I arranged with some friends of mine who wired Mark. He was in Australia, you knew that?"

"Mark!" I felt the anguish of the long night was nothing compared to the shame of wondering what information the two men may have exchanged about me. . . .

"Why did you do it? I never gave you . . ." I clung to the back of the chair as though I were rowing away on a raft.

He sighed. Embarrassment darkened his eyes, as if he felt it awkward that he must explain to me my rapidly shrinking freedom of choice. "You must understand by now that Pinosh will not be coming back . . ."

I tried to shrug, as if it were of little moment to me, as if Pinosh had been a mere diversion to while away eternity with; but it hurt. It hurt that I had not been enough for him *either.*

"And Duncan . . .?"

"Well, Duncan. Duncan is staying at the hospital. The nurses had so much difficulty getting him to leave Pinosh's room, they let him stay. He clung to Pinosh's bedside like a . . ." He rubbed his face with an exhausted gesture.

". . . like a madman," I added with malice. But I knew that was not what he meant.

He said, with a pity that stung me: "If you want to believe that he's mad because he loves the same person you do . . ."

"I never loved Pinosh!" I denied with an intensity which frightened me: why was I so angry about it?

He gave me such a look that I felt ill with shame. It was his look that made me understand my rage: I was angry that he pitied me, and that he pitied me because all these months he had known it was himself I wanted, not Pinosh. I was angry that my feelings should be so transparent to him and that he should be witness to my multiple humiliation: of not wanting (really) to return to Mark; of never having (really) wanted Pinosh; of having wanted (really) him, Carillo, who by some internal revolutionary discipline was denied me. It was as if I had been found wanting on three levels; it was a total self-depletion.

And now, instead of the future—apocalyptic or otherwise—Carillo seemed to be offering my old life back. But on what terms?

"Did you . . . have you . . . what did Mark *say?* I mean, did you speak to him personally?"

"I took the liberty of saying that you would wait for him at a motel in El Paso. I gave him the name of the motel . . . He agreed at once to meet you there . . . It's up to you . . ."

"*Thank* you!"

He pretended not to notice my bitterness. He turned to go. "If you're ready to leave when my friends come, we—my comrades and I—will drive you right to the motel. There you can wait . . . comfortably."

"And Andrea? What of Andrea?"

"That's up to her. You must try to persuade her to leave. To wait here for Malcolm would be . . . suicide." The word seemed extraordinarily painful to him. Suddenly he could barely speak; his lips were cracked and dry. He seemed suddenly a frightened man, I could not believe it.

"You *must* leave—both of you. I will order it, if necessary." Whatever fear or apprehension had overtaken him briefly now turned to rage; he seemed almost growling. Never had I seen him look so angry. "Now I must get ready. I'll need the bath. Do you. . .?"

"Wait," I said suddenly, inexplicably. I put out my hand as if in comradely fashion. Then a terrible need for some gesture at once more tender, more ceremonial and more ambiguous compelled me to say: "Won't you kiss me goodbye? After all, we've been friends for months." My hand in his seemed a small, powerless insignificant hand . . . a begging hand.

"No," he said. "I would only be—for you—another lie. It would only be a kiss . . . how shall I say? . . . in *not even* revolutionary love."

When he had gone, I stood leaning against the wall, my fist in my mouth like a child. In the other room, I heard Carillo's daughter wailing. With a great groan Andrea rose to see what she could do.

"You *must* go," I said.

"But what if he comes back?" She rubbed her eyebrows nervously so that they stood up, odd and bristling against her smooth skin: querulous tufts.

"Malcolm will *not* come back. You know that."

"No, I don't know that. I don't know it at all. What makes you think you know it? You haven't lived with him over twenty years as I have. I know him. I know he needs me. I know he'll come back."

"All right. I understand that. He needs you, but this is no place for him to come back to. We have to admit that this place is wrong. We have to admit that people like us wouldn't survive. We don't know how. . . ." But she was indifferent to that, I could tell. So long as Malcolm survived, she didn't give a damn about the rest of us: a divine mystery.

"I can get along. There's plenty to do here. He's still running those experiments, I can tell—he even left a notebook in the cave."

So, she too had screwed up her courage and visited the cave: only she had come up with completely different conclusions. As if there were some sense in our reasoning by the addition and subtraction of the items Malcolm had taken with him, I said softly. "He took his radio, he emptied his files . . . There was nothing, really, in the cave. . . ."

"But he took our pictures, our pictures of him and me. Of us together. The ones on our honeymoon, at Pisa. Everything like that, he took. He doesn't want to forget me. He'll be back I say. He still loves me. I'm not going."

I decided on cruelty as a tactic: "You're kidding yourself. He doesn't love you. He doesn't give a damn about you and you know it. If he did, he'd *be* here. But he slipped off without even saying goodbye. Without so much as a note. . . ."

"That's not true. He left a note. He did. I found it later when I was cleaning the room."

This surprised me: perhaps there was some rationale for her passionate clinging to a belief in his return.

"What did it say?"

She reached into her pocket, handed me a crumpled note. It was not even signed, it could have been a note to anyone, or even a memo to himself:

Why should I wait for the world to end? I am only fifty-four years old, and have not yet finished my experiment.

"And you interpret that to mean that he loves you and that he's coming back?"

"Where else would he finish his experiment?"

Anywhere. Anywhere at all, I thought. Wherever there were caves and compost piles. But I said:

"This place will be shut down by the authorities when we go. Carillo said the highway patrolmen asked him a lot of questions about his supposed 'hippie commune' we're running here. He . . . Carillo that is . . . says they're the type to run us out of here anyway on the premise that we're practicing communal sex, and to their way of thinking that means we have to be into dope." I tried to make it sound at once convincing and light-hearted, a difficult combination.

She shook her head stubbornly. "Let them come. I'll just tell them my husband's a scientist, that we're doing research here."

"Oh yeah. Like tell them you're out for an evening stroll all by yourself, till your husband gets back." There was no sign that my sarcasm touched her. Strange how people in love lose their sense of irony: love is so deadly serious. I was on the verge of congratulating myself on not being in love with anyone any more, when I thought of seeing Mark and my stomach turned over. Not my heart, I thought (*with irony?*), just my stomach.

I tried another ploy. Firmly I said, "We're *not* leaving you here. You'll die by yourself."

She looked bitterly amused. "So? What's so bad about that? I thought that was what the experiment was all about, for us to get used to the idea. I'm used to it . . ." she added. "In fact, I've grown to like the idea."

Try ridicule, I told myself. "Oh, come off it, Andrea. That's a dumb and very inefficient way to commit suicide. There're lots better ways."

She seemed interested for a moment, like a child caught in the midst of tears by an unusual toy: "Like how?"

"You could try starving to death."

She rose angrily. "Very funny. I'll remember that. I knew you'd all end by finding me terribly funny. Well, let me tell *you,* you may look better, but you've got the morals of a slut. . . ."

Angrier and angrier. *Good.*

"You'd sleep with every man here if they'd have you, and you know it," she said. "But Malcolm never even looked at you. . . ."

She had given me the right clue: "No. He was too busy ogling Jennifer and reading porno books. Face up to it, Andrea, Malcolm didn't care shit about you. He preferred fucking with fanta-

sies to sleeping with you. He was probably masturbating among
the mushrooms. . . ."

Her round smooth face leaped into fragments as though I were
watching a kaleidoscope: pink and white patches appeared in
bright welts on her cheeks. Then she began sobbing, covering
her face with her hands. When I reached over to touch her she
moved away from me with fury, showing me only the curved
expanse of her back, wide and firm as a ship, but not strong
enough to carry her burden alone. I went to pack her things for
her, feeling certain now that she would leave with the rest of us.

Around four in the afternoon two men arrived at our camp
asking for Carillo Vaca. They wore khakis, were strangely thin
and high-strung: somehow they were different from what I had
expected . (But what had I expected?) They gave us orders, not
gruffly, but efficiently: asked questions, reminded us of details to
care of. The goats for instance: enough feed had to be left them
to last till a farmer nearby could come to lead away the small herd
(we now had seven). The same for the chickens. Tikki was to
come along. And so forth: they thought of everything, even of the
jars of preserves put up by Andrea only a few weeks before. It was
as if they had a List in mind of Human Needs, Weakness, Likely
Commodities, etc., and they attacked our problems with the systematic dexterity of soldiers evacuating a village. They've done
this lots of times, I thought, and sighed at my ignorance. I had
learned no survival skills from Carillo after all, and his final judgment of me was to burn in my memory for years. The two men
were particularly clever (even wily) with Jennifer. They managed
to distract her from a sudden rush of anxieties. She had begun
to run a temperature and was now insisting that the van was
going to break down, that she was going to die on the way, that
the baby was going to die. . . . In short, she was exhausted and
hysterical. They seemed so friendly and courteous that I scarcely
realized to what extent they had ignored me until I was safely
seated in the van. They were rather like those baggage men at Le
Havre who handle you with great verve, jollity and wit and a
bright impersonal friendliness because, after all, you're only a
tourist and you're not going to be in their country very long. . . .

They half-dragged Andrea to the front seat of the van where
she and the driver sat alone. I could not help admiring their
instinct in this regard: it kept Andrea insulated, her gaze fiercely

cleaving to the narrow strip of unpaved road on which Malcolm might suddenly appear. . . . The rest of us grouped ourselves as comfortably as we could about Jennifer and the baby for whom the men had created a bunk made of most of our bedding.

The driver raced the engine. "This'll be a rough ride," he apologized over his shoulder. "There's hardly any road between here and the highway."

"We understand that," I murmured dully. "That's why we came here."

"We don't plan to stop till we get there."

At this Andrea moved in a startled way as if she were about to leap from the van. But then, with a great sigh she locked the door, folded her arms and sat squarely in the front seat, like a giant Egyptian sybil facing West.

Michele

The Roadrunner. A Quality Motel. AAA recommended. Approved by Duncan Hines. Air-Conditioned. Color TV. Heated outdoor swimming pool. 7:00 A.M. breakfast served.

What else could I want? Perhaps Duncan's mistake was in not establishing his Colony at a Holiday Inn. We could have watched the end of the world on Color TV. But we of Duncan's Colony had been temporarily, at least, deprived of our neat apocalypse. What to do, as Dylan Thomas's widow had asked, with a leftover life?

Civilized decadent *bourgeoise* that I am *(Carillo listen!)* the first thing I did was have a shower and wash my hair. Then with abandoned narcissism and the luxury of continuity I rubbed cream into my face for nearly half an hour. It was as if I had fallen prey to an illusion (again!) that it would be a shrewd investment to spend a thousand hours keeping youthful. Who knew what erotic experiences might fall to my profit, all for the price of a few shares in Care & Cozening to keep me youthful and desirable? So, a bargain: I shaved the hair from my legs and underarms; I used a fresh deodorant and brushed my teeth. I had bought a new negligée, suitably extravagant and *décolletée* in the shop adjoining the motel (*so* convenient, price-was-no-object to Roadrunners) which I slipped over my perfumed and saunaed body and settled down like a diva to wait for Mark.

As I flipped on the television I told myself that my conscience was perfectly at ease about Pinosh.

The night before last I had called the hospital. A nurse at the desk assured me he was well and resting. I left her my name and the phone number of the Roadrunner Motel. Pinosh was to please call me when he awoke. I waited all morning for him to call me, then I finally decided I was being stupid and difficult—observing false protocol. After all, it was Pinosh who was in the hospital, not I; therefore it was only fitting that I . . . I rang again and this time was connected immediately with Pinosh's room.

Duncan's voice came through, loud and clear and false as Cressid. And extraordinarily self-confident. "Oh! Michele!" he exclaimed with feigned surprise, as if I were calling collect from Mexico or Hawaii and we had such a poor connection that he could barely make out who I was. "We were *wondering* if you'd call . . . Pinosh is in the bathroom just now . . . Would you rather he call you back?"

This from the colonist who had wanted us all to survive a little longer.

"Never mind. I'll call him later. . . ."

"You have our room number here."

"When has the doctor said he can leave?"

"Well, he doesn't really have to stay . . . He's feeling . . . pretty *lively.*" A smothered laugh. "I mean, we're really sort of waiting for some money. . . ."

"I'll call back," I said hurriedly, not wishing to expose myself to any more of his double meanings.

But I knew I wouldn't call back. Instead I switched on the TV again, sat until three in the morning watching an old film in which Gary Cooper crawled across No-Man's Land and single-handedly wiped out an entire nest of German machine-gunners. It was hard to believe that this was the war which everybody had lost. It seemed for the moment very important that Cooper should wipe out every single one of the viperous enemy. At last Cooper had done his duty, had killed off the whole batch of gunners, and I could go to bed. The world had once again been made safe for democracy.

I had hardly fallen asleep at last when the phone rang. I did not need to ask who it was and he didn't seem to think I needed to be told:

"I just wanted to let you know they're all right. The baby . . . Margot is going to stay in the hospital a few days, but she . . . they're all right."

I wanted to ask him to come to the motel to say goodbye to me, but I felt he would refuse.

"Jennifer's not going to return to her parents," he said after a pause.

He didn't have to tell me that; I knew the girl would have
followed him to the ninth circle of Hell: and perhaps that's where
they'll end up, I thought—jealous even of her capacity for suffering, I was weary of suffering. Still, my insatiable curiosity over-
came my pride. Heedless of what he might think, I pleaded:
"Please write to me. Please let me know where you are, what
you're doing."

For the first time, it seemed, I heard him laugh out loud: "I
couldn't ever tell you what I'm doing. But I *will* drop you a card
from wherever we are."

"Yes, please do. Please keep in touch." What the devil was I
begging him for? I became angry at myself. "Well, goodbye," I
concluded, with as much firmness as I could muster: it was as if
he were leaving me in the Colony by myself. In an air-conditioned
colony approved by Duncan Hines.

"The baby's been registered as Margot Vaca," he said with
unexpected irrelevance.

"That's beautiful," I said. Then I stood sobbing by the phone
for a long time after he had hung up.

I walked in the gravel paths alongside the motel; I ate in the
gourmet-approved restaurant; I filed and polished my fingernails
twice; I read the collected poems of three not-yet-dead poets.
Then on the fourth day I walked into the downtown area and
bought all the newspapers I could find so that I could catch up
on what had been happening in the 'Real' world while we at
Duncan's Colony had been waiting for—not the Messiah, but the
Moloch.

They always turn up when you stop waiting for them, I thought dully.
Mark arrived—not while I sat languorously in my negligée reading Verlaine or while I was erotically sun-bathing in my stunning
new white bathing suit, my skin bronzed as a beauty queen—but
while I lay drugged with a sleeping pill during a wretched night:
just when I had finally decided to return to Michigan alone.
Dazed from the pill, blinded by the lights with which I managed
to flood the motel room as soon as I heard Mark's voice outside
the door, I staggered to unlock the door—my mouth full of ashes,
my head swollen and stupid.

I can hardly believe this is the apparition I have been waiting
for so many days and nights. He is not Mark at all but some

stranger, a bearer of ill tidings. He stands, awkward and lean, tanned by the sun, by the beaches of Australia. He is even dressed quite differently from any way I have ever seen him (I remember suddenly with poignance that we used to shop for his clothes together). But this man would not allow me to pick his ties for him; perhaps he would not wear ties at all. At the same time something in me is astonished that I should be thinking about ties. . . . He is wearing a tweed suit with leather elbow patches such as went out of fashion years ago except in academic fastnesses of New England. It is as if he has decided to ignore the last few decades and has cleverly willed himself back to a time when our present means of destruction were part of the Saturday afternoon horror movie.

The tone is set at once by the fact that he does not embrace me. If he had done so, I would have fallen at once into his arms weeping with relief and remorse, and we would have forgiven each other our mutual betrayal in sexual 'reconciliation.'

If his appearance has utterly changed—can less than a year so metamorphose someone one has known a decade?—his voice has not. It is his voice which, like the Sirens of old, now lures, just as it was his voice which hummed in my ear when we first met, when I had asked myself: how long could I resist this man? (In those days we did not yield at once, we were taught to languish a while in desire. . . .) But his voice is no longer in harmony with his eyes which were once shy and hesitant, seeking-their-approval through me which I always gave. So now, although the voice sounds its hypnotic charm, the eyes reflect his impatience with this necessary ceremony. They want me to understand quickly that this trip has been an act of conscience—no more.

"You mean that you've come all this way just to tell me. . . ."

"Eileen wanted to come to the States anyway. She'd heard so much about it."

"It's a little hard to absorb all this at once." I tried to laugh, but I felt as if I were back in Malcolm's cave, only this time the light over my shoulder had faded. "Especially at . . ." I squinted at my travel clock. " . . . three o'clock in the morning."

"I'm sorry," he apologized quickly, like the stranger he had become: he had not meant to intrude on the lady's sleep. He began again. He tried to be friendly, practical: "What we'd like to know . . ."

Ah, the ceremonial *we*, the sandwich board of the ego, the sheltering clamshells keeping the nucleus fresh, eggy, white, alive. . . .

". . . is whether you plan to return to Michigan. In order to file, you know."

It was, really, a kind of charity in him to falter that way, to be unable to use the word *divorce* casually, but only with romantic fervor and tragic awe.

I turned on him a look which moved us back ten years, with words which I, at least, remembered echoed other nights, other words. Then it was I who had used the word—but warily, as a rock whereon I stood, from which I had thought I could move our marriage into a greater depth . . . "On what grounds? Adultery, I presume?"

He moistened his lips nervously. He sat down in a desk chair, not beside the bed. I pulled the new negligée closer to my body, feeling bitter cold.

"Wouldn't . . . desertion suffice? Eileen's a bit sensitive on the adultery bit. On account of the children."

"Oh. She has children, does she?" And in a burst of incredulousness which I regretted long afterwards: "And you're willing to take on all that? You're ready to do the whole bit: kids, Sunday afternoons. House in the city, second home in the country. Churches, sacraments, bicycles, lawns. . . ." All that he had once claimed he could never tie himself down to; he had wanted to be free to travel anywhere, at a moment's notice. And we had travelled extensively. Now he was travelling backward, into security and tradition. Whereas I had nowhere to go except forward, unless I retreated into nostalgia.

"Why did you have to come here to tell me all this?" I was instinctively clinging to the hope of some last-minute reconciliation: the illusion that perhaps he only needed the sight of me to lapse into tenderness and remorse. I was willing to try.

"I thought it would be cowardly not to."

I managed not to say spitefully: *Oh you big brave man you-oooo!*

My legs had begun to tremble so I sat down: not on the bed. I took a chair, and measuring carefully how close would seem a sexual invitation on my part (or rather, sexual assault), I sat down straight-legged—my knees held primly together. My chest was filled with ragged pains that flashed back and forth: a sort of electric shock therapy.

MICHELE

I lit my cigarette, holding my elbow steady in the palm of my hand. He watched as I did this, until I remembered to offer him one. He shook his head. Had given it up: he had will power, then. He had all sorts of secret strengths he had not bothered to use so long as I was there to hold him up.

I finally asked the inevitable: "How long have you known her?" I was totally unprepared for his hesitation.

"Two years."

"Two? Two years? You already knew her. You mean when we were in England?" Shock upon shock, the therapy burning through, destroying old memories, dreams, things you thought were real but were just symptoms of your illness.

"We met at a play . . ."

"I don't want to hear about it. How very chummy it must have been while we were there! Always something to do . . ."

"Don't be nasty."

"Who's being nasty? I'm summing it up. The long walks, just to see London. You said you knew every street in London, you could 'find your way to any historical spot.' And in what historical spot did you find her?"

He looked away. "There's no need for that sort of thing. It won't help any to be bitter."

"What I'm thinking, what I'm now understanding, is that you wanted me to go with . . . Duncan and the others. You thought it was crazy, but you wanted me to go. That you never intended to come back. *Did* you?"

"I wouldn't say that was it, exactly."

"Not 'exactly.' Is it yes or no?" I demanded. "I want to know. I'm tired of these shitty answers, these moral evasions: damnit, speak the truth for once, if it kills you."

"It's not me I'm worried about," he said softly.

"Oh, it's me, is it? Now you're worried about me. Oh dear, how thoughtful. *Thanks.* What I want to know is, and for once in your life, try to tell the truth: did you ever intend to come back? I mean since you didn't really 'believe' in Duncan's little experiment."

He was silent. I thought eventually he would say *no,* if only to cauterize me. Finally, he sighed: "I don't know, Michele. Why do you say *for once in your life:* do you really believe our life together was nothing but a tissue of lies? How can you say that? We had something. It either died, or it was not enough: can't that be enough to know? When I left on the *Hebrides,* it's true I knew Eileen was in Australia: but there were a lot of things I wasn't sure about. . . ."

I mashed the cigarette into the tray; it made a great deal of smoke and yet did not go out; if one wanted to choke to death on it one could still pick it up, puff some air into it, reuse it.

"And now you're sure."

At least he did not look at me supplicatingly. At least he did not expect me to 'give him his freedom,' as they say, and forgive him at the same time. *The bastard,* I tried to think. But I couldn't really think of him in such terms. He had given me much joy and much love and we had laughed and wept together and shared our friends and shared our travels and shared ten years of my life, and unless I wanted to throw that into the ash tray along with the rubbish, I had to accept the reality of those years. We had once been very young, had foolishly married, believing in the Permanency of Things, and now we were no longer even friends. Yet not enemies either. Merely in that emotional limbo left to divorced couples when one of them, at least, still has something to lose.

As if the word *lose* had reverberated through the motel room like a blaring television announcement, Mark said: "There'll be a settlement, of course."

We had some property in Michigan; he'd sell that, divide it up. An equal-rights divorce: a woman of thirty-five left with a paid receipt for the decade she has given to help her ex-husband develop a self-image which will enable him to do the traditional things like marry, settle down and have a home and children. A full-circle of Success.

"No thanks," I said. "I can still get a job." As a secretary, I instantly thought: how many B.A. English degrees were now stalking the corridors as Secretaries to law offices, insurance companies, banking offices, political candidates? I remembered suddenly, as if already my mind were leaping ahead in its attempt to survive, that I had an old friend in the Book Tower, a lawyer who would know other lawyers: I'd get along, I'd. . . .

This cold-water plunge into the future left me trembling— though perhaps it was only the air-conditioning which was set very low. . . . He now noticed that I was shivering with cold: the new negligée, meant to stir and allure, was quite useless if what you needed was body warmth.

"Can I get you something?" he asked.

I wondered dazedly what there was in the world that he might get me that could be of the slightest help. "I think I'll go back to bed," I said with an acquiescent nod, as if he had suggested it.

In the morning it was I who rose early and left him still asleep or feigning. I took a cab to the airport and waited two hours for a flight to Kansas city, with another long wait, they warned me, until the next flight to Detroit. But that was all right: I preferred to wait.